Killing His Fear

John B. Wren

Killing His Fear

Copyright © 2012 John B. Wren

This book is a work of fiction. The incidents cited as well as the names of people and places are not meant to represent any real incident, person or place.

ISBN-13: 978-1478320456
ISBN-10: 1478320451

Cover design By Katie G. Jones

To

Mary Kathleen Wren

'Kass'

My sister, my friend, my greatest cheerleader . . .

by

John B. Wren

To Probe A Beating Heart

ACKNOWLEDGMENTS

The course of writing a book, long or short, can be very time consuming and requires the cooperation and understanding of the people around you. To all of those who stood by as I wrote, to those who read the drafts and those who put forth honest, constructive opinion and advice, I offer this thank you, it would not have happened without their help.

INTRODUCTION

Fall, 2010 . . . *It was his unreal reality . . .* . .

Brandon Croummer had difficulty sleeping. Not just this night, but most every night. He had grown up in great fear of the movie variety monsters that lurked on the silver screen, knowing they were not real, but fearing them none the less. In spite of those fears, he sought out theaters that ran and reran any of the countless horror films that had been generated over the last eighty years. His preference was for the older, black and white films, but the newer variety held almost the same fascination. He was at once excited and terrified in the presence of a character on the silver screen who stepped silently out of the shadows and inflicted pain or death on the unsuspecting. Equally, the villain who wore a hockey mask and brutally murdered the innocent or wielded a machete like a madman also raised his heartbeat and widened his eyes.

The older films depended on lighting, or the lack thereof, to create various shades of grey and that, along with the passing of clouds before a full moon casting moving shadows, gave the impression that something might be there, hiding, watching. A slight breeze moving a loose shutter, rustling leaves or opening a creaking door added to the effect and sent chills down the spines of victims and viewers. Then an almost hushed footstep on a loose floorboard or a creaking stair could elicit a scream from both actor and audience simultaneously. The tension in the theater would increase in direct proportion to the time taken to reveal the source of the sound. A pause, perhaps only three or four seconds could seem an eternity to the terrified. A longer pause

1

might lose its edge and the play of shadows, the timing of sounds and silence made many a movie more effective.

The art of inducing terror began long before the newer films discovered color and special effects. The newer films had the advantage of the earlier works and added to it by spattering blood and scattering body parts about a set. Brandon could sit very still, embedded in his seat and watch these horrific scenes, hardly moving, trying to not make a single sound, just watching. Outwardly he was calm, giving no hint to the turmoil in his chest and in his gut. He could sit calmly as his inner self twisted and wretched. He saw himself as a part of the film, a necessary observer of these events, always a witness in the background, always present but never clearly seen by the villains. He was there to see, not to prevent, there to watch and know, but unable to report. There, all but hidden from the demon driven killers, there and in constant danger of full discovery, but as yet , undiscovered.

The villains or demons who could silently control a victim with a stare, or overpower them with extraordinary strength were equal to the madmen who would rip, tear, slash, and spatter the screen with blood. Brandon was that constant witness, allowed to watch . . . no, forced to watch. It was his curse, to watch, remain silent and hidden in the crowd and be that one witness to all of their crimes. As he watched, Brandon had to restrict his movements so that he could not be seen clearly. He was a shadow to them, one of many in a crowded theater. He could look directly at them on the screen, memorizing every facet of their twisted faces, every gaze, every stare. The demons in turn could only see his eyes. They knew that he was a witness to so many of the killings that he was a threat to them. In each movie, with each viewing, the villains looked out of the screen searching for him. They knew that the more horrific the killing, the closer Brandon had to be, to watch, and the more he had to return to the theater to see it again and again. They knew this and every film was another chance for them to find him.

In those films where blood was cast about the movie set, Brandon could feel it coming out of the screen and hitting his face, his hands, his arms. As he watched, he would nervously claw at his arms and draw his own blood. He sensed that his blood mixed with that of the victims. The experience was so completely real to him that he could feel the heat or the cold of the scene, he could sense the dampness or the dust, he could smell the dirt, the rot, the mold in the earth on which the characters walked, ran, fought and died. When the scene was close in, Brandon could feel the heat of the killer's body and smell his breath. He sensed all that and felt the victims fear and their pain. He was so completely immersed in the scene that he was a fixture on the set in his own mind. As others watched and were occasionally surprised or startled, Brandon was entirely rapt in the script. He could not separate himself from the film. It was his unreal reality.

He sat through film after film, watching, staying hidden in his seat and moving only after the credits had run. After the film was over and the house lights came up, when the demons could see into the world, then he was in danger of being discovered. Then, he could remain safe as long as they could not see his eyes. They hid in the darkened doorways and alleys between buildings, in the shadows behind trees, under trucks and in the sewers. They hid and watched from the safety of the shadows looking at everybody's eyes, searching for him. If he looked at them, they could see him and know he was the witness. As he left a theater, he kept his eyes straight ahead, not looking into the shadows, not giving them the chance to recognize him.

He would walk quickly through a crowd as if pursued by some unknown creature. He knew in his mind that just as the movie was real so to were the dozens of pairs of eyes that lined his route home, looking for that unidentified observer who witnessed their crimes. He knew that they scanned the crowds of people on the street, looking for him. He knew that if they saw his eyes, they would know it was him. As he left a theater, his tall, thin, almost emaciated frame, deep dark eyes, wild unkempt hair, halting speech and his deathly pallor made him

3

almost as frightening as the villains that he feared. People stepped aside as he approached, not wanting to delay this Ichabod from his destination.

Brandon was rarely at peace, his fears were constantly with him and safety was only found in mindless work that busied his hands and his eyes. He found occupation as a dishwasher in various restaurants, working late into the nights and continued with the janitorial duties when he could, sweeping and mopping the floors. On a good night, he would finish his duties as the sun broke the blackened sky and hid the stars that littered the heavens. On those nights when he finished before daybreak, he would tentatively venture into the darkness, clenched with fear and dread at every darkened alley, every turn of a corner. The creatures of the night, the rats, feral cats and unfortunate souls sleeping in cardboard boxes all gave him pause. All were potentially some indefinable threat, possibly an agent of those monsters and demons that he feared . . . something or someone that could expose him to some unspeakable fate.

*   *   *

Had someone told him that they had those same fears, he would have laughed at them, it was not reasonable, there was no logic behind such a fear. But they were his fears. His nights were a constant nightmare and avoiding sleep was his constant occupation This obsession had cost him dearly. Intelligent as he was, he could not concentrate well enough to read a book or add a column of numbers. It had all started when he was ten years old. His mother did not approve of the television programming on the Friday night late movie shows. The movies were about violence, horror, usually some alien, or a particularly nasty villain who reveled in the killing of another human being. She did not approve and his father enforced the rule, turning off the television after the late news and chasing the children off to bed. Then Brandon turned ten and his parents allowed him to watch his two younger sisters, instead of hiring a babysitter, while they went to a neighborhood party. The festivities went on into the late evening and Brandon decided to take advantage of the situation and watch one of those movies that he had only heard about and had been forbidden to watch. The film was preceded by a brief lecture discussing the merits of the actors and announcing the fact that the main character, Boris Karloff had died in 1969, but would live forever on the screen as his most famous character, the announcer continued, Colin Clive was the infamous Doctor Frankenstein and Boris Karloff was "The Monster". . .

The film is not one in which blood is spattered and bodies are ripped apart, in fact the monster was in some ways a sympathetic character. Sympathetic, but frighteningly real to a ten year old boy who had never seen such a movie before. The lighting, the cast of shadow and the absolute lack of color leaving everything in some shade of grey gives the film a special character. The movie held his attention throughout, surprising and scaring him to the end. Then, when the film was over, he shrugged and told himself that "it wasn't all that scary," and he went off to bed. That night brought the first of countless nightmares. The thought that "he will live forever as The Monster," repeated over and over in his mind as the haunting face gazed closer and ever closer into Brandon's eyes. He woke in a sweat, not crying, not screaming, but repeating over and over, "No — no — no —," louder and louder and soon waking his father.

"Brandon, what's wrong, are you alright?"

He came fully awake at the question. "I — , I was dreaming, a man was chasing me — , it was scary. I couldn't run and he was going to get me. He was so close, he saw me and — he was coming closer — ."

Anton Croummer put his arm around his son sat on the edge of the bed and said, "Was this man big, — bigger than me?"

"I think so, he was huge," Brandon said as he looked up at his father's full four inches over six feet and then nodded, "Yeah, he was bigger than you."

"Well what did he look like?"

"He was all grey, — and he had on a dark suit, — and his head was too big, — and he had stitches all over — ."

"Sounds like someone that I know, or that I know about. Did you watch television last night?"

Brandon thought he might be in trouble, but he answered, "Yeah, I saw a movie — ."

"Was it a Frankenstein movie?"

"Yeah, it didn't bother me when I was watching it, not too much — , I mean, it wasn't that scary. It was old and not so good."

"Listen to me now, what you watched was just a movie about people that really did not exist. There was never a man named Frankenstein, and there was never a monster — ."

"Are you sure?"

"Yeah, I'm sure, and another thing, you are in control of your dreams. If you ever have a dream about some else like that again, you can just ask me to come and help you."

"I can?"

"Absolutely, and I happen to know that most actors in those movies are not as big and strong as I am. I could whip a bunch of them at once, if I had to — and Boris Karloff, he was actually a very nice man, but he pretended to be scary for the movies."

Brandon thought about that for a moment. "Dad, can I sleep in your room tonight?"

"Tell you what, I have a book that I want to read. I'll go get it and sit here with you tonight while you sleep, okay?"

"Thanks dad."

Anton went back into his bedroom and his wife was awake. "What's wrong, Anton?"

"It seems as though our little Brandon watched a scary movie last night while we were at the party. It was bound to happen sooner or later and curiosity was going to get to him eventually. Well it scared the hell out of him and now he's paying for it. I'm going to sit in his room while he goes to sleep."

"Don't yell at him, he's a good boy."

"Not to worry, I think that I went through something like this myself at about his age, and yeah, he is a good boy. You go to sleep, I'll be back."

Anton went back into Brandon's room and sat in a chair near the bed. Brandon was covered up to his neck with the heavy blankets and his eyes were closed, he looked as if he were asleep. Anton smiled and started to read when Brandon said, "Good night Dad."

He smiled again and said, "Good night son."

The sun peeking through the curtains at 7:00 am was Anton's Saturday morning wake-up call and he could smell the coffee brewing in the kitchen. Brandon was fast asleep and Anton walked quietly to the kitchen joining his wife for coffee and a heated bagel.

*   *   *

O~NE~

Sunday Morning ... *The wind seemed less biting* ...

It was a Sunday morning, about ten minutes before four, Brandon was mopping the last of the floors in the kitchen area. He had worked an additional eighteen hours this week and that was going to be enough to justify buying a new DVD player. Karen walked into the kitchen with her coat on, ready to go home and her one day off. She was an old 35 plus, a bit overweight and tall for a woman but her five foot ten was still almost a foot less than Brandon's six foot eight. She had rarely spoken to Brandon in the five months that he had been in her employ and he always felt uncomfortable around her. She saw Brandon near the back door and approached him, handed him an envelope and said, "We will not be needing you anymore. So please take all you belongings with you when you leave here tonight." She did not wait for a response, but brushed past him, walked out the door to the back alley and her car.

Brandon stood motionless, staring at the envelope, allowing her words to sink in and then wondered why he was being let go. He saw Phil, the bar manager just finishing his inventory and making notes as he came into the kitchen. He approached Phil and said, "Excuse me Phil, are we cutting staff, I mean, I wonder if I have done something wrong?"

"Not that I am aware of. What do you mean — done something wrong?"

"Karen just told me that I was no longer needed. She told me to take all my stuff home. I don't have any stuff. Who's going to wash the dishes, and mop the floors?"

"I don't know what to tell you, Brandon. I have no idea who's gonna' do the dishes? — and I have no idea who's gonna' mop the floors? I just do not know. You're gonna' have to ask Karen, she's the boss and she didn't tell me squat."

"Don't know — , I do not know — ." Now Brandon was angry, mostly at Karen, but also at Phil and everyone else at "Rizzonte's Restaurant". He dropped his mop to the floor, took his coat from a hook on the wall next to the back door and continued out into the alley. He had everything that he had ever brought to the restaurant during his employment there. It was in his pockets or on his back. He had brought nothing extra to the restaurant, no pictures of family or friends, no souvenirs of vacations or special events . . . nothing. His life was his work, the movies and the terror filled times in between, there was nothing else. As he stepped off the last stair to the broken and pitted pavement about to start down the alley, he paused, looked around the alley for Karen and heard the back door dead bolts slam closed. Phil had bolted the rear door and now he would immediately go out the front, locking that door as he left. Brandon did not see Karen or her car.

"She must have run to her car and got outta here before I coulda' come out to talk to her," he muttered to himself. He started to walk down the alley and paused again below a dying light, opened his envelope and counted his money. "Son of a bitch — , that little —"

The extra eighteen hours that he had worked this last week were not paid. He turned again toward the alley door, but there was nobody there to tell. He would have to wait until Monday when Karen was due back in. Angry and hurt, he turned again into the alley and started to walk toward home.

The alley was dark, windowless and poorly lit. Small separations between the old red brick buildings and indentations for doors were the only interruptions in the dirt stained walls where the demons and their minions could hide and watch him. Watch and whisper, trying to gain sight of his eyes. A slight breeze made small noises moving paper about the ground and rattled a loose window. A screen door moved open, it's spring pulled it closed and the critters of the night scurrying about in search of food made more noise. Brandon's mind magnified the entire symphony to a deafening roar. He hurried his pace and saw the end of the alley only four more buildings away. As his breathing began to relax and the noise began to subside, a rat crawled out from under a dumpster. Both Brandon and the rat were each stunned at the sight of the other. Brandon stared at the enormous rat, and the half grown rat stared at the huge ugly human bearing down on him. Brandon paused, the sounds grew louder, the rat bared its teeth — .

Brandon, still angry with the situation at the restaurant, looked at the rat and said, "You want a piece of me too?" Then he took two steps toward the stunned rat and swiftly brought his steel toed boot into contact with the rats yellow teeth. The boot won. The rat flew backward against the dumpster and left a bloody smear where it's shattered head made contact. The collision of rat on metal seemed to quiet down the noise. The wind seemed less biting, the alley fell still save the mild breeze and the dark nooks and passages between buildings were not as dark and appeared to be empty. The demons had all left. Brandon's boot had sent them away. He stood straight and panned the alley. All quiet, he relaxed a bit and started to walk, silence, a gentle breeze, little movements of paper caught in the wind, a car with a bad muffler, but no demons, no threatening creatures whispering, no symphonic booming in his head. The night was now calm and he walked out to the main street and four more blocks to a corner where he turned for home, no longer holding his coat tightly about himself. He walked all the way home, tall with his head up at an easy pace. Easy and angry.

*　　　　　*　　　　　*

His Father had consoled him, given him a weapon to use against the nightmares and it had worked. He did not watch those films any more, but the billboards and commercials on television were enough to keep the fear alive in him. When he dreamt of one of these demons or monsters, Brandon simply called on his father to help. His dreams were his and he controlled them. So when a predator tried to grab him, he thought of his father and Anton would appear. Anton was a large man and Brandon's dreams made him even larger, much to the chagrin of the bad characters in the dream? It worked very well until Brandon was sixteen. Just two weeks after Brandon's sixteenth birthday, Anton Croummer was run down by a hit and run driver as he was walking home from the drug store on a dark street with prescription for one of Brandon's sisters. He never regained consciousness and died in the hospital three days after the incident. Brandon's mother cried constantly saying, " that bastard, that monster — ," and that driver was never identified. She was so hard hit by the tragedy that she required psychiatric help. She spent three months in the concentrated care of a psychiatrist and then regular weekly, then monthly sessions for the next three years. During that time a large part of the responsibility of caring for Brandon's younger sisters fell to him. He was still a very young man and had the entire world in front of him, but there were differences. His father was more of a pillar holding Brandon up than anyone ever assumed. Anton was now dead, his mother was collapsing and Brandon assumed the overwhelming responsibility of being a parent. He made a few mistakes and some bills did not get paid on time, he missed several days of school at a time and his grades began to slide. The pressure increased and he did not react well.

His dreams continued, but now, his father was dead, murdered, in his mind by some Monster, and Anton could no longer help him. His mind was burdened with the worry of caring for his sisters while his mother was being treated by the psychiatrist. His imagination, fueled by the tragedy of his father's death, encouraged by the absence of his father's strength and fed by his mother's constant cry, " . . . that monster," led Brandon to opening the mental doors that allowed him to see demons in dark places and allowed his fears to grow. He was drawn to the theaters, to the movies that scared him the most. He was looking for relief and he found more to fear. He returned over and over and each time he hesitated, then moved ahead. Each time he thought, "I shouldn't do this," then he went ahead anyway. He had to watch, he was compelled to watch, to look for the evil, see it, recognize it and then fear it. His attendance at the movies did not help him deal with his fears, it made the fear greater.

The movies that affected him were not always the bloodiest. Often when a theater ran old movies or they were played on television, Brandon watched. The most frightening were often those in black and white, like the first one he saw. It stayed with him, the shadows, the shades of grey, the hint of violence and not the spattering of blood.

It came to the point that Brandon was either in a theater or in front of his television, watching a movie with some horrific scene more often than not. It was his drug and he was addicted. Addicted to the disadvantage of everything else in his life. When his mother was finally through her psychiatric treatments, Brandon was definitely in need of the same. Any mention of psychiatry and Brandon would fly into a rage, "No, I want nothing to do with them, look what they did to mom, and they won't bring dad back. No, I will not go."

Brandon felt that watching the movies in a theater was safe, it gave him an edge, he knew they were there, he knew what they looked like and he knew how to hide from them. As he watched the silver screen, he was in control, he was safe. When he left the theater and walked the darkened streets, then he was in danger. Then they could see him, if they could see his eyes and identify him as the one, then they could watch him and then they could plot how to kill him.

The sun was a relief. The bright light of day drove the creatures into hiding, the day was safe and he could rest, sleep. Sleep but also dream and those dreams were no longer under his control. The car that had killed his father was in practically every dream, following him as if it was not sure that it was him, waiting to be sure, waiting for the opportunity to run him down too. The shadowy figures that lived in the shades of grey moved closer and ever closer. They turned their faces toward Brandon, closer and closer to seeing his eyes, but never quite getting there. He was still safe, just safe on the edge of danger, but for how long?

Brandon went to more movies, often seeing the same one repeatedly. The movies distracted him, instructed him and allowed him a strange peace as he watched. His life became a series of little crises that he addressed as they appeared and his release was the theater, the violence. Then he saw a movie in which a man, walking home late at night, was intentionally run down by a car driven by the madman, a serial killer. The killer's objective was to get him out of the way so that he could attack the rest of the man's family and murder them. It pushed him over the edge — and his dreams returned in full force. He was completely distracted, he could not concentrate, he could not sleep, he could only stare and worry.

Brandon never graduated from high school and college was a lost hope, no longer even a dream. At the age of nineteen, he had alienated any friend he ever had and his mother and sisters lived in fear of him and his outbursts. He had grown to a height of six foot, eight inches, weighed something less than two hundred pounds and due to lack of sleep and poor eating habits, he appeared more dead than alive. He wandered the streets at night, walking with long strides wearing faded blue jeans that were to tight and to short, working boots with steel tips that bulged at the toes and a torn black raincoat that was missing all of its buttons and was noticeably short in the sleeve for Brandon.

When he finally left his home in Michigan, just outside Detroit, his mother and two sisters were relieved. Brandon had announced that he was going to Florida and would come home after he had shaken the demons that pursued him. It was unspoken, but accepted that they would never see him again. He was on a downward spiral, they could do nothing for him and he was not helping himself.

*   *   *

TWO

Sunday Morning . . .   There were no whispers in dark alleys . . .

For some reason, killing the rat had relaxed his fears and that morning when Brandon arrived at his apartment he was feeling more alive than he had in years. He stripped off his clothes and stood in the shower, rinsing away the dirt and grease of the night's work and his walk home. He stayed in the shower for about ten minutes, changing the temperature of the water from hot to cold and back to hot again, wondering why he was as relaxed as he was. When he finally stepped out and began to dry his boney body, he thought about food, he was hungry. He finished drying and pulled on clean jeans and a clean tee shirt. As he was about to put his boots on again, he looked at the toe that broke the rat's face, "I should at least clean off the remains of the beast that dared roar at me," he muttered. He used a wet paper towel to wipe off both boots, then thought about polish . . . it was a passing thought and he settled for the quick wipe down.

Dressed and mildly energized, Brandon walked outside, the sun was about to rise, the wind had eased and birds had begun their chattering as they prepared to begin the days search for bread crumbs, insects or other edible bits that littered the city streets and walkways. He walked into the nearest McDonald's and ordered one of their standard breakfast meals to go and slowly ambled outside again. He sat at one of the outdoor tables in a small grassy area next to the restaurant and delved into his bag of fast food. The birds gathered in anticipation of a crumb or two hitting the pavement and bounced about chirping, begging and looking. He accommodated several of the foragers by tossing a few scraps their way and smiled as they argued briefly over the crumbs.

The air was still cool from a long night without the heat of the sun, but the promise of a warm afternoon was in the gentle breeze and a cloudless sky. Brandon shook out a few more crumbs for the birds and rose to begin his short trip home. He was still hungry, so he bought a second breakfast and returned to his apartment, taking a long round-about route, enjoying the morning air and the noticing the trees, the leaves and the bushes for what they were, the life that grows and gives life to so many creatures, not the dark hiding places for the demons and other creatures that he so often feared were there watching him. When he arrived at his apartment, he turned on the television and sat in his overstuffed chair to watch the news or whatever was interesting as he delved into his second round of breakfast.

As hungry as he thought that he was, and as small as the fast food meal was, he could not finish, so he put the remains of his second meal in his otherwise empty refrigerator and returned to his chair. The television programming on a Sunday morning was limited. It was 8:15 and a minister was talking about recognizing who was truly important . . . he woke at 2:30 in the afternoon to someone kicking a field goal. He was hungry again and he retrieved his bag from the refrigerator. Sitting in front of the television, he turned the channel several times and found a weak movie about an overgrown crocodile and watched, uninterested for an hour. Then he decided that the movie was not worth the watching and he turned the channel again settling in on a football pre-game show. The Houston Texans were in town, the game would begin a little after four and he found that he was more than happy to pass up his usual night at the movies to watch the game. He wondered why he had more interest in a game that had never meant anything to him before. The game began well enough with a pair of field goals in the first quarter. The Texans scored a touchdown in the second quarter, putting them up by one and Washington answered with two touchdowns in the same frame. Halftime and the score was 20 to

15

7. Brandon found himself getting excited by the game and feeling good about the score. He had never watched a game all the way through before, but now there was no thought of doing anything else. The third quarter began with the Texans booting a field goal, cutting the lead to ten points. Washington came back with a touchdown and the lead jumped to 17. Brandon thrust his fists up over his head and growled an "Alright, way to go." Houston came back with 17 unanswered points and forced an overtime.

"Sudden death, that sounds rather harsh — death," and his mind drifted to the rat and the kick that shattered the animal's head and sent the demons away. His mind was wandering, he looked at the television, Houston kicked a field goal, suddenly his team was dead. The game was over, the Texans won. He turned off the television and walked out into the night, to walk and to think.

The night was quiet, the demons were not around, there were no whispers in dark alleys, no low growls from darkened doorways, just the low murmur of people talking as they walked and cars passing by. He found a theater showing another new version of a vampire movie. He went in and watched for a while, found it to be boring, left the theater and walked home. Again, the streets were quiet and Brandon was tired. He thought about the game as he sat on the edge of his bed, kicked off his boots, he leaned back with his feet still on the floor and drifted off into a deep, peaceful sleep.

*   *   *

When Brandon left Detroit, he took a Greyhound bus to Washington, DC where he intended to stop to earn some more money before continuing on to Florida. He found work as a dishwasher in a restaurant on Capitol Hill and initially intended to sleep on the street to save as much money as possible. As the months passed, he became more comfortable with the Washington area and thought he might spend the winter. This meant finding some shelter for the next few months. He found a third floor walk-up, single room with minimal amenities. This he could afford and it gave him shelter and a degree of safety from his constant demons. His apartment was a single room with a small bathroom. His one window faced another dilapidated apartment building about twenty feet away. Directly opposite his window was another window into a similar single room apartment. The other window was normally closed and a heavy drape pulled across. He saw into that apartment once when it was being cleaned or fumigated. At one time these were efficiency apartments intended to house the numerous people who came to Washington for frequent short visits, mostly people connected with some political organization or an elected official. They were economical then, today, they were cheap. Today the dirty, cracked plaster over lathe was constantly in need of patching and painting, but repair was more a concept than a fact. The plumbing fixtures in the bathroom were old, leaky and noisy, but that meant higher water bills from the utility and the building owners were gradually replacing the fixtures with the cheapest parts they could find. There was a small kitchen counter with a sink, a two burner range and a microwave oven. Luxury . . .

After two years in this apartment and working as a dishwasher in five different restaurants, Brandon had established a routine. Work through the night, walk the streets through the darker early morning hours, sleep for four or maybe five hours and catch another movie on television or in a theater before getting back to work at seven in the evening. He avoided the dreams when he slept in the day light hours, usually, but not always. As he discovered his neighborhood shops, he found one that dealt in used videos. They had both the VHS tape films and the DVD formatted films. He could buy a cassette player or a DVD player, but not both. Knowing that the DVD was the way of the future, Brandon splurged on both a television and a DVD player at a Salvation Army store on route 236 in Virginia for under fifty dollars. He managed to purchase a few of the classical horror films including Frankenstein, Dracula and the Wolfman. Each month he would go to his used DVD shop and select another film. After two years, Brandon had about forty five different DVDs that he had purchased, found, traded for or had stolen.

*   *   *

T HREE

Monday Morning ... Here I am, ready if you are ...

Monday morning was the beginning of a new phase in Brandon's life. He slept until a little after 9:00 am and did not dream, at least he did not remember a dream. He felt energized and was determined to collect the rest of the money that he was due from Karen. Showered, shaven and dressed Brandon walked outside with a feeling of confidence. Initially he intended to beg Karen for his job, but now he just wanted the money he was due and he would find another restaurant that was in need of a dishwasher. As he walked toward Rizzonte's, he stopped in a Starbuck's and bought a bagel with cream cheese and a medium coffee. He walked, ate his bagel and drank his coffee. A unique feeling, relaxed and eating, not looking in the doorways he passed or at the other unfortunates like himself on the street. He finished his bagel, tossed the wrapper in a waste basket and walked at an easy lope sipping his coffee.

The street was a succession of restaurants, coffee shops, shoe stores, book stores and smattering of cell phone shops. Brandon looked in each window as he had never done before. Not checking the reflection to see who was behind him, but to see what was inside, for him a novel experience. Then he saw a sign in a restaurant window. "Help Wanted," with the word "Dishwasher" in smaller print. He looked up at the sign over the door, "Stewart's Pub", gave a satisfied nod, tossed his empty cup in a waste basket on the street corner, walked in the door and spotted a man checking items on a clipboard and talking to another man leaning on a dolly.

The man turned toward Brandon, "We're not open yet, pal. But please come back at 11:00, that's when we start serving lunch." The man was almost six feet tall and built like a prize fighter. His hands and forearms stood out. They were huge. His sandy hair was short and neatly cut. A thin moustache was the only facial hair and steel blue eyes were friendly, but dangerous.

Brandon stood tall and spoke with confidence, "I'm here about your sign in the window, is now a bad time?"

The man signed the clipboard sheet and handed it back to the delivery man. "You lookin' for work?"

"Yeah, and I have experience in the kitchen, washing dishes, sweeping and mopping up."

"Well, yeah, okay. When can you start? I mean it's not as if I have twenty people beating down my door, lookin' for work."

"Well, I have an errand to run and that will take about an hour and the rest of the day is open."

"Okay, but first I have to ask you a few questions."

"Sure, go ahead."

"Well, let's start with what's your name and where do you live?"

"My name is Brandon Croummer and I have a room at the Exeter Apartments on Third, it's small, but I don't need much."

"Okay, do you have any disease that would or should keep you out of a kitchen?"

"No."

"Good, how about a police record, anything that we should talk about?"

"No."

"Anybody after you, like the IRS, or an ex-wife?"

"No," he answered with a slight laugh.

"Okay, how about $10.50 an hour to start, and you get something off the sandwich menu for every eight hours that you work. Payday is every Friday at the end of your shift and it's one week behind."

"Works for me."

"Great, my name's Stu Bricker, this is my place and I could put you to work as soon as you can be here, so an hour from now is great," he mumbled to himself looking at his watch, "So I'll see you around 11:30?"

"I'll be back, maybe less than an hour, maybe 11:00, maybe earlier."

"Okay, see you then, oh — come around to the alley door, we usually don't open the front until 11:00, and if you have some kind of identification with a photo, like a drivers license . . . "

"I have my Michigan license and a Social Security card, will that do?"

"Perfect, see you in an hour."

Brandon hustled down the street not looking in anymore windows. He wanted to get back and start earning money as soon as possible. He covered the six blocks to Rizzonte's in just over ten minutes, but Karen was not in when he arrived. "I thought she usually came in early on Mondays, when should I come back? "

"She should be in around noon — had a dentist thing today," said Phil, "I'll tell her you were here and you want to talk to her."

"Thanks Phil," and Brandon was back in the flow of human traffic going back to "Stewart's Pub". The sun was still in the sky, the breeze was still calm and the normal cacophony of whispering demons was

21

silent. This was turning out to be a pleasant day after all and he didn't fully understand why, but he was not about to ruin it by questioning his luck. He arrived back at Stewart's Pub at about 11:30 and paused outside to catch his breath. The street was filling up with the lunch crowd and Brandon noticed the people, their clothing, their faces and practically everyone was on a cell phone or involved in conversation with a companion. He looked in the widow to the pub and saw Stu talking to an attractive woman and the bartender. He mumbled, "I hope this place is better than the last one," and he walked around the corner to the alley, then down to the door that was labeled "Stewart's Pub" and walked in. He was in a vestibule that led to the kitchen on the right and a second door that was open to stairs to a basement directly ahead. Brandon walked into the kitchen where he saw a tall man wearing an apron and a Washington Nationals baseball hat. "I'm looking for Stu . . ."

The man pointed to a pair of doors and said, "I think he's in there . . . talking to Brenda . . ."

"Thanks . . . " He went into through the doors, saw Stu still talking to the woman. As he approached the three of them, their conversation ended and they were getting back to work. "Stu, my appointment didn't happen, she wasn't there, so here I am, ready if you are."

Stu looked at Brandon with a little question still in his head, nodded and said, "Great, you have your ID?"

Brandon pulled out his wallet and retrieved his old Michigan drivers license, "Is this okay, I don't have a car and never bothered to get a new license?" He pulled out a second card from his wallet, "This is my social security card," and handed it to Stu.

"Yeah, these will do, but you should get a new license, even if you don't drive."

"Never felt the need, but yeah, I should."

"Okay, I'll copy some information from these and give 'em back to you and you can tell me the rest, but first — let's walk around the joint." He gestured toward the bar with his left arm saying, " The bar can sit sixteen people and there are six, four tops in the same room," and his right arm waved at the opposite side of the room. Stewart's Pub occupied three store fronts in a recently redeveloped commercial building. The bar area and main entry were located in the first of the three, a corner suite glassed across the twenty foot west front and the first sixty feet along the north side. The entry was angled between the north and west walls and the bar filled the majority south wall.

"The dining areas are this way," and Stu walked along the bar toward the front door. At the end of the bar he paused, looked to his right and said, "This is the hostess station," pointing to a short counter with a cash register, a bowl of mints and a stack of menus.

Brandon looked around the room and nodded toward the bartender as Stu led him to the left through an opening into the first dining room. "This room has twelve four tops and nine two's." Brandon was impressed with the count thus far and was about to comment when Stu said, "Now, come on this way," as he led Brandon across the room and through another opening to another room that was the same size as the first dining room. "We have another four two tops in here and ten sixty six inch round tops. Those can sit eight each, but we are happy to get six in and usually end with four at each. So all in all we can sit one hundred seventy four people at one time. Think we dirty a plate or two to keep you busy?"

Brandon grinned, "How many turns do you do on average?"

Stu looked slightly surprised at the question, grinned and said, "We have done three nearly full turns at lunch and the same at dinner, but that's a damn good day. Usually it works out less except on the weekends, there we may do a few more. We are closed on Sunday, so that's when we get a lot of the heavy cleaning work done and I like to see the windows washed weekly. Monday, Wednesday and Friday mornings we get deliveries from our meat and bread suppliers and we inventory the bar on Wednesday mornings, restock on Thursdays. That usually means a lot of lift and carry work for all of us. So now let's check out the kitchen." Stu led Brandon back to the waitress station next to the opening to the kitchen. "Brandon, this is Lisa and Melissa, and I think that Barb is also working this room today."

"Hi," and he hurried after Stu as he turned left into the first dining room. The two girls smiled and said something that he completely missed.

"Okay, this is Brenda, she's our Hostess and she is in charge of the waitresses. Brenda, this is Brandon, he's gonna' take over the wash station."

Brenda was the woman he saw earlier and her smile had Brandon instantly wanting to say yes to anything she said. She was about five foot six, probably in her thirties, but could pass for less, slender with brown hair and big brown eyes. Brenda could have been a model and her looks alone could sell Fords in Tokyo or Toyotas in Detroit. Brandon assumed that Brenda and Stu were somehow attached.

"Brandon, my pleasure," as she extended her hand, "We have been a little scattered since our old washer ran out on us. But I must say, Stu has been getting pretty good at the wash machine. Hope you like it here," she said with that magnificent smile.

"Thanks, I think I will, I like to stay busy."

"You have come to the right place. Come back out before the action starts and meet the other waitresses."

"Okay, I'll do that." Stu led him through another opening back into the bar area.

"Ah yes, Brandon this is Steve, he is our lead bartender and will be working the first shift today."

"Hi Steve."

"Brandon, come on back here and see what we have," and Steve led Brandon down the length of the bar. "These glasses are all clean and the used ones will go in that tray. Usually we can handle the wash up here unless it really gets busy, then we will fill a tray or two and you get to pitch in."

"Easy enough." Brandon looked at the other two empty trays. "Dishes and utensils?"

"You got it, and after we finish with everything, close and lock the doors, the bar is closed. No free drinks. You can drink all the water and soda you want, but we lock down the hard stuff. Are you good with that?"

"Works for me, I haven't had a beer since I left Michigan a few years ago. Just never appealed and the hard stuff, well I never developed a taste for it."

"Great, we do get our share of guys who think that working in a bar means free drinks — not here. We sell our booze, and don't drink it. If you start, it's tough to quit."

"I haven't started yet, been doing this kinda work for about five years now and I don't have the desire to drink."

"Well our last dishwasher got lost inside a bottle. Seems as though he does that every once in a while. Hank is a good guy when he's sober and a nice guy when he's drunk, but drunk he can't work so we gave him a choice. He went with the bottle."

Stu was talking to Brenda and returned to take Brandon to the kitchen. "Okay, the kitchen crew is run by George, he's somewhere around here. Ah —, this is Frank, he does prep."

"Hey Frank," they shook hands.

"And this is Bill, one of our cooks."

"Bill."

"George, there you are, this is Brandon, he is going to join us in the kitchen, he will handle the dish wash station, and maybe more, we'll see."

George was the man Brandon met earlier, he extended his hand, "Brandon, glad you are here, I drive the bus back here, so you come to me with questions, when will you start?"

"Show me where to hang my coat and lead me to the dirty dishes."

"Great, Stu if you have finished with the tour and intro's, we got work to do back here. Brandon, this way," and George walked to the far corner of the kitchen where there were a few dishes, silver and pots needing attention. "Do you know how to run the machine?"

Brandon smiled and started loading the trays to run through the machine, "I think I got this."

George grinned, "Okay, you got it . . . " He looked at Stu and nodded, "We're good in here."

"Okay, when there's a break in the action I have a few questions for our new man for the files."

The lunch hour was busy and no problem, Brandon did his job and helped out lifting and carrying deliveries from the back door to the basement and other shelving in the kitchen.. The dinner hour also went well and he seemed to be settling into his new job with no problems. After the restaurant closed the doors and the last patron left, it was time to sweep and mop. Brandon automatically began to wipe and stack chairs to clear the floor for a sweep. Stu came in and said, "Brandon, you did good today, the sweeping is more than I intended, but if you want it, it's all yours."

"Thanks Stu, I can run the vacuum in the dining rooms then sweep and mop the hard floors and finish in the kitchen after they wipe down the equipment. I should be done before 12:00 and be back in by 11:00 tomorrow morning."

"Okay, this is going to work out good, but first I have those few questions that I mentioned earlier. We want the files on all our people to be complete and we can talk about our benefits package. Actually, Brenda is the benefits person — she actually understands that stuff, insurance and taxes. Let's go downstairs to the office and run through everything."

"Okay, you lead."

Brenda was sitting in the small basement office, tallying up the day's receipts on the computer. "Hey y'all, I was going to ask if you were ready for the final bits of paperwork, but here you are , so let's run through it. Stu have you copied his ID and social security card?"

"Ah, right here kiddo, I was coming down to do just that."

"I'll take it from here," she said. "Brandon, pull up a chair. Stu, this will take about twenty minutes, everybody can go home and we can lock it up for the night."

"Okay, I wanted to check on a few things in the coolers and I'll be ready to go," said Stu.

"I have to do the floors yet and that will take a little while. If this is only 15 to 20 minutes, I should be done by 1:00," said Brandon.

"I'll check the coolers and start the floors, and let you finish," Stu said to Brandon and turned toward the walk-in units.

Brandon pulled up a folding chair and said, "He must have a heavy date tonight."

27

Brenda smiled and said, "Let's run through this and we can all go home." She had a package all ready for Brandon with the insurance and benefits information. "So let's do the questions first."

As he had predicted, Brandon finished all his chores by one am. Stu and Brenda had a brief meeting with Steve immediately after Brenda finished with Brandon, then walked out together to the alley. Brandon put the brooms and mops away, George let him out and locked the doors. Brandon was still feeling good, no whispering in the shadows, no unidentified noises from the darkened doorways and he walked home in the dark at a relaxed pace. Home before 1:00 am, he draped his coat across the back of his chair, turned on the television and scanned for a movie. He flipped the channels for a few minutes, pausing here and there, but nothing drew his attention. He turned off the television, walked over to his bed and sat down to remove his boots. As he sat there on the edge of his bed, he thought about the day and the people that he had met.

"I met Stu and Brenda, then Steve and George and Bill and Frank and . . ." As he was trying to remember the names of the waitresses, he lay back on the bed and fell into a deep sleep. The night passed without a sound or dream and he awoke at 7:30 Tuesday morning completely refreshed, his feet still on the floor, still wearing his boots.

*   *   *

F OUR

Tuesday brought a new sunrise and a second day starting with peace and quiet. Brandon stood and shook the webs from his head, walked into his bathroom and looked in the mirror. "Not bad for a guy forty years old . . . but I'm only twenty seven." He hung his head for a moment, then looked in the mirror again and said, "Time to start living." He kicked off his boots, stripped and stood in the shower as long as he could stand the hot water. Somewhat reddened by the shower and the toweling off he dressed and walked to the coffee shop at the corner and bought a bagel and a large cup of coffee. Life felt good at that moment, and he was anxious to get going, see what the day may bring. He walked down the street feeling good, enjoying the sun, looking at the other people and he arrived at Stu's Pub as he finished his cup of coffee. He flipped his empty cup into the waste basket and headed around to the alley entrance.

Stu was fumbling with some papers and talking to another deliveryman when Brandon stepped through the door. "Morning Stu, is it okay if I'm a little early . . . no charge?"

"Brandon, bull — , I could use some help, so if you're game, you're on the clock."

"An extra buck never hurt, what are we doing?"

"I've got about twenty packages here and we have to check 'em all and get 'em into the store room. Open that one next to your foot and give me a count."

They worked for an hour opening packages and stacking the store room shelves with salt, pepper, sugar, coffee, filters, stir sticks and napkins.

"So what drew you this way this early?" asked Stu.

"Nothing special, got a good night's sleep, got a bagel and coffee and started walking. I just wound up here and thought that I might relax a bit before the onslaught of dirty dishes."

"Well I'm glad you did, saved me a bunch of time. Hey, its pushing 10:30, let's get a couple of sandwiches and have lunch before the crowd arrives."

Brenda was standing at the waitress station talking to a couple of the waitresses and walked over to Stu, "You gonna' have a little lunch, both of you?"

In unison they replied "Yes." Stu continued, "How about a ham and cheese for me, and — ." He looked at Brandon.

"The same please."

"Comin' right up gentlemen."

Stu looked at Brandon as they sat at the end of the bar and said, "Service in this joint is pretty good." They sat and talked about the weather, then Stu mentioned the current baseball season and before a new topic opened, lunch arrived. At five minutes to opening, fed and ready for the day, Brandon went to his dish station and Stu stepped behind the bar to check the cash register. Brenda looked at Stu and said "Time in?"

"Yeah, let's get it started," and Brenda unlocked the front door allowing three patrons in and showed them to a table.

A normal day, busy but not too busy and at midnight, Brandon was again finished and ready to head home. He went out the kitchen door.

The alley was wide enough for a full sized truck to access the rear of each business on either side. The buildings formed a dirty red brick canyon with doorways, dumpsters and an occasional parked car. Single incandescent bulbs over the doorways provided the minimal lighting and a recent rain shower made the walls and pavement glisten. Puddles in potholes in the pavement were shallow but all to frequent and Brandon was watching where he stepped as he walked toward the main street. A strange moaning sound that he did not recognize sent a slight chill up his spine, but when he turned, there was nothing there. He upped his pace and felt the cold as he walked and his foot splashed the water out of a small chuckhole. The wind stirred a few papers and again drew his attention, but he continued down the alley at a slightly quickened pace.

Once again home and safe, Brandon tried to regain the relaxed feeling of the previous day. He turned on his television and flipped the channels till he found a movie. As he watched, he felt the discomfort ease away and he fell asleep in his chair.

*   *   *

F IVE

It was dark, he could see a dark brick wall with a window and in the window was a figure moving out of the shadows. It was a large man with a sad, grey face. He was wearing a dark shirt and coat and as he moved across the window, he turned and looked directly at Brandon. The face was old, wrinkled and scarred. There were dark lines from his deep set, almost black eyes that disappeared halfway to his mouth. His thin , pale lips moved very slightly as if he were talking to himself, but emitted no sound. The man paused in the window and calmly watched Brandon.

"He saw me, I know he saw me," Brandon mumbled and turned to his left to walk away but there was another dark, brick wall, another window and another man stepped out of the dark corners within. He looked the same as the first man, large, grey faced and he too turned and looked directly out through the window at Brandon. The mouth was moving and again, there was no sound. Brandon turned to his right again to try to walk away. He saw yet another brick wall, the same as the first two. As he looked in through the window, he began to breathe heavily, to perspire and as the fear rose to an almost unbearable level, Brandon awoke suddenly, sat up straight in his chair, the television was on and some reporter was describing the traffic entering the city. It was 6:37 am. He had slept for over five hours. He stood, turned off the television, kicked off his boots and lay down on the bed. He spent the next two hours trying to fall asleep again, unsuccessfully. He decided to shower and get ready for the new day. Clean shaven for the second day in a row, showered and dressed, Brandon set out for his morning coffee and bagel. His step was not as light as the previous day, but still he felt freed of the fears that usually plagued him in spite of his dream. Early to work for a second day, Stu was again pleased to have some help setting up for the day. They again shared time at the end of the bar and had a little lunch before starting the regular work day.

Brandon went to his station in the kitchen and Stu was again checking the cash register when Brenda unlocked the doors. She walked over to the bar and sat on a bar stool and said, "Brandon seems like a good find. He has come in early, works hard all day, doesn't complain and he is very polite. I like him, Stu."

"Yeah, so do I. He seems too smart to be a dishwasher though, makes me wonder what his story is."

"You know the saying, don't look a gift horse in the mouth, but I would wonder too."

"I know, we may have a prize here or he may crash and burn, we've seen a few of them over the years." He was smiling at Brenda, looking at her and holding her hand.

"We can talk about this later," she said, then gave Stu's hand a firm squeeze and walked over to the waitress station picking up a pile of menus and turned toward the front door.

Steve was giving the bar a final wipe down and said to Stu, "You know how lucky you are?"

"Yeah . . . yeah I do."

*   *   *

The day again ended at about midnight and Brandon again left through the kitchen door. The alley was dry, some water remained in a few of the chuckholes and a slight breeze moved the loose papers in the alley. Again Brandon heard the moaning noise, this time a little longer and a little louder. The breeze picked up and some critter moved behind a dumpster. He again sped up his pace and as he passed a separation between two buildings, he heard a whisper. He moved faster, the end of the alley was not getting any closer. He heard another whisper and he all but ran to the end of the alley. The main street was lit and he felt safe again. People were still going from place to place and he felt himself hidden in the crowd. He hurried his pace and then slowed. He at once wanted to be at home and at the same time knew that a man rushing through the streets would stand out. Keeping his head down and not looking at others, he moved with the crowd, not through it, his eyes hidden from view.

Finally home, Brandon pushed himself into his stuffed chair and stared at the television. The host of some late night talk show was interviewing some actor or politician, he stared but never heard what they were saying. He could not remember what was on after the talk show, but he remembered his dream.

It was night, he was standing in a street that that ended with high dark brick walls on three sides. He could not turn around to look behind. There were no trees, no lights and nobody else was in sight. He was starting to feel closed in, unable to move. There appeared to be no way out. Then he noted a window in one of the walls. When he looked again, each of the three walls had a similar window. Initially, there was nothing there and he was starting to relax. Then something moved in a window. A large man seemed to step out of the shadows behind the wall, bend forward and look out, scanning the area. His dark eyes settled on Brandon and he stood straight, with those eyes locked on him. Another man in the window to Brandon's left appeared, leaned forward and looked until his eyes were directed at Brandon. The man stood and kept his gaze on him. The window to the right was still empty and Brandon heard a low moaning sound. The man in the middle window was moving. Brandon looked at the wall to his left and saw a door next to the window. The center wall now also had a door and as he turned to the right a door was opening and the moaning sound grew louder. The doors were now all open and the sound was getting louder. The doors moved slightly and to the right, the large man was coming out, his head slightly bowed to clear the door frame. Brandon was again breathing hard, sweating and shaking.

*   *   *

SIX

Thursday Morning . . . *Why do I let these dreams control me* . . .

He woke sitting straight up in his chair, it was 3:45 in the morning. He tried to sleep again, he closed his eyes, but he knew that he was awake. Then he was again in the street and he saw the middle door move, then the door to his left moved. He sat up right again, he was in his apartment, there were no doors with windows, no men with grey faces, just a television with some infomercial running, "Buy it now and save another 20%." It was now 4:15 am, he turned off the television and undressed, walked into the bathroom and stood in the shower as long as he could. Dried and dressed, Brandon looked out his window. It was still dark, but the sun would come up in a few hours.

Far too early to show up at the restaurant, Brandon bought his coffee and bagel as the sun broke the day and sat on a park bench watching the people hustling to work as he ate and drank. He wondered about the face, who was it, why was he seeing it? He continued to watch the people and he dozed off.

"Hey, buddy," said the policeman as he touched Brandon's shoulder, "Are you alright?"

Brandon was startled, he was suddenly wide awake, "I must have fallen asleep, rough night officer, I'm okay."

"Just checkin', have a good day."

"Ah, do you know what time it is?"

"Yeah, I make it just ten after ten."

"Thanks, I have to be at work at 11:00 am. Better get going."

Brandon picked up his cup of now cold coffee and the wrapper for his bagel and hustled toward the pub. He tossed his trash in the waste basket at the corner, walked quickly to the alley and arrived at the Pub to see Steve and Stu checking the liquor stock and adding bottles to the under bar storage area. Stu saw Brandon and said, "Good morning, you ready to lift and carry some cases of beer, we got a bunch?"

"Sure," and he helped stocking beer for an hour.

"Okay guys, that's the last of 'em. Now let's grab some grub before the attack of the lunch crowd," said Stu as he headed for the bar.

Steve looked at Brandon and said, "Well c'mon, eat first, then we work."

"I'm with you," he replied as they followed Stu to the bar. The lunch crowd was sizable, but not record breaking and the break at 3:00 in the afternoon was very welcome. As he approached the bar to get a cold drink he saw Stu take a bag of day old bread out the back door to the alley. "Something for the home front — " he said to George.

"Not quite, he gives the bag to the first hungry looking bum he sees out there. Tells 'em to spread 'em around," said George with a look of disapproval and he turned back toward the range and continued his cleaning.

Steve noticed Brandon coming out of the kitchen and said, "You look like you could use a tall cold one," as he filled a frosted beer mug with root beer from the soda gun. "You and about two other people drink this stuff," he added with a grin.

Brandon sat at the end of the bar drinking and asking Steve questions about mixing drinks until it was time for him to return to the dishwashing station. The day progressed without event and ended again at midnight when Stu approached him and said, "Brandon, I told you that payday is every Friday and it's always a week behind. You got enough to carry you through the next week?"

"Yeah, I'm good. The rent is due next Friday and I have enough to fly on till then."

"Okay, just checking. I'll see you tomorrow."

Friday Morning . . .

Brandon was a bit tentative about walking out into the alley but he could not bring himself to admit to his fears, especially to these new friends and co-workers. At the appropriate time he ventured into the alley. The pavement was again damp from a brief shower, not enough to fill the chuckholes but damp across the pavement and up the canyon walls. A slight mist hung in the air and a gentle breeze rustled the litter on the ground. An occasional rat or a feral cat in pursuit of a mouse interrupted the silence for a moment till the mouse found safety, or became a meal. Brandon walked carefully at first, looking both left and right as he passed doorways and dumpsters. He again heard the whispers, the moan and movement behind doors. He looked for windows, but there were none. No windows, no large men with grey faces. He hurried as the symphony again grew more intense until at last he reached the main street. Breathing heavily and feeling the damp cold penetrate his jacket, he proceeded through the slowly moving crowd, bumping into people and apologizing as he went. He finally reached his apartment, went in, locked the door and turned on as many lights as he could. He sat in his chair still breathing heavily and turned on his television set. The same type programming was on as the night before and he eventually fell asleep shivering and still wearing his wet jacket.

He saw the open door and the grey man was standing outside looking. His face was scarred and stitched, his eyes were half closed and as he opened his mouth, he made a terrible moan as if he were in pain. Brandon turned and the second door was open, another man was standing there looking from left to right, he turned again and a third man had taken a few steps in his direction and Brandon could hear the moan the third man made as if replying to the first. Each man seemed to be staring at Brandon, as he looked from one to the next, they seemed to have moved closer. Their grey faces twisted in evidence of a great deal of pain, they drew closer, making those terrible sounds, each a low moan, together a frightening sound that made him try to run.

Brandon sat upright in his chair, again breathing heavily, he stripped off his wet clothes and turned on his shower, as hot as he could tolerate it. He stood in the shower turning red from the heat, but feeling safe as he washed off. He turned off the water, grabbed a towel and dried himself.

"Why do I let these dreams control me?" he muttered as he dried and dressed. It was 3:45 in the morning and he knew that he was not going to sleep again this night. There was nothing of any worth on the television and he noticed that the misting rain had stopped. He put on a dry coat and ventured out into the night. He walked aimlessly on the empty streets, thinking about the grey men in his dreams. He had lost complete track of time, but it was morning, almost sunrise, the sky was turning lighter and the stars were turning off. He stopped and surveyed the landscape, deciding where he was, he turned toward home and started to walk at a slightly hurried pace. The dreams still plagued him, his mind was running down all sorts of dark alleys and fighting his way back to safety. As he walked the dreams became darker and darker, the sounds became louder, the wind got colder, and his mind worked harder fighting off the thoughts of grey men. The moaning, he heard it again, a cat in heat or a man in agony, he didn't know. Then he heard a footstep behind him, then another, a little closer. He couldn't look, he hurried his pace and turned into an alley much like the one behind the Pub. Again he hurried his pace and again he heard the heavy footstep behind him. Then the moan again, louder — and he stopped suddenly about fifty feet into the alley, turned and found himself face to face with a man with a knife. A rather small man, but the knife served as an equalizer. He wore a thin fake leather jacket over a bright red shirt that was open half way down his chest. His shades were riding on top of his grease saturated hair, thick and disheveled, a gaggle of gold colored chains were leaving green stains on his neck, his eyes were reddened and his breathing betrayed a heavy smoker's lungs. Both men stared at each other, breathing heavily and the little man finally spoke.

"Give me your money, or I'll cut you open and let your guts hang out." As he waved the knife in front of himself, he leaned forward as if he was going to attempt a slash at Brandon's mid section.

Brandon remembered the rat baring it's yellow teeth and without any further thought he stepped twice toward the man and kicked at him as hard as he could. Brandon's six foot eight frame moving directly at the man froze him where he stood slightly bent forward and Brandon's kick with his long leg impacted the little man slightly below his solar plexus. Brandon's boot broke a number of the little man's ribs, pushing shattered bone into the man's lung and rupturing his spleen. The sound of cracking ribs and the gasping for air accompanied the man as he fell backward into a pile of trash against a dark brick wall. He lay spread on the trash heap, his shades broken against the wall, his face twisted in confused pain and the knife still in his right hand. Brandon stood over him uncertain about what he should do next. The man moved his hand with the knife, trying to ask for help but seemingly continuing his threat. Brandon brought his heavy boot in another kicking motion directed at the knife. His boot struck the man's wrist with a bone cracking sound and the knife spun away up against the wall. The man looked at his broken arm with wide eyes, unable to utter a sound. Brandon stood over him and watched as the little man struggled to draw a breath and finally stopped moving. His eyes bulged, his tongue looked swollen and blood trickled from his mouth. Brandon felt nothing, he knew the man was dead, he knew that he had killed him. He knew that he had defended himself and probably would not be charged with a crime. Then he noticed, it was quiet, the whispers had gone away, the moaning sounds had stopped and Brandon was again at ease. He looked around the alley, no one was there, no one saw what had happened. He leaned in closer to the dead man and opened his jacket. The man had five twenty dollar bills in his shirt pocket. Brandon took them out and without looking at him he muttered, "You can't spend this, but I can." He put the money in his pocket and casually walked away from the dead man laying in the alley. He felt no remorse, no pity for the dead man, no feeling of any kind, nothing. The man was dead, Brandon was not. The demons seemed to go away, Brandon was at ease. As he walked away, never looking back on his attacker, he was already putting the little man out of his mind. The man meant nothing, he was insignificant, Brandon was at ease, relaxed and safe. That counted, that mattered. Brandon's step had slowed, relaxed, eased. He walked back to the main street where he encountered the first flow of people hustling in both directions with the blank faces of under caffeinated worker bees all heading somewhere specific. It was just after 5:00 am and the world was starting another day. Such chaos, yet, such organization. Traffic lights turned colors and the masses responded. No leaders, just bees or ants hustling an un-programmed rush to somewhere. Brandon felt comfortable, at ease walking into the middle of this slow stampede and loping along toward his favorite coffee shop. He walked through the crowded main streets with a slight smile, nodding at people coming at him in a pleasant greeting of sorts. He did not appear at all threatening, just another young man on his way to or from work, perfectly normal.

* * *

SEVEN

Friday Morning ... Mutt and Jeff...

Philip "Pills" Decker was a small time criminal who had already done two tours through the prison system in as many states and was not considered a loss to society in general. He had no known relatives and nobody claimed him as a friend. "Pills" was not going to be missed. His death, as brutal as it appeared to be, did not stir anyone's inner being, did not generate a single tear. The only people who seemed to care were the patrol officers who responded to a dispatcher's call about a body in an alley, the coroner's minions who had to pick him up out of a pile of odiferous trash and the two detectives who wound up with his file.

Dan Carney pulled his patrol car into the alley, blocking entrance by any other vehicle. "Dispatch, this is car 4075, we are 10-23 in the alley. Time in is 06:05, please advise ETA of ME." He looked at his partner and said, "You want the guy or the gate?"

Frank Tollar took a final drink from his coffee cup, and said, "I'll take the gate — ." They got out of the car, Frank opened the trunk, picked up a roll of yellow 'Crime Scene tape' and walked toward the entrance to the alley. Dan took another roll of tape and walked slowly toward another man standing in the alley.

As Dan approached the man he said, "Are you Anthony Reyes — ?"

"Yeah — Antonio — Tony — and that's the guy I found. I called 9-1-1 right away and I didn't touch nothin'. Was that okay?"

Dan looked where Tony was pointing and said, "Yeah, you did good. You didn't touch anything, or pick anything up — ?"

"No man — look this is scaring me a little . . . I mean being here with a dead guy, you know ?"

"Yeah, I understand, you go over to the car and give me a minute, I'll be right there." Dan whistled over to Frank and indicated that Tony would be coming his way then turned and looked closely at the man laying in a pile of trash. He was apparently dead, but Dan felt for a pulse anyway. "Nope, you're gone buddy. You do look familiar —," he mumbled. Dan walked down the alley a bit farther looking for a place to limit the crime scene. There were no obvious signs of unusual activity and he tied his tape to a post about 100 feet from the body. He then crossed the alley and tied off the tape to a dumpster. He turned, looked at the scene from the tape line, thought for a minute and walked back toward the car. He was about to check again on the ME's team when their van pulled into the alley entrance. It was now 06:12.

Frank turned and Dan said, "I'll move our buggy, then you take a look at our vic, I think that we have met before." He moved the patrol car enough for the ME's van to pull into the alley, then moved it back to block the entrance again.

Sal Benito and Freddy Knolls got out of the van and stood about twenty feet up wind of the victim in the trash heap talking to Dan. The CSI lead came over to Dan. "You Carney?"

"Yep — ."

"Name's Chuck Barasso, I'm gonna' walk the scene first, then I'll look at the vic."

"Okay Chuck, I set the tape down there," said Dan pointing down the alley. "Let me know if you want it moved."

Chuck was a big guy, probably 6'-2" and well over 200 pounds but he carefully moved across the scene in a grid like pattern looking for detail everywhere. Finally after about 15 minutes he raised his head, "Hey Freddy, you can start shooting this one up. Not much to see, and I'll get on the vic."

Frank brought Tony back to Dan and continued to the victim. Dan pulled out a notebook and said, "Okay , let's take it from the top, Your name is Antonio 'Tony' Reyes, any middle name?"

"Oh yeah, it's Carlos, like my dad's name, you know Carlos Reyes —," he said nervously.

"Tony, relax, you're not in any trouble, this is all just for the record, okay?"

"Yeah, okay."

"Give me your address, phone number, e mail address, where you work, all that stuff."

Tony answered each question relaxing a little more with each answer. And Dan continued, "Now, do you know the victim?"

"No man like I said — ."

"That's okay, these are all standard questions, now relax, please," Dan said as he made notes in his pad.

"Yeah, okay."

"Now tell me what happened, I mean how did you find him?"

"I'm on my way to work, I do construction and I cut through this alley a lot."

"Uh huh, and where do you work?"

"The job they got me on today is on 'K' Street a few more blocks down."

"You work for a contractor?"

"I work outta the hall, they send to different jobs all the time."

"Okay, and who are working for today?"

"Ah, it's called Hammel Construction."

"What time are you supposed to be at the job, Tony?"

"We start at 6:30, but I try to be a little early, you know make the boss happy."

"Okay, that's a good thing, now what time did you find him, our victim?"

"Oh, I don't know man, but I called 9-1-1 right away, like maybe two seconds after I seen him laying there lookin all kinda dead, you know."

"Okay Tony. Now have you ever seen this guy before?"

"Oh man, I don't think so, but you know maybe he looks different when his face ain't all blue like that."

"Good point," said Frank as he approached the little gathering. He took Dan aside and quietly said, "I think this is 'Pills' Decker, we have had him in the station a few times. I'll call in, check on the D team and put Pills name in the magic box. Be right back."

Dan took Tony over to the patrol car and opened the back door, "You hop in and relax, the detectives will be here in a few minutes and they will have a few more questions for you, okay?"

"Hey man, I gotta get to work, you know, I mean the boss ain't gonna' be happy me bein late and all."

45

"Not to worry Tony, we are gonna' give you a ride to your job and explain everything. So relax."

*   *   *

Sal was a tall, strong lad and Freddy was shorter and very thin. They were often referred to as a 'Mutt and Jeff ' team because of the difference in their sizes. Sal had wanted to be a cop, it was in his family, but he had bad knees and passing the physical was not in the picture. Freddy was quiet, more likely to sit on the fringe of a group and listen, rather than to talk. He seemed to be happy just to be alive and able to walk around. Some mistook this as an indication that Freddy was not very bright. A skinny non-athletic kid who grew up in southeast Washington, managed to avoid the neighborhood gangs while in high school and never went to college, but he was bright and he had a talent. Freddy allowed people to think that was not the sharpest scalpel in the M.E.'s office, but he made an effort to be seen as a good kid a hard worker. He was new to this line of work, picking up bodies, moving them around the Morgue, doing a bunch of menial tasks that all needed doing. The strength that he played on was his talent was with the camera and his ability to see things that many others might pass over. He took very good crime scene photos, capturing the position of the body as well as the crime scene in all its magic. His photos were very much appreciated by the detectives handling cases where Freddy had photographed the scene. He also worked with the M.E. during an autopsy, capturing details that were determined to be significant.

Freddy had checked his camera, he was ready to do his photo shoot, as soon as Chuck and the detectives could do an initial survey of the site. He and Sal couldn't do anything until the detectives did their initial look around. Lake McLarry and his partner Kat Murano arrived at 6:18 am, parked outside the alley and walked in.

"Yo, McLarry, you and Kat caught this one?"

"Yeah Sal, I gotta talk to Chuck and you can have 'em, unless he found something interesting."

Chuck was packing up his bag and looked at Lake, "Not much here, Freddy has some shooting to do and his pics may catch a detail or two that we don't see on first pass."

Lake turned toward Freddy and Sal and said, "Give me a second or two guys."

"Hey man, no rush, we got all day, Right Freddy?"

"Yeah, right."

Lake approached the two patrol officers and said, "Hey Danny boy, how have you been?"

"Lake, good to see you. Who's your friend," asked Dan as Kat wandered over to the victim.

"Detective Katrina Murano, and no, she is not married and again no, you cannot have her number," said Lake as he took a notebook from his pocket. "Now what do we have here?"

"What we have is one dead guy in a pile of trash and the fella that found him in the back of our patrol car. I don't think he had anything to do with our vic being dead, but that's your call."

"Did you get his specifics . . . ?"

"Yeah, you wanna' copy em?"

"Yeah, then we will talk to him."

"You and the pretty lady detective?"

"Back off Danny boy."

"You said she was unattached — ."

""Yeah, well she's too old for you — "

Lake walked over Kat and looked at the victim laying in the trash pile."What do you think Kat?"

"I think that I know this guy. 'Pills' Decker, I think his name is Phil."

Lake handed her a pair of latex gloves and they both pulled them on.

"That's what we think Detective," said Dan as he joined them. "We've run him in a few times for pestering people. He's a seller when he can raise a stake and buy a supply."

Lake was checking the body, "This looks like a boot print on Pills' shirt, the guy was kicked or stepped on."

"Hey Freddy, do your thing over here so I can move the guy's shirt."

" Yeah, Chuck told me about that one Lake, gimme a minute." Freddy walked around in a modified spiral pattern, starting about ten feet away from the body, circling back and forth getting closer with each pass until he was next to the victim. He moved slowly inward noticing the body, the dirt , the trash, the puddles, all the while shooting. He walked quickly around the scene, getting different angles, adjusting his flash, sometimes taking several shots from the same perspective with different settings, like he knew what he was doing, he did. He knew exactly what he was doing. Every so often Freddy would point at something on the ground and Sal would bag it and number the bag, talking into a recorder.

"Done Lake, you move him, or his clothes and I'll get anything that looks interesting as you roll him around." Freddy watched and shot several more as Lake and Kat carefully moved Pills' shirt and moved the body. "Got it."

"Got what?" said Kat.

"The bruise on his chest and his stomach," said Freddy, "and his wrist, it's broken."

The detectives both looked at Pills' wrist then at each other and then at Freddy. He shrugged and said, "Chuck told me about those too," and he photo'd the two of them staring at his camera.

Lake and Kat checked his pockets, bagged his wallet, his watch, neck chains, a ring, some loose change and a few scraps of note paper. They counted two hundred thirty five dollars in his wallet and eighty four cents in change. The notes in his pockets included a few phone numbers and a list of drugs. Probably his wish list that he intended to turn around and sell. They made some notes, looked around for anything else unusual and joined Dan and Frank at their patrol car.

"Hey Murano, how you doing?"

"Frank, I thought you retired or died," chided Kat.

"Nice, real nice Murano. And you still look like the back end of a horse," Frank retorted.

"You two know each other," asked Lake?

"Yeah from back a few years when this little spitfire Marine first started playing cop."

"You were in the Corps — ," said Dan?

"Yeah, I did a turn back in 2000," she answered.

Dan looked at her and said, "Semper Fi, who were you with?"

"I was with the 2nd Marine Expeditionary Brigade, got a trip to Greece for a NATO exercise. Didn't have to shoot anybody and when I got out, I thought that I had a shot at the DC Police Force. Where were you that year?"

"In 2000, I was with the 31st Marine Expeditionary Unit. We went to Thailand on a little exercise. Didn't have to shoot anyone there either. Got out in '04 and decided to get into the family business," said Dan with a thoughtful gaze.

"Is your whole family is on the force?" asked Kat.

"It's more like the main business of the clan." Said Dan.

"What the KKK?"

"No, not Klan with a K — Clan with a C, a traditional Irish Clan. Ask Lake."

"Lake, what's the story here?"

"A clan, like a bunch of families that are related."

"So you two guys are related?"

"Yeah, we're related, like distant cousins and as our Uncle Sean used to say, "We don't carry cards, have picnics or wear T-shirts bragging about it, but we are family and we do look out for one another.""

"You both have the same uncle?"

"Yeah, Sean Daugherty, he lives in Cleveland, or he did. Last time I checked he was talking retirement and something about North Carolina." said Lake.

"Ah guys, can we get moving here," said Sal.

"Keep your shoes on Sal, we'll get it done. I thought you had all day."

"Just got a beep from the house, looks like we got another customer."

"I think we got everything that we need, Sal. Kat, you need anything else?"

"No, we're good you can wrap this one and we'll check in this afternoon or in the morning, see what you guys have for us," said Kat as she peeled off her gloves and threw them in a bag with Lake's.

Lake had a few more questions for Tony while Sal and Freddy put Pills in a body bag for transport to the morgue. Lake signed off on the M.E.s team and caught up to Kat. "This one is going nowhere. Two plus in his wallet, this was no robbery. I think Pills tapped the wrong guy and we probably will never know who. No way this Tony character did it and I'm not exactly heartbroken over Pills suckin' dust. Let's check in and do the paperwork, maybe we will finish by noon and grab another jacket or check on some oldies."

"Okay Lake, I'm with you."

"Danny boy, you can let our friend go to work and head back in. Get your paperwork done and let's talk after we see the ME tomorrow. Most likely and we can put a nice little bow on this one and shelve it."

Kat and Lake got in their car as a slight rain was trying to get started. Dan and Frank gave Tony a ride to his job and walked him in to help explain why he was late. Back in the station, Lake pulled Pills' record and was making a final entry when his phone rang. "Homicide, Detective McLarry — , yeah, we'll be there around one, okay." He hung up and looked at his partner. "That was quick, the M.E. wants to run this one with us now, so when you finish your write up we can grab lunch and head over there."

Kat was not enthused, "Yeah, what can he have for us that matters?"

"He probably wants to get this one out of the way, get on to more important things — . One way to find out for sure."

They finished the paperwork on Pills and put his file in the active drawer.

*   *   *

Detective team Martin Lake McLarry and his partner Katrina Maria Murano had been a team for the last six years. They were several years apart coming out of the academy and initially Lake had tried several times to have the Detective Sergeant change his partner assignment.

"Come on Lake, she'll grow on ya', 'fore you know it you two will the best of friends."

That was about how long it took, Kat was a fast learner and a hard worker, but at the same time, she could melt a guy's knees with a batting of her large brown eyes. After she had done her tour in the Marine Corps, she went straight into the police academy. Kat would not hesitate to stand up to a room full of obnoxious drunks. She might even have them lined up and saying please and thank you in very short order.

"She's a tough little broad," the DS had told Lake, "And someday you're going to appreciate her being around." Since then, Kat and Lake had worked together and proved to be a solid team. They had a decent solve rate, high enough to keep them near the top performing Homicide teams in the department. They had just finished a rather long and time consuming case and the killing of a small time hood in an alley was a relative vacation following their last assignment. The victim was a two time loser who was probably done in by his intended victim, and there was no feeling of sympathy for Philip "Pills" Decker. He was a some-time drug dealer when he could get enough money together to buy a supply from another equally small time but still higher up the food chain criminal. It was assumed that that was his objective in being in the alley.

*   *   *

Eight

Friday Morning ...   Hey man, relax, I'm not going to hurt you ...

Brandon walked back to his apartment, it was far too early to show up at the Pub. He doffed his coat, draped it across the back of his stuffed chair and turned on his television. "Weather and traffic reports, I really don't care," he said as he navigated through the several channels available to him. "Ah, news, what's happening in the world today?" he muttered to himself as he settled into his chair.

The reporter announced that a body was found in an alley in northeast, "Hmmm, kinda close to here —, " then he remembered, "Oh, I guess that I should watch, it might be that little man — " It might have been, but as the reporter stated, "The man's name is being withheld pending notification of family — " and he continued, "Further developments as they come available — ." Brandon continued to watch and as soon as the next story was on screen, he forgot about the funny little man that couldn't breathe.

He watched until the weather report came on and he turned the channel again. The early morning talk shows held no interest and after an hour he turned off the television, checked the time and decided to head toward the Pub.

A stop in the coffee shop, a bagel with cream cheese and a tall cup of coffee had Brandon back on the street, walking through the sea of people going everywhere and nowhere. He felt confident, relaxed and pleased with himself. No feelings of guilt about the little man, no concern for the man's family or their loss. He walked, drank and ate, and as he finished his bagel, he found himself standing at the corner next to the waste basket in front of the Pub. He finished his coffee, tossed the empty in the basket and turned toward the alley. As he entered the alley and stepped toward the Pub's door, he heard a slight noise, a movement of cardboard and papers. Brandon stood straight, thinking that he may be attacked again. He turned to see an older looking man at the side of the dumpster covered with cardboard and looking terrified. Brandon relaxed, stood tall and looking down at the man said calmly, "Hey man, relax, I'm not going to hurt you."

The old man cowered and tried to cover himself with more cardboard as if it would protect him. Brandon put his empty hands up, stepped backward and turned toward the Pub's entrance. George was in the kitchen checking a list of meats as Brandon entered. "Mornin' George — ."

"Hey Brandon, wanna' give me a hand here?"

"Sure let me dump my coat downstairs and I'll be right there."

"Actually, if you could go into the big cooler down there and start by giving me a count on the meat? The steaks are lined up on the left hand side as you walk in, top shelf . . ."

"Gotcha'," and he danced down the stairs to the basement. The walk-in coolers were at the bottom of the stairs and after hanging up his coat, Brandon flipped the light switch, walked in the cooler and began counting the steaks. "Yo, George, there are five packages of 'strips', three packages of sliced roast beef, two labeled 'R steaks', five packages of burgers and a small package of fillets. Those are all unopened."

Then on the second shelf there are pork chops, ham steaks, cutlets and — this next one is not labeled —."

George yelled down, "Okay, I'm gonna' toss you a note pad, write 'em down then come on back up we'll sort them out up here. Oh, and bring me two packages of burgers when you come up."

Brandon went to the base of the stairs and George tossed him the note pad and a pen. He was enjoying the work. He actually felt a part of the business, as if he were on a team, working together with Stu, Brenda, George, Steve and the others. A team, a family . . . Brandon was truly home.

*   *   *

Brandon wandered aimlessly for about an hour, looking at the people, peering into store windows and feeling very relaxed. He had no urge to hide in a theater, rather he wanted to see the faces of others as they laughed, cried, talked and sang, he was enjoying the human experience and did not want it to end. Want one thing and do another, Brandon directed his steps toward home. He got to his small apartment, turned on the television and did not look to see what was on. He walked directly to the bathroom, stripped off his clothes and stood in the shower. Hot then cold then hot then cold again. He turned off the water, dried and pulled on a loose fitting sweat shirt and matching pants, laid down on his bed and promptly fell asleep. The sun breaking through his single window woke him at a little past ten that morning. He had slept for only two hours and a few minutes . . . No memory of any dreams, no grey faces, windows or doors. He was rested, invigorated, alive. He returned to the bathroom, shaved, showered and dressed for the day. Once again he felt completely alive, he looked forward to his day, to seeing others and working. He walked to the coffee shop and bought a large coffee and started across town toward Stewart's Pub.

*   *   *

Nine

Saturday . . .   I killed that man and the demons left . . .

The day passed without significant event, Brandon arrived on time, worked through a relatively busy day, finished up sweeping and mopping the floors and left the restaurant around 1:15 in the morning. The streets were empty and quiet. Very quiet. At about this time, with very little light, the sounds of the night would magnify in Brandon's head and drive his fears to the front. He would normally feel compelled to run through the night to home. This night, Brandon was ambling along with only the pleasant music of the wind playing in the trees and an occasional car passing by. As he walked, he thought back to the previous night. To the confrontation with the little man and how his violent reaction to the man's threat drove all the whispers, the moaning and the footsteps away.

"I killed that man and the demons left." He walked and thought. "I killed the rat and they went away for one, two, four days." He continued, an occasional person of the night approached and passed by, no whisper, no threat. He felt a great relief, maybe this was what was needed. Show the demons who is to be feared, he Brandon should be feared or at least respected. He walked on at the slow easy pace until he arrived home. His apartment was warm and inviting. He tossed his coat over his stuffed chair and looked in his refrigerator. Bread and peanut butter, better than nothing, he made a sandwich and turned on the television. Again lame infomercials and very old reruns of very poor television programs. He finished his sandwich, turned off the television and stripped. Ten minutes in the shower, shaved and dried he stretched out on his bed. It was just after 3:00 am. He woke seven hours later, completely refreshed, rested and ready for a new day. He rose, dressed and headed for the coffee shop. It was Saturday, the temperature was in the low seventies, Atlanta was in town for the second of a three game stand, the weather was perfect for shopping and the restaurant was going to be busy at lunch and dinner. He hurried to work and arrived in time to once again help move cases of beer to the cooler behind the bar.

*   *   *

McLarry and Murano arrived at the M.E.'s office and traipsed up to Dr. Arthur Colburn's office. Colburn was intent on some document in front of him as the two detectives entered his office. "Hey Doc, What's happening?"

"Lake, it's been a while, almost three days," Colburn said with a big grin.

"Never long enough, eh Art. What'cha got?"

Dr. Colburn looked at Kat, "And a very good morning to you Detective. Colburn turned again and picked up a file, pulling out a print of a shoe print. "What I got is a foot print of a boot, a work boot, one of the steel toed variety."

"How can you tell it's a steel toe type?" asked Murano.

He smiled at Kat and stepped closer to her, "May I show you?"

She smiled, Kat got a lot of that treatment. People liked Lake, but teased him because they could and he was good at the parley of words, Kat was good looking lady and the same people that razzed Lake, treated her like a princess. "Please do, we are hungry for more information, so tell me about steel toes."

"The tread pattern we found is unique to this boot," Colburn said as he held up the picture of a pair of boots that he had just pulled from the

57

file. "And the damage to the sternum and ribs indicate something harder than the average leather toe, definitely a steel toe."

"Anything else?"

"Yeah, the bruising around the broken radius, right arm, was again a match to this boot. The same boot, right foot, size fourteen, this guy is big, at least his foot is big and he probably has long legs. Long enough to build up a lot of speed, enough to dislocate Mr. Decker's sternum, break those ribs and snap his arm."

"And?"

"And the boots are or were black, now some faded shade of black."

"And?"

"And nothing, took this poor slob a few minutes to die after being kicked. He was awake, musta' hurt. If the guy kicked him in the chest first, and he did, then he kicked the arm, probably because he was holding this — knife," he said as he pulled another picture out of the file. "The prints match, placement after a kick lines up right, thanks to Freddy on that one, and he was alive when the guy kicked the arm. I give it about three minutes minimum and six max from kick to lights out."

"Big guy, size fourteen boot, like a football player, a kicker?"

"I can't tell you that, I don't think kickers are all that big, as a rule."

"Big feet, long legs, more like a basketball player, if he has a sport."

"Again, don't know, but bring in the boot and I can match it to the footprint. He's had these boots for a while, there are some very distinct wear patterns. Here is a pic of the footprint."

"Thanks Art, I owe you again."

"That you do Lake, and some day I may collect, now get outta here, I have three other guests downstairs and they all get equal time and attention. You can take those pics with you, I got more."

"Thanks again Doc, and thanks to Freddy when you see him."

McLarry and Murano took the pictures and headed back to the car. "Think the guy watched Pills die?" asked Murano.

"I'd say yes, the first kick did the guy in, he was not going to get up after that, it's amazing that he held onto his knife and I'd guess that the guy was watching when Pills moved that hand with the knife. Got him another swift kick. Yeah, this guy coulda' walked away, but he was close, close enough to watch and close enough to feel a threat from that knife, yeah he was watching."

"I'm with you on that, but he didn't take anything, money, watch, nothing."

"Not a robbery not by the killer?"

"Nope, but Pills tried."

"Tried, and died."

*   *   *

The lunch crowd was large, Brandon was busy and in great spirits. He joked with the bus boys about cleaning tables quicker and finding dirtier dishes. He hummed some silly version of a tune that seemed stuck in his head and laughed at everybody's jokes. He hadn't this pleasant a day in years. The fears the plagued him every day of his life seemed to have melted into nothing and he was seeing the better side of everything and everybody.

The dinner crowd was as large as the lunch crowd and the restaurant was about to experience it's best day since opening several years before. Stu was happy, George was happy, the tips were running higher than usual, everybody was going to win today. At 6:00 pm, George called Brandon over to the prep table. "Brandon, you ready for a little dinner?"

"Sure, I just ran a load and there's not enough the start another one yet."

"Well then, take off that apron and go sit at the end of the bar, next to Stu."

"Really, okay," he walked out to the bar and Stu pointed at the stool next to himself.

"Come on over here and sit down, Brandon."

Brenda came over with a napkin roll and a glass of soda. "Good evening sir, your dinner will be here in a second or two."

Brandon looked confused and looked at Stu. He was smiling and said, "Don't worry, sit down and enjoy." Brandon sat and looked confused, Stu was laughing, "Brandon you have been with us only a week and we are thrilled with your help. This is just a little thanks for the extra help that you give almost every day." Brenda came out of the kitchen with a large steak dinner and placed it in front of Brandon. "I believe that you said a proper steak has a slightly pink center, enjoy."

Brandon sat up straight, smiled, looked at Brenda and Stu and said, "You guys are great, thanks."

Stu held out his hand and said, "If you will excuse me, I have a load of dishes to wash while our regular guy is goofing off."

Brenda laughed and said, "Don't you let that steak get cold, eat."

Brandon finished his dinner as Stu was coming out of the kitchen. "How was it Brandon?"

"It was perfect, thanks."

"Brandon, it's a two way street, so thank you."

"Stu, I'd better get back in there, the line is already out the door and we're just getting started with dinner."

"Go get 'em," said Stu as he walked behind the bar and poured himself a short glass of orange juice.

Brandon picked up his plate and silver and went back into the kitchen. "Hey George, you do a beautiful steak, thanks."

George smiled and gave him a thumbs up. The night went along with the same feeling, everybody was in great spirits and when the waitresses were settling up, Brandon wound up with just under fifty dollars from the tip pool. Bill and Frank were talking about going to the baseball game the next afternoon and they asked Brandon if he would like to join them. He had never gone to a baseball game and it appealed to him. "What time is the game?"

"We like to get there a little early and watch the batting practice, so we will be there about noon," said Bill.

"Yeah, and their record is like 66 and 89, so the crowds are getting smaller all the time and tickets are easy to get. We get the cheap seats and after a few innings, we get down closer, sometimes right behind the dugouts," said Frank.

Brandon felt very relaxed and a bit excited about the game, "I'll try to make it, is there a chance of rain?"

"Yeah, but so what, a little sprinkle won't hurt", Bill grinned, "It's being there and havin' a few beers and seein' all the people."

They talked for a few minutes and Brandon learned that Stu picked someone from his staff every Saturday night to have dinner at the end of the bar. "I was lucky to find this place," he mumbled to himself as he was saying good night to Bill and Frank. He ventured out into the alley and turned toward home. It was now Sunday morning and he had a full day to himself to enjoy. The thought of the baseball game came was appealing and he hoped that it would not rain. The night was quiet, the normal gentle breeze rustling loose papers in the alley was the only noise he heard as he pushed his hands into his pockets and easily strode down the alley toward the main street.

*   *   *

T EN

Sunday Afternoon ... I was lucky to find this place ...

Lake was off on Sunday and had taken his wife and kids to church. They stopped after at a McDonalds for breakfast and were home in time for he and little Marty to watch the ball game.

"Is it gonna' rain, Dad?"

"Looks like it could, but that may not stop the game, let's see." He tuned in the television and they snuggled in on the couch to watch. The weather was a little cloudy, but the game started with Hernandez on the mound. He got through the first few innings without giving up a run and getting help from his own team in the form of a run in each of the first two innings.

"Dad, why do they wear the red shirts sometimes and the white shirts other times?"

"Well the teams want to look different. It used to be that the traveling team wore white and the home team would wear a colored uniform. Now, I think they talk before a game and as long as they tell the teams apart, they wear which ever uniform they want. So for our team, red shirts are usually what they wear when the team is at home and the white is usually when they are playing at somebody else's park."

"Oh, okay."

*   *   *

Brandon was standing with Bill and Frank at an entrance above the third base dugout as Bill explained the shirt colors to Brandon.

"Oh, okay."

"Keep your eyes open for seats that stay empty, we can usually get 'em if nobody comes along, the ushers don't care, it's easier on them too if everybody is down closer." Hernandez gave up a home run in the fifth and faced two guys in the seventh giving up another run. Brandon was having a great time, just being there with no thought of grey faces or dark places. His mind was taken with the game, the crowd, the excitement, he was in heaven.

A foul ball came screaming into the crowd, causing the three amigos to move quickly out of the way and not get hit. A high school kid several rows back and to their left put his glove in the way as much for self defense as anything and caught the ball. The cameras zoomed in on the kid and replayed the catch several times noting the diving spectators and the kid standing firm with his glove at the ready.

*   *   *

"Nice catch," yelled little Marty, "Dad did you see those guys jump out of the way?"

"Yeah, look they're playing it again."

"Dad, Look at that big guy jump. He went upside down with his feet in the air."

"Marty, that ball would make me jump outa the way, and I used to play short and third . . . that ball was movin'." They played it again, and the tall guy looked a little silly jumping out of the way.

*   *   *

"Wow, that was close," said Brandon. "Close but cool." The game was tied going into the bottom of the seventh and with the bases loaded,

Desmond pounds a single up the middle bringing in two runs. Four to two, and that's how it ended. "That was so cool, I want to do this again, when's the next game?"

"We get the Phillies on Monday, Tuesday and Wednesday."

"You don't sound excited about that, are they any good."

"The Phillies, yeah, they're good, damn good and Halladay is scheduled for tomorrow."

"Halladay?"

"Yeah, Roy Halladay, pitcher for Philly, the guy is tough to beat."

Those games are all here, but we'll be workin', then I think they go to New York for three games with the Mets and that's the season."

"Wish I had done this earlier, that was great," said Brandon.

"Yeah, it's great when you win, but we seem to have lost more than we won this year so we don't go to the post season."

Brandon was still on a high cloud. "There's always next year."

"Yeah we've heard that before," Bill frowned.

"Yeah, a few times," Frank grinned.

As the three were leaving the ball park, a vendor was coming their way with a box of hats announcing that all hats were now 50% off. Brandon walked over to a vendor and came back with a new blue baseball cap. "I offered him five bucks for this and he took it. What'a ya think, do I look like I could play third base?"

They made their way to the Metro for a ride home laughing about Brandon playing third and diving out of the way of every line drive that might come at him. *   *   *

Eleven

Sunday Evening ... Hey you're that guy on the news ...

Brandon got home at a reasonable hour and sat up watching television. When the late news came on he was watching one channel and the coverage of the game was brief and no film. He changed the channel and missed the reports on the other two major stations. He was hoping for some film of what he had seen and maybe even catch a glimpse of himself. No such luck. He finished off a bag of chips and a soda and decided to get a good night's sleep. Monday was going to be a new day and he was still feeling good about himself.

Monday Morning ...

Morning came and Brandon was up by eight and ready for the day. He stood in the shower, shaved and dressed and stepped out to meet the world. The sun was somewhere behind a cloud, periodically peeking out and casting beams of warmth and light in his path. He walked to the nearby Starbucks, bought his usual coffee and bagel with cream cheese and moseyed toward Stewarts Pub. He noted a shoe store across the street and he walked in. "Do you carry large sizes?"

"I think that we can help you, we get some basketball players in here and they usually take the larger sizes."

"Let's take a look." He found a pair of fourteens that he thought might fit. "A little snug at the toes — . Do you have anything larger?"

"We don't carry anything over fourteen, but I think that I got a couple returns in the back. You got a few minutes, I'll go get 'em?"

The salesman went into the back room and returned in a few minutes. "These two are fifteens and these are fourteens, but a different manufacturer. Sometimes the different brands are cut just a bit different and they might work. You should try all on and then decide."

Brandon tried all three pairs and the white fifteens won out. "These work, are they the same price as the sale shoes?"

"Yep, these are twenty five plus tax. How about the other pair, the black ones, for you, they are knocked down to fifteen? That would be forty total."

Brandon checked his wallet. He had $87 and thought for a second. Okay, I'll take 'em."

"Should I wrap them up for you?"

"I'll wear 'em and you can put these things in a bag, you keep the boxes." He walked around the store with a light step noting the difference in weight immediately as the salesman rang them up and returned with his change. "I should have gotten some of these a long time ago." The Brandon noticed a rack with some bright colored knit shirts and another 'SALE' sign.

"How much are the shirts?"

"Those are ten each, the rack behind is fifteen apiece."

Brandon had about twenty that he figured he could afford so he found two on the ten dollar rack that were his size. "I'll take these too."

"Hey, we got jeans, tees, socks, belts, —."

"Naw, I need the rest of my cash to eat. I'll come back again when I get paid"

"We run a sale every other week here, till we get rid of the overstock, so in two weeks, try us again."

"Sounds good to me," said Brandon as he went back out into the flow of human traffic buzzing to work or meetings or where ever people buzz to.

It was just after 10:15 when he arrived at the restaurant and Stu, Brenda and Steve were already there.

"There he is, TV star, Brandon," said Steve, "I saw you on the news last night, you moved pretty fast for a big guy, getting out of the way of that foul ball."

"Was that on TV? Wow."

Stu was smiling, "Yeah, I saw it too, you looked good."

"Pretty cool, Brandon," said Brenda, "I missed the news but I have heard about it from everybody else here, you're famous."

"Yeah, for about two minutes and then I'll be just one of the crowd again, hey anybody want and autograph?"

They all laughed and Stu said, "No but you can help me stock the cooler downstairs."

Brandon smoothed his hair back, turned his face up towards the ceiling and said, "Physical labor, well, after all I am famous." Again everybody laughed. Then he turned toward Stu and said, "You think I could milk this for more than two minutes?"

Grinning, Stu replied, "Nope."

"Okay, then, let's stock the cooler." He walked out of the bar area and into the kitchen with his nose almost straight up and his hands on his hips. Again they all laughed. The day was fun for Brandon, being playfully teased about his being on the news. Several customers were sitting at the bar having lunch and talking about the game. Steve asked if they had seen the foul ball hit into the crowd, and once again Brandon was in the spotlight. He had reacted as anyone would have wanted to, getting out of the way of the ball. Not everyone could have moved that quickly or gracefully and each time Steve mentioned it to a customer, Brandon was invited out to take a bow. His life had been one of hiding from unknowns, avoiding contact with those whom he didn't know, living in dark theaters and staying awake rather than allowing the dreams to play with his fears.

This was fun, this was life and he was beginning to feel alive. The baseball game was exciting, not because of the play of the game, but rather because of the crowd, the people and Brandon being one of them. His mind wandered to football, hockey, basketball all games that drew large exciting crowds. He wanted to go to each one, he wanted to experience the thrill of the crowd again and maybe even get on television again. He wanted to be with Bill and Frank again, eating pizza, drinking beer and being a bit goofy. He wanted to stand and cheer when his team did well and he wanted to boo when the officials blew a call. He wanted to be one of the crowd.

*   *   *

Lake and Kat had two new cases tossed their way that morning. One was a domestic squabble that ended with the wife's new boyfriend planting a knife in her husband. Had they called for an ambulance as soon as it happened, the guy might have made it, but they chose to argue about their story while he bled out on the floor between them. When they did call, "It was an accident," and "I didn't mean to do that" and "I wasn't thinking" and "I didn't know it was that bad" the two were arrested and booked.

Kat leaned back in her swivel chair and looked at the ceiling, "Some people —, I've been doing this job for what, nine years now and it still boggles my little mind when people don't recognize how much danger that a guy like that was in . . . they could'a called it in immediately and saved all that 'I didn't do it' crap after makin the call and the guy might still be alive. Then they're lookin' at an assault, now they're looking at some serious time for murder — and the guy is DEAD."

"Kat, I hear you and no argument, people are strange and do some really dumb things." Lake opened the other file and said, "Here's another one — guy kills his girlfriend because he THINKS she is cheating on him —. Does he ask her first, NO. Does he ask anybody anything first, NO. The dumb son of a bitch sees a situation from one point of view and he goes off, now we have a dead girl, seventeen and a dumb kid almost eighteen, going to prison for a long time, he may never come out."

"You could'a got a job sellin' used cars," said Kat.

"Aaww —, what about Pills, anything new on him?"

Kat picked up another file and browsed through it. "No, word is he was trying to build up a stake, a pile of cash to buy a supply to pedal on the street."

"And he picked on our steel toed rib kicker," Lake quipped.

"So it seems, but if it were a regular citizen that he picked on, you would think, one swift kick and 'Steel Toes' would have run for it, try to find a cop."

"Yeah," said Lake, "so who wears steel toed shoes at that time of night, in that part of town? Not likely another drug pusher like Pills, and not someone up that food chain. It's gotta be Joe Citizen, drinking late and on his way home, or on his way to work, some construction or industrial type work where steel toes are required?"

"Maybe works in a warehouse, but most likely not on office worker type."

Lake tossed the file on his desk and said. "We may never know, and very few people will ever care. Pills did not have any family or friends. Lets visit the scene when this rain stops and see if there are any construction sites nearby."

"Or warehouses."

"Yeah, or warehouses."

*   *   *

The day passed to night and Brandon did an uncounted number of bows in the restaurant. He had a wonderful day and as the hour approached 12:00 midnight, he was wearing down, he was getting tired."

"Hey, TV star." said Bill, "You look beat, it must be rough taking all those bows. Why don't you let me finish up here and you head on home, get a good night's sleep."

Stu and Brenda were finishing up the counts and agreed.

"Both of you guys get outta here, I didn't go to the game, so I'll sweep up, and I'll see you guys tomorrow," said Stu.

"No argument there," said Bill as he grabbed his coat and turned toward the door.

Brandon truly looked beat, "Thanks Stu, see you in the morning." He took his bag with his boots and walked out the door into the alley. It was dark, it was chilly and there was a gentle mist just short of a rain shower. Brandon walked toward the main street and thought about the day, the jokes, the teasing, the laughter and the applause from the customers as he took his bows. He was happy, tired and happy. When he reached the main street, he turned left to go home and almost walked into three men coming the other way.

"Whoops, excuse me", said one of the men, Brandon smiled and was about to say "No problem" when one of the men said, "Hey you're that guy on the news, nice move buddy."

Brandon grinned, turned facing the three and shrugged his shoulders, then turned again and continued on his trek home.

*   *   *

T WELVE

Tuesday Morning . . . There's a guy sleeping next to the dumpster . . .

The walk home was uneventful after his encounter with the three men on the street. Brandon was very tired and looked forward to getting a good night's sleep. He stopped at an all night convenience store and picked up a bottle of soda and a bag of chips, his late night snack, and continued home. The soda was warm and he had not filled the ice cube trays in his freezer, so he put the bottle in the refrigerator and laid the chips on his small table. He sat on the edge of his bed, took off his boots and thought about turning on his television. "Maybe a rerun — of —" and he fell backward sound asleep.

No dreams, no whispers, no strange sounds at all, this was the fourth night in a row that he slept through. Four nights, he had control, he was the big man now. His father's words "just think of me and I will come into your dream." Now Brandon felt in command, he had killed the rat and scared the demons. Then he killed that man with a knife and the demons retreated farther into the darkness, maybe forever. He started to think about how long the demons would stay away.

It was almost 9:30 and Brandon started to move, shower, shave and dress. He had to hustle, get back to the Pub, the people, his friends, the laughing, the work. He was out the door before 10:00 and at the coffee shop five minutes later. Coffee and bagel in hand, Brandon walked quickly with a light step, eating and sipping. He arrived at the Pub a bit before 10:45 to a warm "Good Morning," from Brenda.

She was writing the specials on a dry marker board said, "Stu's in the kitchen, he could use some help with a delivery."

Brandon responded with a smile and a "Good morning" to Brenda and he went to the kitchen tossing his empty coffee cup in a trash can. "Good morning George, is Stu back here?"

"Yeah, he's taking these cartons down to the cooler," as he gestured toward a pile of cardboard boxes.

"Okay," and Brandon picked up the top carton and went down the stairs to the basement. Stu was unloading another carton and stocking the shelves.

"Hey Brandon glad to see you, I could use some — , I see you have already started, I was going to say help."

"I'll get the rest of the cartons first and then we can stock the shelves and the cooler."

"Yeah, great."

They worked for the next twenty minutes finishing up the unloading and shelving. Brandon picked up the torn open boxes and started up the stairs. "Do these get recycled or pitched in the dumpster?"

Stu was grabbing a few scraps and following Brandon up the stairs, "Well, sometimes there is a green dumpster out there for recycling, otherwise just pitch 'em."

" Okay," and Brandon took the remainder of the stairs in pairs and was outside before Stu got to the third step. He found the blue dumpster but no green one and was tossing the scraps when he saw something move next to the dumpster. He closed the lid and walked around the end of the blue box and came face to face with a man trying to stay dry under a large cardboard sheet. The man could have been eighty or more likely sixty with a lot of rough mileage. He was wearing two coats that Brandon could see and a pulled down knit hat that had been clean at some time long ago. His beard was weeks or maybe months old , his face was dirty and his shoes had holes in them.

The old man squinted and raised a hand as if defending himself and said, "Please don't hurt me, I don't got nothin', I jus' wanna' sleep, please."

Brandon was used to seeing people like this, he was himself one or two steps from that life and had never given much thought to how pitiful they were. Homeless, alone in the cold, the wet, the wind. Open to abuse or attack by rats, bugs or any passerby. "I'm not going to hurt you," and he turned away and went back inside the restaurant.

Stu saw the look on Brandon's face and said "Hey, what's the matter, you okay?"

"Yeah," he thought for a second then continued, "There's a guy sleeping next to the dumpster, surprised me, kinda feel sorry for the guy."

"Old guy, squints when he talks?"

"Yeah, sounds like him."

"Probably Lew, don't know his last name. He's been sleeping out there on and off for about a year, nice guy, afraid of everything and everybody. He thinks the world is going bad and everybody wants to kill him," Stu smiled and continued, "He sorta trusts me, I'll go see him." He started towards the door and turned toward George.

"Yeah, I know, here's three," and George picked out three hard rolls from the bag of yesterday's leftovers and handed them to Stu. "You know, you should run him outta here."

Stu took the rolls and walked out the back door. George looked at Brandon, smiled and said, "He would feed the entire alley if we let him. Guy has a heart as big as the state of Georgia."

"That's not a bad thing," said Brandon.

"Never said it was, I just raze him so he doesn't give the store away. That and I worry that he is drawing a bigger crowd out there than we need."

The lunch crowd started to come in and the kitchen was busy for a few hours. Brandon noted a bag of trash and volunteered to take it out to the dumpster. "I got this," He walked outside and saw Lew sitting up finishing one of the rolls. "Hey man, you okay?"

Lew looked at him and squinted, "I saw you before."

"Yeah, I was just wondering, are you okay?"

"Yeah," he said as he staggered to his feet and started to walk away.

"I won't hurt you."

"Okay," and he kept moving, slowly but steady.

*   *   *

Kat walked the length of the street that backed to the alley where Pills had met his end and Lake went around the block to the front of the other half of the block. They were looking in windows and checking the activity inside as many stores and offices as they could without stirring up any curiosity from the inhabitants. They met at the corner of the alley and together walked its length checking everything. Lake looked at Kat, "Let's go at least one block each way and see what's happening."

"Split up or stick together?"

"Same routine as this block, we do the fronts alone, but walk the alley together."

"Works for me," Kat grinned and said, "North first."

"Let's do it."

They covered two blocks each way and were about to pack it in when they saw two uniformed officers walking toward them.

"Can I help you folks," asked the taller of the two.

Lake squinted looking at the taller cop, "Hey Danny boy, what brings you to this alley?"

"Dan Carney", he said as he extended his hand toward Kat, "We met Saturday morning at the other end of this alley."

"I remember — , Clan with a 'C' — ."

"Yeah, with a 'C' — . We were just walking the alleys, keep in touch with the locals and you never know what you might find."

"Frank chimed in looking at Lake, "We were just about to step into that coffee shop and grab a bite, you want to join us?"

Kat smiled, and said "Yeah, we'll join you," and the four of them walked in the alley door to a small coffee shop, found an empty table and ordered a little lunch.

Lake was checking his notes and said, "We did a walk about here when Pills met our man. Now this time we wanted to get into it a little deeper. The ME has given us something to chew on, a size fourteen steel toed boot, older, well worn probably a faded shade of black."

"Fourteen, " said Frank, "Is this guy some kinda monster?"

"No, probably just tall," said Lake, "I don't think our little friend would take on a linebacker, so the guy is probably tall and thin, not threatening looking."

Kat set her coffee down and added, "Doc Colburn figures he is tall, able to get his foot moving pretty fast to do the damage he did to Pills."

"So you are looking for a tall man — , like six- four, six -five, maybe more — ," posited Dan.

"You understand, this is all guess work, but yeah, probably more than six-five, size fourteen steel toed boots, well worn, faded black — and he was walking through this alley at two or three in the morning," replied Kat.

"So he may be a vagrant, living on the streets, maybe a stock broker out looking for a pack of cigarettes, we don't know," said Lake, "But if you put it all together and look at the simplest explanation what we get is a construction worker, or maybe a warehouse worker, someone who would be likely to be wearing steel toed shoes."

Dan thought for a second and asked, "What is he doing at two or three in the morning?"

"I don't know Danny boy, maybe he stopped for a few drinks, closed the bar and was walking home. After all, it was a Friday night. Maybe he was heading for the Metro. Anyway, we want to check out the obvious first, so Kat and I checked the places that have exits into this alley both north and south of this location."

Dan looked at Kat with a raised eyebrow, "And you got zip?"

"Right, so we will expand the search another block each way after we finish here," said Lake as their lunches arrived.

The conversation wandered to the weather, the end of another disappointing baseball season and touched on the football game against Philadelphia coming the next weekend. Kat looked at Dan and asked, "So you have family in Cleveland, is that where you are from?"

Dan sensed an opening and replied, "No, I was born and raised here in the DC area, actually in Northern Virginia. We have family all over the country. There are McLarrys, Carneys, Rynnes, Dixons and more — all connected through the Clan, with a 'C'."

Lake was about finished and said, "Yeah all connected and this connection has to get back to work. You ready to hit it Kat?"

"If you're ready, you could get us a refills on our coffee to go and I'll be right back —," as she stood up and turned toward the restrooms.

Lake looked at Dan, "With a 'C' — ?"

Frank said, "Speaking of refills —," as he took his cup over to the counter to pay the tab.

Dan said, "C'mon Lake, she's nice, I like her — ."

"Yeah, and she's my partner," said Lake as he turned toward the counter with their coffee cups in hand.

Frank took his coffee and walked out to the alley again, waiting for Dan to join him. Lake filled his and Kat's cups and stepped outside to wait with Frank and Dan started to refill his cup when Kat came out of the restroom. She walked over to Dan and said, "I remember something about Lake going to Cleveland years ago to help look for a missing girl. I think it was a cousin."

Dan's face grew serious, "Yeah, that was in '91, I was just a kid about nine or ten and my dad wouldn't let me go. He went, with Lake and a couple of others from around here. All family, they looked for days before the search was called off. Her name was Annette. I met her once at a wedding in Pittsburgh, but can't for the life of me remember her face, just her name."

"So they never found her?"

"Turned out to be a serial killer case. Annette was one of his first victims. Made some of the papers down here recently when they found the bad guy."

Kat perked up, "Yeah, I kinda remember that one, wasn't he a salesman?"

Dan picked up his coffee and the walked out to the alley, "Yeah, he was a salesman." Dan seemed a little uncomfortable discussing his cousin and quickly asked Frank if he was ready to get moving.

Frank stopped and asked Lake, "Have you guys been looking at all the remodeling jobs in these buildings. There are always little remodeling jobs going on around here. You know, when a store goes under or moves and a new outfit moves in, they tear down walls, put up new ones, paint, do carpet, stuff like that."

"So any tall construction workers?" asked Lake.

Dan said, "Who knows, right now we got nothing that helps, but we'll keep our eyes open and if we see or hear something, I can very easily dial your number." He was looking at Kat as he spoke.

She smiled and handed him one of her cards. "That number rings at both of our desks, the cell, that one is mine alone."

Lake rolled his eyes and said, "We gotta get back to work. You guys see something, call either one of us." They left Dan and Frank in the alley and walked back to their car. "Were you making eyes at that poor guy, Kat?"

"Hey, he seems like a nice guy, I'm allowed."

"He's a little young, don't you think?"

"Thanks Lake, that's just what I need to hear." They got into their car. "Only a coupla years differece."

*   *   *

T HIRTEEN

Tuesday . . .   She wanted me to stay . . .

The Tuesday lunch crowd was average and the dinner crowd was weak. Not unusual, Tuesdays were not ever the best day unless it was the night before a holiday. Brandon's fame was fading fast and he didn't get any curtain calls that evening. The last of the customers left around 11:30 and with all dishes, pots and pans cleaned and stowed, Brandon had swept the barroom floor, ran the vacuum in the two dining rooms and mopped the kitchen all by midnight. He was sitting with Stu at the bar, talking about the baseball team and the structure of the play offs leading to the World Series.

"Not much happening now, If you want to hit the road early, I promise not to tell Brenda." Brandon laughed, Brenda kept track of everybody's time and checked the time cards every week before they were sent to their accountant.

"I'll take you up on that, I'm still a little tired and another good night's sleep would be great. I'll see you in the morning," and he went into the kitchen, grabbed his coat and walked out into the alley. As he turned to head to the main street, he saw Lew trying to hide behind the dumpster. Brandon put his head down and walked down the alley, as if he did not see him and when he was about twenty feet passed the dumpster he said, "Good night Lew, see you tomorrow." He smiled to himself, kept his head down and continued to the end of the alley.

The walk home took Brandon twenty blocks north and another four east. The air was crisp, clean after a mild washing rain and the sounds of the city were pleasantly quiet. He was thinking about Lew, the poor guy living in the alley, eating scraps of other people's meals and constantly in fear of being beaten and killed. He thought about the baseball game and going to another one next year, and ducking out of the way of another foul ball. He thought about Stu, Brenda, George, Steve and he smiled again. "I guess I'm a lucky guy, they are nice people," he mumbled as he walked. Then he thought about Karen. He felt a chill, the wind picked up a bit and he heard something move behind him, he looked, nothing was there. He remembered the rat, and the wind died down, the sound was no longer there. He was almost home. He never gave thought to Pills Decker. When he got home he opened his bag of chips and poured a glass of soda, cold soda.

*   *   *

Five blocks south and four more to the west of Brandon's apartment, Dan Carney and Frank Tollar were walking through the neighborhood where Pills had met his end. They made a point of noticing people's shoes, especially the taller people. As they covered the immediate territory, they also looked for recent construction sites and wandered into a few, just looking around. Neither the contractors nor the workers seemed to mind their presence. It was a subtle signal to potential vandals and thieves that the police were in the area and it might just keep them from tagging walls and stealing tools or whatever else was not nailed down. Several times they were told that they had to have hard hats, eye protection and a reflective vest to go into certain areas. Steel toed shoes were not always required but a number of people said that they were recommended and, "Most of the guys wear 'em."

No unusually tall men with work boots were found, mostly a shorter variety of people who may or may not have been in the country legally. Neither Dan nor Frank was one to stir the pot. If the customs people wanted to run these guys out of the country, that was their problem. These two officers were interested in peace and quiet. Finding a tall, steel toe wearing man so he could call the cute detective was also on Dan's mind.

*   *   *

Brandon woke early, before the day had gotten started. It was a minute or two past six thirty and the sky was still dark and clouded over. A cool gentle rain was falling as little rumbles of thunder were rolling in the western sky. Brandon stood and looked out his window into the alley between buildings and up toward the dark murky heavens. Dark and somewhat forbidding, promising to keep raining for the time being. He felt a slight chill and dressed quickly, pulling on his new white shoes and an old beat up Carhart jacket and a baseball cap.

"A fine day for a walk, take in the morning air," he said to himself as he stepped out into the misting morning. He walked for an hour as the sky lightened but the rain continued. He noticed the fall flowers standing tall as if to soak in all the rain they could and the leaves on the trees glistening as the dirt and dust was washed away. The rain gave the thirsty plants another brief drink and they were all responding with brighter colors and a clean smell. Life was all around, drinking. Even the birds, chirping away as they hopped along the sidewalk poking at bugs and seeds seemed to be enjoying this gentle bath of energy. Brandon was feeling confident, happy and ready for an full week of whatever may come his way. As he was passing a bookstore, he thought about coming back when it was open and buying a book. He had never read a book all the way through and it was now on his list of things to do.

"Coffee, yes coffee," it was almost eight o'clock and time for his coffee and bagel. He aimed for the nearest coffee shop, a Starbuck's directly across the street. The people coming into town for the day were amassing in the shop and Brandon was lucky to squeeze in through the door.

"Let's have a little cream cheese on the bagel today," and he spied an empty chair in a corner adjacent to a large window. He sat in the coffee shop, looking out the window, watching the people hustling between rain drops and dancing around puddles. He was amused, pleased and still very happy. His life had not been this relaxed since his father was run down. It had been almost eleven years since that day and every day since had seen fear, pain and misery. Now there was peace, now the demons, the grey men were keeping their distance. Brandon had shown that he was not to be threatened, not to be pushed. He was a force that could strike back with power, with confidence. He was in charge of his life and the demons were now powerless.

As he finished his bagel, Brandon noticed the time was fast approaching nine and knowing that it would take about twenty minutes to walk to Stewart's Pub, he thought about taking the rest of his coffee with him as he walked. Then he noticed an attractive young lady who seemed to be looking for a place to sit with her breakfast. "Excuse me, miss, I'm done here, you can have the table."

She smiled, one of those sunshine smiles that make a man feel years younger, "Oh, thank you," as she sat and batted her bright blue eyes at Brandon.

"Stay dry and enjoy," and he walked out the door thinking to himself that she wished he would stay and talk. That was a common fantasy of men who are too old, or too poor, too out of shape or too married —, don't look back, don't say any more, leave them wanting you more than you want them. He knew full well that if he were to look back, the young lady would probably not be looking after him, but would rather be looking for another chair for someone else to join her. But, that was the trick, don't look, just imagine and enjoy the scenario that would never play out in reality. The remainder of the day would fly by with that thought, 'she wanted me to stay.'

The rain continued, misting not pouring. No break in the clouds, no bright sky on the horizon, but a beautiful day non-the-less to him. He walked and drank his coffee, felt the mist on his face and imagined standing at the tiller of a sailboat with the young lady in the coffee shop huddled behind him. It was just after nine twenty five when Brandon arrived at the Pub. Steve was getting ready to open boxes and restock the bar when Brandon walked in and said, "Mornin' Steve, do you need a hand with the boxes?"

"Brandon, your timing is perfect, yeah, I could use a hand."

"Give me a minute to hang up my coat, pitch my empty cup and dry off some of this rain and I'll be right with you."

Steve leaned against the bar and picked up his orange juice. One big drink and Brandon reappeared from the kitchen, wiping his head with a hand full of paper towels, ready to pitch in. They carried in three boxes of new bottles, emptied the boxes and lined the new bottles up on the bar.

"Brandon, grab those empties below the bar and match 'em up with the new soldiers."

"Okay, that's easy enough." He pulled nine empties out from below the bar and matched them with nine new ones.

Steve was looking at the remaining liquor in bottles behind the bar and pulled six other bottles out with very little left in them. "Okay, now let's match these up with new guys."

"Okay, why do you do this?"

"It's a check on what we buy and what we have sold. Very simple method and we tell Stu exactly what empties we are tossing out. He tracks the booze in and out, matches it against the sales figures and we see if we are making or losing money. See, simple."

"Yeah, I get it."

"So we take the pour spouts off the empties and put them on the new bottles, the empties go into the boxes and the new bottles go behind the bar."

"So should I rinse out the pour spouts, before they go into the new bottles?"

"Yeah, then I will place them behind the bar, every bottle has a location that Russ and I are used to."

"Gotcha, you don't want to pour bourbon in someone's gin and tonic."

"Right. You change out the spouts, I'll put 'em away."

"Okay." Brandon was feeling better every minute. He had never worked behind the bar and as he was helping out , he imagined himself mixing drinks, pouring drafts and talking to the customers."

Steve was watching Brandon as he moved around behind the bar. "You want to learn the bar business, Brandon."

"It seems like it would be fun, dealing with people directly, rather than scrubbing their dirty dishes. Oh, but I'm not complaining, happy, yeah, I'm happy doing the dishes."

"It's cool, Brandon. We like to see people move up. If you want to learn this stuff, I'll talk to Stu, see what we can work out. Don't worry, you will still have your dishes."

They both laughed and Brandon said, "Thanks Steve, I appreciate the open door."

"No problem, let's put the other box down in the store room and take the empties to Stu. Then you can hit the dishes again."

*   *   *

Frank and Dan were on foot. The rain had all but stopped and they had parked their cruiser and were checking a pair of shipping and receiving docks in an alley. As they approached a gathering of men, one of them turned and walked quickly away, almost running.

"Excuse me guys, you can tell your friend to relax, we're not after him," said Dan. We are looking for a tall fella, wears steel toed boots. Maybe you could help us out here."

One of the men said, "We don't know no tall guys, with or without boots. Why you askin'?"

"Just want to talk, no trouble, just talk," said Frank.

"Yeah, we hear that before."

"So why did your friend run, is he illegal?" asked Dan. "Do you think I should call ICE and see what they say? Maybe they would like to talk to him."

"You don't gotta do that, man. He was just runnin' cause he had to take a leak. You know."

"Yeah, everybody does now and then. So you want to think about what we're lookin' for? Maybe we'll come back later and ask again. Maybe your friend could help us. We'll see you." Dan and Frank walked a bit farther down the alley and approached another group of men. "Good morning guys, I have a few questions for you," said Frank.

*   *   *

Kat was pouring her third cup of coffee when Lake walked into the squad room.

"Is that a fresh pot, Kat?"

"Just brewed it myself, knew you were comin' and did it just for you."

"You're a good human being, and I appreciate that." He rinsed out his mug and reached for the pot. "So, nothing new on our rib kicker. Like I said before, probably a one-time thing. He'll blend back into the

86

landscape and if he has no qualms about cracking Pills' chest, that'll be that. Over and done with."

"You hoping or what?"

"Hey, a collar is a collar and each one we tally up is only good for us. So I wish we coulda' found something that we could chew on, but hey — nothing."

"Drink your coffee, I'll go grab another jacket, maybe we'll get lucky on the next one and the perp will walk up to you and beg to be heard."

"Yeah, whatta' thought."

*   *   *

Fourteen

Thursday . . .   I'll stand a little closer to my razor in the morning . . .

"Another day, another dime," Brandon mumbled to himself as he cleaned the last load of dishes from the lunch crowd.

Stu came into the kitchen and asked Brandon to join him at the bar when he was done.

"Sure, give me about five minutes and I'll be out there," and he lifted another tray onto the belt feeding the washer. When the last load had run through, Brandon dried his hands and walked out to the bar. Several patrons were finishing their extended lunch at the bar and Stu asked Brandon to join him at a table in the dining room.

"You want something to drink before we sit down?" asked Stu.

Brenda walked by and said, "I just brewed another pot of coffee for anyone interested."

Brandon said he would take some and Stu said, "Brenda, be a doll and bring us a few mugs and the fresh pot. Oh make that four mugs and why don't you and Steve join us."

"Sure thing," and she set four mugs on the table. "Hey Steve, fresh coffee — ."

"I hear and I am there," he came around the corner and sat next to Brandon. "What's up Stu?"

Stu waited while Brenda poured coffee in each mug and sat next to him. "Brandon, Steve tells me you may be interested in learning the bar business."

"Well, sure, I mean, yeah. Yeah, I would."

"Good, the more you know and the more jobs that you can do, the more valuable you are to this place and any other joint where you may work. I started in the kitchen years ago when I was in high school. Then in the army, I started cooking. After, when I got out, I wanted to learn more and went to a Community College and took some courses. I bounced around from one restaurant to another. Learned a little here and a little there. Then about eight years ago, I tried to do a place on my own. It was tough and the location was no help. So I sold out to some guy who turned it into a 'shot and beer' place. Then I met Steve, he was working at a place over on K Street. We got along and started talking about what we would like to do. A lot of agreement between us. So, we found this joint and started to plan it out. We had the ideas, and we had the background. What we didn't have was enough money. I had some dough from the last joint and Steve had a few bucks, but we were still a little short. Then I met Brenda. She had the missing pieces. Not just the bucks that we were short, but the restaurant business sense and accounting background that made this team complete. The three of us have experience in different facets of the business. We were given breaks over the years and now we have this place. I own the biggest piece, but both Brenda and Steve are partners. We run this business our way and we like to see guys move up. So, what I want to do is have you work with Steve when your load in the back is light. You will start by pulling drafts, popping bottle tops and washing the glasses behind the bar. It's all part of the job. Whenever Steve is going to mix a drink, you watch, ask questions and learn. Steve is a damn good barman and he can teach you a lot, so listen."

Brenda chimed in, "Brandon, you have a personality that seems to enjoy people and behind the bar that is very important. Like Stu said, watch Steve, he is very good at this and he will help you develop your skills."

Steve added, "This is a business, we are here to make money. No money, no restaurant, no job. So it is important that the people that we put in front of our customers, make them want to come back and spend their money here. I think you have a natural ease with others and I am anxious to get you started."

Stu sat up and said, " A couple of things about working in the front of the house. You have to be neat and clean and dress the right way. We are a business oriented place, our customers are business men and women who come here not only to eat and drink, but also to meet others, have informal meetings or continue a session through lunch or dinner. We know this and make it appealing for them to be here. The tables are a little bigger, so they can open a notebook or a computer. The music is a softer variety that does not interrupt or overpower a conversation. The lighting allows the customer to read or write with ease and we do not push people out the door when they finish a meal. It often means another round of drinks and a healthy tip."

Brenda smiled and said, "Brandon, we would like you to bring in a change of clothes, so that when you are behind the bar, you can be dressed properly. Like Steve, he wears a shirt and tie once in a while, but usually a collared knit shirt and slacks. Oh, and comfortable shoes."

"Okay, I'll bring in some things and be ready. I guess that I should get a haircut and I'll stand a little closer to my razor in the morning."

Stu then said, "Listen, tomorrow is payday, but I don't expect you to run out and blow the paycheck on stuff for here. If you need a few bucks for a new shirt or shoes, we'll help you out. The important thing is having what you need when you need it."

"I just picked up a few things, so I should be okay for a while, but thanks anyway."

Stu pushed away from the table and as he was standing said, "There will be a lot of questions in the next few weeks, and any one of us that can, will help you out, so don't hesitate."

Brenda said, "Okay, that's that, now let's get ready for the dinner crowd."

*   *   *

Dan drove into another alley and parked the patrol car where it would not deter delivery trucks and construction vehicles. The air was relatively clean after the recent rain but the constant odor of rotting restaurant trash was ever present. "Let's walk this alley and see what's happening."

"You still hope to find something to take to that Detective?" asked Frank.

"I've had worse ideas and who knows, maybe we will find something." Dan picked up the radio, "Two four seven five, we are in the 4000 block near Jefferson. Going to do a walk about in an alley or two."

A crackling "Roger that," came back over the speaker.

"C'mon Frank, let's take a walk."

"Okay, but chances are somewhere around slim that we will find anything . . . but it is a nice day and a walk kind of appeals."

As they walked and talked about everything and nothing, looking at different people and their shoes, Dan noticed the same man who ran from them the previous day. "Hey, you c'mere, I want to talk to you."

The man was all but frozen, there was no way out from this encounter and he was determined to appear as legitimate as possible. His thoughts ran from saying that he left his papers in his apartment to, "I lost them . . ."

Dan approached the man, "What's your name?"

"I — I am David . . . "

"Well David, I just wanted to ask you a few questions yesterday, you didn't have to run away."

"I had to take a leak, you know . . . like real bad . . ."

"Yeah, sure you did. Now you don't, right?"

"Si — I mean, yes, right."

"Relax David, I am a district cop, not immigration, not customs . . . and I just want to talk. Okay?"

"Sure, okay, we talk."

Dan pointed at a crate and said, "Let's sit down, relax and talk."

David was still very nervous as he sat on the crate and took off his hard hat. "I don't know nothing to tell you . . ."

"Let me ask you a few questions and we will see what you know, okay David?"

"Si, yes, you ask . . ."

"Okay, now, what is your name?"

"I told you, I am David — ."

"Yeah, what is the rest of your name?"

"Oh, si, my name is David Jorge Juan Carlos Gonzales."

"That's a lot of names David. My name is Daniel Patrick Carney."

"I have three uncles when I am born — ."

"Jorge, Juan and Carlos?"

"Si — yes."

See how easy this is?"

"Si — easy."

"Okay, now, you work here in these offices, what kind of work do you do?"

"I put the drywall and I paint . . . most times I put the drywall."

"Okay, do you do the taping also?"

"Si, yes I do the tape when it is all up, then I do the tape."

"Okay, now you work with a lot of different people, right?"

"Oh . . . yes . . . lot of people."

"And you see a lot of other people too?"

"Yes, a lot of people."

"Do you remember a tall man, very tall man who wears boots like yours?"

David thought for a few seconds, "I don't know any very tall man . . ."

"But do you remember seeing a tall man with boots like yours?"

David paused, thinking, "No, I don't remember anyone like that."

"Okay David, that's what I wanted to ask you yesterday. You didn't have to run away from me. I am looking for a tall man who wears steel toed shoes and has been in this area. I don't know if you are a legal or illegal worker and I don't care. If you are a good man, don't break the law, I don't care about your immigration status. That's somebody else's problem. The tall man is my problem. You see? Now I have to get back to talking to other people. You be a good man, work hard and don't break the law."

"Thank you Mr. police, I will be good."

"My name is Dan, remember, you call me Dan, okay."

"Okay Mr. Dan."

As Frank and Dan walked out of the alley, Frank kiddingly said, "Okay Mr. Dan."

"Don't be a wise ass Frank, that guy may be illegal, but then, look around . . . probably most of these guys are, but we have to be able to talk to them when something happens. I think that the legal / illegal alien thing is a mess and there are too many illegals in this country, but I can only solve one problem at a time."

"So why not call ICE and turn the guy in?"

"Then next time we need a little cooperation, we won't get it. No, to do our job the most effective way, we need the ability to talk to these people, legal or otherwise and not scare them away."

"Well, I would'a turned him in . . . "

"Yeah, but now you won't, and maybe we have another friend."

"Maybe, Mr. Dan —, but I doubt it."

"You doubt, I'll trust — ."

"Trust . . .?"

"Si . . ."

*   *   *

FIFTEEN

Saturday . . .   The three men were slowly moving toward him . . .

Another bright morning, the sun was up, the streets were full of people with more smiles than usual. "Saturday, it's Saturday," mumbled Brandon to himself as he left the coffee shop. "They're not going to work, they're out enjoying the sun and spending their hard earned money." He strode along, coffee in hand thinking about being one of the masses. "What can I buy?" He continued walking, pausing to look in a window or two when he stopped in front of a book store. The inside of the book store was as foreign to Brandon as the streets of London or Paris. He went in, walked between the stacks of books, marveling at the number of different books and the categories . . .

Mysteries, Romance, Science, Medicine, the signs over the stacks went on and on. Brandon was overwhelmed, "Maybe this was a bad idea . . ." Then he saw a book on a rack labeled 'Bargain Books'. The title was partially covered by the Reduced Price sticker, but the word Bartending was obvious."Four ninety five, this is it." He took the book to the check out, placed it on the counter and dug out his wallet.

"Will that be all sir?" asked the young lady behind the cash register.

"Yeah, I think so, thanks." He handed her a ten and she rung it up, handed him his change and was about to put it in a bag.

"I don't need a bag, thank you, I'm going to start reading it now."

She smiled, he almost giggled and walked out into the sunshine again. As he walked, he fluttered through the pages, pausing more at the pictures than the verbiage and nearly crashed into several people as they passed. He was excited and kept walking toward the Pub.

"Good morning Brenda, ready for a new day?"

"Hey Brandon, whatch'a got there?"

"Oh I stopped in a bookstore a few minutes ago and saw this book on bartending . . ."

"Let me see — , hmm, I think that Steve has that one behind the bar, must mean it's a good one to have."

"I hope so, it cost me almost five bucks," he said with a big grin, "and I'm gonna' read it cover to cover."

"You should ask Steve about it, he may have some tips . . . "

"I'll do that. But right now, I gotta get the day started . . ."

Walking home, Brandon heard noises in the doorways and alleys between buildings. Low noises, muted voices and whispers. Nothing distinguishable, just murmurs and hushed whispers. The demons were watching again and he dare not look at them. That would allow them to see him, to know him and pursue him. He turned his collar up, hiding a portion of his face, lowered his head and increased his pace. As he covered the distance to his apartment he was tempted to vary his route, but he didn't, he quickly entered his building and climbed the three flights to his room. Home and safe, Brandon bolted the door, took off his coat and turned on his television.

"A movie, I'll watch a movie, maybe one of Karloff's, that will keep them away." He inserted his most watched DVD, the original Frankenstein, pushed himself into his stuffed chair and pulled a woolen blanket up to his neck. As the movie progressed, Brandon dozed, woke and dozed again. The film finished with Brandon missing more than half to sleep. He finally fell into a deep sleep for a few hours. He opened his eyes to see a dark window to a dimly lit room. There was the shadowy figure of a man moving slowly from right to left looking out the window, looking directly at him. The man stopped, stared, his face a grey space with dark, sunken eyes, hollow deeper grey cheeks and a black line where his mouth should have been. The man slowly moved his mouth, emitting a low monotone sound. Not a voice producing words, but a low moan, bespeaking of pain, great pain. His clothes were black and several shades of grey in his face moved giving more definition as he leaned closer to the window. Brandon turned away, looking to his right. There was another window, another dark figure of a man, another moan. He turned again not looking at the first window but quickly turning his head to the left. Another window, another grey man, another moan. The three together made a sound almost mimicking his name, *"Brandon . . . "* He looked straight ahead again at the first window, the man was opening a door next to the window, he looked right, another door was being opened, then left, the man was outside the door staring at him. Brandon's head turned quickly from left to right to center and again left. The three men were slowly moving toward him. The windows and doors faded to some dark grey abstract and the men came closer moaning louder and louder. *"Brandon . . . Brandon . . ."*

He sat up in his chair, he was alone in his room, no windows, no doors, no grey men, but a very low moan in the distance, outside. He pulled the blanket closer and looked at the static snow on his television. His eyes burning, his heart pounding and his blanket absorbing his sweat pouring from his head and arms. Brandon passed the next two hours dozing, waking and dozing again and again. At around seven in the morning, he staggered to his feet and made his way to the bathroom.

*   *   *

Sixteen

Sunday . . .   Excuse me, may I join you . . .

It was Sunday, his day off and he was determined to make it a good day. "I can have a life, a real life . . . and the demons can all stay in hell . . ." he mumble to himself. A brief stand in the shower, dressed and ready to start his day, Brandon looked in the mirror and tried to imagine a pep talk. He thought about the opportunity that was being presented to him. He was going to be a bartender. To Brandon this was a whole new life, he should try to be positive, stand tall and not let the dreams and demons run him down. Looking in the mirror, he took a deep breath, straightened his back, nodded to himself and turned toward the door.

The sun was warming the morning air, birds were busy foraging, people and cars were making their way through the streets and Brandon ventured out into the flow. He kept his head up, walking with confidence and made his way to the coffee shop for his morning repast. He ordered a larger coffee than usual, a cinnamon-raisin bagel, toasted with cream cheese and picked up a small fruit plate from the cooler. Sunday, breakfast, or by this time, brunch and he was going to enjoy the day. The Nationals were playing their last game of the season in New York and the Redskins were in Philadelphia, so neither of those were an option. The Capitals were playing their last preseason game against Nashville, but tickets would not be cheap and as he was waiting for his bagel, he overheard someone mention going to the zoo with their children to see the pandas. "Never been to the zoo," he muttered to himself. He collected his bagel, fruit plate and coffee and spotted one of the several open tables near the window. "Perfect," and he sat down to enjoy the view and his food. Then he noticed the front door opened and the same young lady that he met on Thursday came in. His mind drifted into that same impossible dream world . . . "She wanted me to stay . . ." and he realized that he was staring at her. He turned his head and eyes toward the window quickly and continued his dream, "She wanted me . . . "

"Excuse me, may I join you?" said a pleasant young voice.

He turned and was looking at the same sunshine smile and bright blue eyes he had seen on Thursday. "Sure . . . That would be very nice." He reached over and moved a chair for her to sit and noticed that there were a number of empty tables. He looked at her and said, "I remember you, from the other day . . "

"Yes, that was nice of you to let me have your table . . ."

"I was finished and I had to get to work, you were . . . "

"Thankful, it was crowded and I was about to get a bag and take my coffee to work in the rain."

"My name is Brandon . . ."

"Oh, hi, I'm Suzanne . . ."

Brandon had never been able to establish a close relationship with anyone, but he was determined that this was going to be different. She could be everything that he could have wanted in a friend, a woman. "Do you live around here?"

"Yes, I share an apartment with two friends, we all work at the same office on K Street."

Brandon forgot about his bagel and again caught himself starting to stare, "Excuse me, I — I work at a restaurant, I'm — I'm going to be a bartender. Just learning now . . ."

"Which restaurant?"

"Stewarts Pub, over on . . ."

"Oh I've been there, not for a while though . . . Have you been there long?"

"Just two weeks, so far. Hope to be there a long time. They are really nice there, giving me the chance to do more than just wash dishes."

Suzanne laughed, "Wash dishes . . . that's all I could get when I first got here."

"Where did you come from?"

"Well, I was raised in Winchester and when I finished High School, I wanted to try a Community College, but that didn't work well either, I guess I'm just not a student . . . So, I came to DC to find a job. I was going to give it a few weeks and see what I could get and I was staying with an old friend from high school and another girl temporarily. They were both working at an ad agency and waitressing a few nights a week and they got me a job bussing tables and washing dishes at the restaurant while I tried to find a regular job. Deanna, that's one of the girls, not the one that I went to school with, she does modeling and she got me into a modeling school. We get little side jobs at the conventions and industrial shows. Then they got me into A.J. Wiggins and Associates, the same office where they work and I've been there for two years now."

"What do you do there?"

"I'm an administrative assistant. I have four guys that I work for and I finished the series of modeling classes and now I get some of that work too."

"You mean like for magazines . . .?"

"Well there are a lot of different things that we can do. I can continue to work at Wiggin's and do these little gigs on the side. Like this week, Monday — we have a casting call for a show at the convention center. I usually just stand next to the salesmen and hand out brochures to all the people passing by. The people at the agency said that I would be very good at that, and all I have to do is smile, say 'Hi,' and hand them a brochure."

Brandon was stunned by the outpouring of information and was grateful for the pause. As he was about to speak, Suzanne looked a little embarrassed and said, " I'm sorry, sometimes I talk too much, like I don't know when to listen and not talk."

They sat quietly for a minute sipping their coffee and Brandon said, "Have you seen the pandas at the zoo?'

Suzanne looked a little confused at the question, smiled and said, "No, I haven't been to the zoo since my dad took us years ago."

"Well, I have never been to the zoo here and they have these pandas . . . I've never seen a panda, I mean a real live one and I was thinking about going today."

Suzanne smiled and said, "That kinda sounds like fun — ."

"You wanna' come with me?"

Suzanne paused, smiled and said, "Yes, I'd like that."

Brandon's first date, he was twenty seven and had never taken a girl anywhere. They finished their coffee and walked together to the Metro. He had an old Metro ticket with a few dollars left on it that he added another five to and put in another five on a new ticket. Suzanne was reaching into her purse to get her Metro pass, saw him buy the second ticket and paused. Brandon handed her the second ticket and she took her empty hand out of her purse, smiled and said "Thanks."

They went through the turnstiles and down the escalator to the platform, chatting about the zoo, the different animals, and when Suzanne said, "It's so neat that the Smithsonian doesn't charge to get into their museums or the zoo."

Brandon said, "I didn't know that," and breathed a sigh of relief. He was prepared to spend whatever he had in his pocket to make this a great day and free was a pleasant surprise.

They walked from one end of the zoo to the other talking about the animals they saw and not once did Brandon hear the whispers, or footsteps behind him. He was completely relaxed, happy and so was Suzanne. They left the zoo, walking down Connecticut Avenue and had no idea what time it was. After an hour, Suzanne said, "I live down there, about three blocks from here. I had a wonderful day and I don't want it to end, but, I have to get home and be ready for tomorrow."

This was not the end for the day that Brandon was hoping for, the promise of other day to come made him smile and say, "I don't have a phone, never needed one, but you can reach me at the Pub — if you wanted to."

Suzanne took out a pen and wrote a number on a piece of paper, "This is my cell phone, I'm usually home in the evening if I'm not doing a job. You can call me any time."

They walked down her street to an apartment building and Brandon said, "I'll call you tomorrow night to see how the casting call went. Good luck." He was very uncomfortable , not knowing what he should do next when Suzanne leaned forward, pulled his head toward her and kissed him.

"It was a beautiful day, I loved every minute of it," and she ran up the stairs into the building.

Brandon was once again on top of the world. He turned around several times walking in the general direction of his apartment and dreaming about another date with his new friend. He walked all the way home, not hearing any whispers or footsteps behind him. When he arrived home, he turned on his television in time for the early news, the Redskins won in Philadelphia, the Nationals won in New York but the Capitals lost their last preseason game to Nashville.

"Oh well, three out of four, not a bad day."

*   *   *

Seventeen

Monday . . .   Better put them on too . . .

A new week, the beginning of another new phase in Brandon's life. He felt that he had a chance to have what others had, someone special. His mother and father had something special, something he never thought he would have, but now that could change. Stu had Brenda, Steve was married and had a girl friend, and George was married with a couple of kids. As he walked out of his apartment and started for the Pub, he dreamt of sharing his life with someone like Suzanne. It could happen, he was going to learn to tend bar. He would become one of the hundreds and thousands of people that he saw every day coming and going to and from work, or lunch, or shopping or dinner. He would find a nice woman, get married, have children and live to see his grand children marry and continue the cycle. He was going to be happy.

Walking to work that morning, Brandon again passed a store with cut rate clothing. A pulled thread here, a missing button there and therefore less than half normal price. "That works for me," he said quietly as he entered the store.

"Good morning," said the little man with a cloth tape measure draped around his neck. "Can I help you find something?"

"I'm a little tough to fit, everything has to be a tall size and extra tall if possible."

The little man fingered his tape measure and said, "Yes, I see, tall and slender."

"Very tall and skinny would be more accurate," laughed Brandon."

"And shoes, oh boy you got some canoes there," chided the little man.

"Yeah, they have always been the bigger problem," Brandon said with a grin.

"Okay, you follow me to the tall section and we will see what works for you."

Brandon followed the pleasant little man to the far corner of the store and was amazed at the selection of clothing that looked like it could work.

"You want tall, I got tall — ," said the little man with a big grin.

Brandon found another knit shirt, a pair of khakis and much to his surprise, a pair of white size 15 running shoes. He paid the little man, took the bag with his new clothes and said, "Pay day is Friday, I will be back on Saturday."

He left the store feeling excited about life again and covered the distance to the Pub with his head at about 20,000 feet. He went directly to his locker in the basement and stowed his new clothes with his old jeans and work boots. "I should pitch those things," he mumbled as he closed his locker. He bounded up the stairs and saw Steve

The rain at mid day and again around the dinner hour meant for a slow day at Stewart's Pub. The dinner crowd was scant and they did less than a full turn on the tables. "That happens once in a while and we have to take advantage of these opportunities," said Stu. He and Brenda were holding their coats and talking to Steve at 7:30 as Brandon came out of the kitchen.

"Brandon, it looks like a slow night, so you come out here and handle the bar," said Stu, "Steve is going to manage things while Brenda and I sneak out. We'll be back tomorrow bright and early and hope for a better day tomorrow."

"Sure, I'll change and be right back."

Steve looked at Stu and said, "We got this, you guys enjoy the evening and we'll see you tomorrow."

Brenda and Stu walked back through the kitchen towards the back door and called down stairs to Brandon, "We'll see you in the morning, Brandon. Pay attention to Steve and enjoy the bar." They headed out into the rain and Stu's car parked in the alley.

Brandon came back up the stairs tucking his shirt into his trousers and hurrying to get behind the bar. He was excited and nervous. The bar was going to be his. Steve would coach, but Brandon was going to run it.

No one was in the bar except Steve. "Okay Brandon, what should you do first," he asked.

"Um — , I don't know, I guess that I should figure out where everything is kept, like — the stir sticks — and — "

"Yeah, get a feel for the bar, look over the stock and try to spot the most asked for brands, or ones that you know and like. Then you will start to remember what is next to those and so on . . . it'll grow on ya' after a bit and before you know it, you'll know where they all live."

With a semi stunned look, Brandon said, "Okay, I guess . . . "

The evening was not one of the best in the Pub's history, but Brandon was thrilled. He had the bar to himself and the twenty plus customers that he took care of were none the wiser. Steve was pleased, he had another back up bartender and he knew that Stu would be pleased also. Business had been slow, but that added to the opportunity to teach Brandon more about tending bar. He was a quick study and was not only picking up what Steve laid down, but he was animated, talking to the customers, making the Pub a pleasant experience. The evening had several very slow spots and Brandon took advantage of one to call Suzanne. She didn't answer, he left her a message. The next opportunity to call was after 11:00 and he decided that he would try again in the morning.

"Brandon, you did a couple of things right, the drinks were good, the customers were happy and you didn't scare anybody away. For an off night, I think that you made us a few bucks and we are going to do this again, if you're willing."

"Oh yeah, I had a great time. It went by fast."

"It can be that way when the crowd is good, the conversation is positive and we are making money. You did alright for your first time back there."

"Thanks Steve, but if you were not here, I would have been in deep stink when it went beyond pulling a few drafts. The beer is easy and a shot of bourbon or a gin and tonic doesn't strain my brain, but I've seen you back there when the names of the drinks are ten words long and you fly around keeping everybody smiling. I got a long way to go."

"True, true, true, but time and experience will address most of that. You keep checking in that little book that you bought and soon you'll find yourself knowing what to pour and the book will start gathering dust next to the register."

"Well, now what do we do? It's almost twelve and nobody is here — ."

"Tell you what, you take the rest of the night, go get a good night's sleep and be ready for tomorrow. I'll finish up here."

"But I can still — "

"No, no, you had a good night behind the bar and I want you to remember that, so take the little time left and get home before that rain comes down any harder."

Brandon looked out the window, it was coming straight down in a steady, but gentle rain. "Don't have to ask again, I'm gonna' grab my coat and get outta here."

"I'll see you tomorrow," said Steve as he moved behind the bar.

Brandon was already going through the kitchen door and said, "Bright and early — " He half jumped down the stairs to the basement to grab his coat when he thought, "I should change out of these clothes, may need them tomorrow . . ." As he quickly changed his shirt and pulled on his jeans, he spotted his boots. "Better put them on too . . . " Changed into his old working outfit and wearing his black raincoat, Brandon hustled up the stairs and out into the alley.

Steve was occupied counting up the money in the till and didn't notice that Brandon had taken the time to change before he left. Finished behind the bar, Steve locked the front door, took the cash and receipts into the kitchen, locked that door and went down the stairs to the office. He put everything away and locked the safe, turned out the lights and went back up the stairs to the kitchen. "An interesting night," he muttered as he walked through the bar and dining rooms, turning off lights and again checking the front door. By the time Steve had locked the door and run to his car, the rain had picked up some energy and a slight wind. As he wiped the rain from his face and cleaned his glasses, he said aloud, "Damn, I shoulda' told Brandon to wait a few minutes and I coulda' driven him home . . . where ever that is." He started his car and drove out of the alley into the light city traffic, and headed for home.

*   *   *

Eighteen

Tuesday . . .   Just what you owe me . . .

Brandon had started toward his apartment and thought, "It's early, I might catch Karen if I go over there right now. Eighteen hours should be about $150 and I know exactly where I could spend it." He turned another corner in the direction of Rizzonte's and hurried his pace. The rain was slowing, then picking up and slowing again as he walked and he was soaked through to his skin. A gentle breeze seemed to cut right through his raincoat and shirt and stab him repeatedly in his chest and shoulders. Not a novel experience for him, cold, wet and hurrying through the night. All that was missing were the whispers, the movements in the shadows, the footsteps behind him. As he walked he remembered the noises and as if on cue, a whisper — then another — and another. The night was turning on him. The rain slowed again, almost to a stop and he heard movements in the shadows. They were there, they were following him. His mind went to the extreme. As he turned another corner, he glanced in a large shop window and saw a figure, a tall, heavy set man with that blank grey stare moving as he moved and staring at him. Brandon quickly turned his face away, looking at the pavement a few feet in front of himself. His reflection in the window did the same. He heard the whispers again, the movement as if someone was walking through dried leaves.

"It's raining, they can't be coming . . ." He lifted his head slightly and glanced ahead halfway toward his right shoulder into another window. "Nobody . . . nobody." He lifted his head and slowed his pace. "I'm alright, nobody is there in the window." He did not turn full right to see his reflection. He estimated that he was about ten minutes from Rizzonte's and stepped ahead.

As he walked, Brandon thought about what he would say to Karen. "You owe me for eighteen hours, bitch." He walked on. "Hey Karen, can you pay me the rest of what you owe me?" Another several steps, "Excuse me Karen, but it seems that my pay envelope was about $150 short last time." The rain seemed to start again and then stop all together. "Hey, Karen. I wanted to ask you if you had the rest of my pay. It should only be about $150, but that's a lot to me." He ran several more scenarios through his head as he approached the final turn into the alley behind Rizzonte's. The alley was littered with paper and cut-up cardboard box pieces, some soaked and some relatively dry.

The night had been bad for business all across the District and people were leaving Rizzonte's through the alley. He saw the clean-up crew including a new face walking out the back door and his reaction was to step into a darkened doorway as they approached. Unseen and starting to get nervous again, Brandon stepped out of the doorway after they passed and moved slowly up the alley. "Maybe she's gone already, and I will have to come back again . . ." Then he saw her car, "No she's still here." He waited a few minutes and approached her car wondering if this was all a mistake. Then thinking, "No she has to pay me, she can't say NO. She will probably say that she doesn't have it this week and I'll have to come back."

The back door to Rizzonte's opened. Karen stepped out onto the small landing, turned back toward the door and said something to someone inside.

"Probably Phil," he mumbled and started toward Karen.

Karen turned and started down the stairs as the bolts were pushed closed inside. She paused at the bottom of the stairs still in the light of the bulb above the door and pursued her keys in her purse. Brandon approached and she looked up seeing him about twenty feet away. "What the hell are you doing here?"

"Hey, I just wanted to ask you — "

"What, to ask if you could have your job back?" She said it in a mocking manner, angering Brandon.

"No, you owe me for another eighteen hours, that's about $150 and I want to know when you're gonna' pay me."

"I owe you nothing, and that's exactly what I'm gonna' pay you — nothing. Now get outta here." She turned toward her car and delved into her purse again.

"C'mon Karen, I worked for that money and you have to pay me."

"No, I don't have to pay you. I didn't ask you to clean up, you did that on your own and I'm not paying you for it. I fired you because you scared the waitresses and the cook. Now get outta here. Go find a job you worthless piece of crap." As she spoke, she brought a small can of Mace out of her purse and pointed it at Brandon. "Go on, get out."

Brandon stopped and stared. Karen took a step in his direction and pressed the nozzle on top of the can. The Mace got about half way to Brandon and seemed to fall out of the air. Brandon stepped toward Karen and said, "I didn't scare anybody, you do you fat old witch."

Karen pressed the nozzle again and this time the Mace reached Brandon's face and chest. Mostly his chest. As he brushed at the little bit that reached his face, Brandon heard the moaning sounds that had plagued him before. He was trying to keep the Mace from his eyes and backing away from Karen. The moaning sounds got louder and Karen seemed to attack him with her spray can. Brandon tripped moving backwards, falling into a pile of trash and a broken pallet breaking his fall with his left hand.. Karen had him cornered and unloaded the can toward his face. Brandon brought both of his hands up in a defending gesture and deflected most of the Mace but enough reached his eyes to make them redden and swell. He now looked like a movie villain, wild hair, blood red eyes, a bleeding hand and angry. Karen moved toward her car and Brandon found his feet, stood and took four steps in her direction when he realized he was holding a piece of the broken pallet in his left hand. His eyes were burning, his head ached and the moaning sounds were all around. He moved the stick to his right hand, leaving a large splinter in his bloody left hand. The whispers and movements behind dumpsters and in doorways were deafening and Brandon never heard Karen's cries as he struck her twice on her back with the piece of wood. He was losing control, the sounds were louder, the moaning drowning out the whispers and the noises of movements. He spun around fully expecting to see a man with a grey face and saw nobody. He turned again as Karen staggered another step toward her car. Brandon raised the piece of wood and with both hands, struck Karen again on her back. She rolled to her right, falling on the pavement pleading for him to stop.

"Please — stop, please . . . "

Brandon did not hear anything but the ever loudening moaning. He turned around again like a wounded rat looking for his tormentor. Karen half crawled toward her car and pulled open the door. Brandon spun around again and saw her as she leaned into the driver's side door. He stepped toward the car and kicked the door all in one movement. Karen's head was in the way and prevented the door from closing, opening a gash in side of her head as she fell to the ground.

Brandon hesitated, the moaning noises stopped for a moment, and he started to relax, to breathe. Then as suddenly as they stopped, the moaning sounds started again, growing louder and louder. Karen was hurt, stunned, almost unable to move. A slight wind started, the moaning continued increasing to a fever pitch, all but deafening in Brandon's head. Karen started to scream at him and even though he could not hear her, he told her to be quiet. Karen picked up a small piece of the asphalt pavement and weakly threw it at Brandon. It bounced harmlessly to the ground and he raised the piece of wood as high as he could, then brought it down on her head. Karen rolled to one side, not moving.

Brandon stood up straight, the noises stopped again. "I only wanted my money. I didn't want this," he said as she began to open her eyes. Brandon once again caught his breath and noticed that Karen had the money pouch in her purse. It was almost falling out on the pavement. "Just what you owe me, nothing more," he said as he looked around, saw no one and bent over picking up the pouch. "Just what you owe me . . ."

He took out a wad of bills and started to count out his $150 when Karen stirred, got up and stood with one hand on her car. She was disoriented, dizzy and did not intend to move toward Brandon. As she stood, her balance demanded that she move her feet to stay upright. Her shuffling drew Brandon's attention and he turned facing her as she staggered a step in his direction. The low moaning sounds began again and Brandon reacted by stepping toward Karen and kicking her as hard as he could in her mid section. She fell backward against her car and slumped toward the ground, her breathing stopped and a choking, cough replaced the respirations. Brandon leaned forward listening to her breathing and showing no emotion. Karen was slowly dying, not able to inhale and Brandon watched. The sounds of the night stopped, no moaning, no whispers, no shuffling of feet.

"I just wanted my money — money that I earned," he said as he took exactly $150 and threw the rest in her face. Karen didn't hear his words this time and didn't see the money fluttering into her face, she had finally lost all sense of the world. Karen was dead.

Brandon put the money in his pocket, turned his back on Karen and began to walk out of the alley. As he moved toward a dumpster he stepped in a large chuckhole filled with water. He threw the piece of wood in the dumpster, stomped the water off his foot, wiped the blood away from a cut between his thumb and forefinger and scratched at the splinter in the palm of his left hand. He calmly walked out of the alley kicking several pieces of cardboard aside, keeping his thumb against his forefinger and scratching at his palm as he went.

*   *   *

Nineteen

Tuesday . . .   Lookie here what I found . . .

"Yo, Freddie, wait till the suits get here — "

"Be cool, Sal, I'm just gettin' a closer look . . . it's gonna' rain again soon and I wanna' be sure to not miss anything — " said Freddy as he snapped off a few long distance shots looking the length of the alley. As he was snapping pictures, Kat and Lake walked into the alley. They approached the patrol officer and Kat started asking questions and taking notes. Lake wandered slowly toward the body lying next to her car.

 Sal said, "Hey Lake, it's gonna' rain any time now so I suggest that we hurry this one up.

"Give us a minute or two," said Lake "and the scene might be yours. Where's the Doc?"

"Right here," said Chuck, standing up behind Karen's car. This is a nasty one. The lady was hit a number of times with something across her back and then her head. She has a large gash in her forehead where it hit or was hit by the car door." Chuck was making notes and shaking his head, "This one makes no sense. The money scattered about says 'Not a robbery', no sexual assault, no hint as to why — ."

"Maybe somebody didn't like her, well that's our part of this —, like a husband, a friend, family . . . we'll run 'em all. See what stands the tallest," said Lake.

Freddy walked over to Sal as Kat moved toward the body joining Lake and counting the money scattered about as she walked. "This sure doesn't look like a robbery, look at all that money blowing around."

"Yeah, I noticed — we oughta — ," Lake paused, stood and turned toward Sal and Freddy, "Hey, Freddy can you shoot the scene and start collecting the money flying around this alley?"

Sal grinned and said "Can we keep it?" as he and Freddy moved into the alley. "You shoot and I'll collect he said as they began.

As Sal collected the last of the bills, checks and several scraps of paper that seemed to be charge receipts and an adding machine tape, Freddy was looking for anything interesting to shoot. He paused at the front of Karen's car, looking at the front door.

"Hey Lake, check out the driver side door, I think it was kicked and put that nasty cut in the nice lady's head."

"Kicked — ?"

"Yeah, kicked, see the smudge on the door . . . I wanna' get up close on that." He took several shots and backed away shooting as he went.

"How many pictures are you gonna' take Freddy," asked Sal?

"I don't know, I don't count 'em. Shoot till the card is full or I think that I got everything."

Freddy turned back toward the M.E.'s van and put his camera away to help Sal get the gurney and a body bag. "It's gonna' rain again, Sal. We gonna' get wet."

"You gonna' want more time to shoot up any more of the scene?"

"Yeah, a little, but we almost done."

It started to rain and Sal said, "Hey guys, this rain gonna' ruin everything. Let us bag her and Freddy can shoot the rest of the scene."

The rain increased in intensity and Lake looked at Chuck and said, "Okay guys, She's yours."

Chuck nodded, "I'll work on this with the ME. He likes to get at these right away and keep our lockers empty."

"Chuck, I don't think we have any empty lockers. This nice lady is going in the big cooler," said Sal as he positioned the gurney and unfolded a new body bag. "C'mon Freddy help me get her into the bag."

They lifted Karen into the bag, zipped it up and placed her on the gurney. As Sal was pushing her into the van, Freddy grabbed his camera and ran to Karen's car. "I gotta get this," he said as he took a number of additional shots around the smudge on the door. Then he went back to the van took out a second camera and panned the alley. He walked it's length, holding the camera steady, filming the north side and returned filming the south side. Standing again at the van and looking into the alley he again picked up his first camera. He looked at the dumpster and as he moved closer he pulled a paper towel out of his pocket and raised the lid. "Well, well, well — lookie here what I found."

Sal walked over to the dumpster and looked in, "What, what do you see Freddie?"

"Hold the lid up while I shoot this."

"Okay, shoot what, that piece of wood?"

"Yeah, see the little stain on the skinny end — ?"

"Okay, yeah, what . . . blood?"

"Maybe, on both ends, see . . ." as he snapped off another shot.

"Both ends of what, Freddy?" asked Kat as she and Lake approached.

"Hey guys, just snooping around before we give up the scene," said Freddy as he stepped aside for Lake to peer inside.

"That stick, Freddy?"

"Yep, I would bet even cash that the stain on the big end is your vic and the little stain on the narrow end is your boggy." Freddy took several more pictures of the dumpster and looked at both Kat and Lake watching him.

"You keep this up and we will have to get you a shield, Freddy," said Kat.

Freddy grinned at the two of them and quickly snapped a picture of them looking at him and holding the dumpster open. "It's rainin and you gettin wet, me and Sal goin' back to the barn with the nice lady. See you guys later," and he ran to the van covering his camera.

Kat looked at Lake and said, "I'm gonna' to ask if I can trade up to Freddy as a partner — ."

"Yeah, yeah, yeah, the kid is good, let's bag the stick give it to Chuck and get outta here."

*   *   *

T WENTY

Tuesday . . .   This is looking familiar . . .

Brandon woke at 9:30 am, looked out his kitchen window at the clouds in the sky and walked into the bathroom to take a shower. He scratched at his hand again, checked his cut and tried to pull the splinter out. The cut had stopped bleeding and was not as bad as it seemed the previous night, the splinter was in too deep and he was not able to move it. He looked around his apartment for something to help him rid himself of his splinter. He found a safety pin. "Eureka . . . ," he muttered as he bent it as straight and proceeded to scratch an opening in his palm, exposing more of the splinter. Then he used the pin to raise the end of the splinter and was able to pull it free. A little blood flowed out and Brandon made sure no more of that damn stick was still in his hand. He turned on the shower, stripped and stood in the water fall until he was fully awake, got out and dried off, glancing in the mirror and grinning. "It's going to be a good day, I can feel it," he mumbled to himself. He looked at his hand, no more bleeding, just a ragged scratch where the splinter used to be and a small cut that was already healing.

He noticed that the rain had slowed to a gentle misting and the sun would soon be in command of the sky. He pulled on dry jeans and a shirt and hung his wet clothes from the previous night in the bathroom. Noting the time, he mumbled, "I have to get to work," as he put on a jacket, then walked out the door and began thinking about his bagel and coffee. He gave no thought to the lady that he left dead in an alley. He knew that the whispers had gone away, he had his overtime money and his future was looking up.

"Tall coffee and let's do a cinnamon raisin bagel with a little cream cheese today," he said to the girl behind the counter. She called out the coffee order, pulled a bagel from the tray and said, "Toasted — ?"

"Sure," as he turned and scanned the population in the shop. No sign of Suzanne. "I should try to call her again when I get to the Pub," he mumbled. Turning back to the girl behind the counter, Brandon paid her, collected his breakfast and headed for the door. Coffee and bagel in hand, Brandon ventured out into the mass of moving people and aimed for the Pub.

*   *   *

Freddy sat at a computer reviewing the photos of the alley where Karen Maria Pavia had met her end. He gathered all the photos of the car door and lined them up, scaled them to the same size and traced out a print of a larger size shoe or work boot. "This is looking familiar," he mumbled to himself as Dr. Colburn was passing by.

"What'cha got there Freddy?"

"Give me a minute here Doc, I want to compare this to another boot print we collected at another scene a little over a week ago."

"You got a match?"

"Don't know yet Doc, but how many 'Bigfoot' characters do you think are kicking people and cars in alleys this month?"

"Good question, who's case is this?"

"Same team, McLarry and Murano."

"You wanna' give em a call?"

"First I wanna' check the rest of the photos and see if anything else lines up."

"Go get em Detective . . ."

"Don't say that around them — , " said Freddy as he punched up his photo file on the Decker case. He browsed through his pics until he had the composite boot print that he had assembled from the several shots taken at the Decker scene. "This is starting to look real good. The first one is a composite and the second is just an outline, but I gotta ask again, just how many 'Bigfoot' kickers are out there?"

"You ready for the Detectives now?"

"Almost, just a few more things to check out."

"Okay Freddy, when you are done, come in and help me with Ms. Pavia."

"Okay Doc, can I have just a couple of minutes?"

"Make it ten and then we have work to do, where's Sal?"

"He went upstairs to get us some coffee, he'll be right back. You want one?"

"That would be great, black, no sugar — "

"Okay Doc, straight up." Freddy picked up his cell phone, pressed a button and said "Hey Sal get one more for the Doc, straight up."

His phone crackled and Sal came back, "Who's buyin — ?"

"You are, dump the cigarette, get the coffee and back here, he was askin' where you were."

"Okay, I'm movin'."

*   *   *

Lake and Kat drove over to the Pavia scene at 10:30 when the employees would start showing up for work. As they arrived, Phil was fumbling with his keys, holding several newspapers under his arm and a paper coffee cup in his teeth. Kat walked up to him and said, "Excuse me, what time does this restaurant open?"

Phil found the right key, inserted it in the lock and took his coffee out from his teeth, "Well, actually, it should already be open. I mean she usually unlocks the front door around ten, I get in around now and the kitchen guys are already at it in the back doing prep. We don't start serving for another half hour though, so you can come in and wait if you'd like — the coffee should be on, but like I said, we don't start serving until eleven."

Lake chimed in, "We'll come in now," as he held up his credentials.

Phil pushed open the door, "Oh, okay — ," as he stepped inside.

Al and Linda were sitting at a large round table near the kitchen entrance, looking very somber.

"Mornin' guys, what's going on, you look terrible, Karen's late and these two people are from the police — ." Phil hesitated, thinking about what he had just said. "What happened?"

Lake said, "Why don't you sit down and we can talk, okay."

Phil put his newspapers on the bar and set his keys down behind the bar then walked to the table with his coffee and sat down, "Yeah, okay."

The three of them were sitting together an Kat sat next to Phil. Lake walked around to the opposite side of the table and sat facing Kat.

Lake started by asking, "Is anybody else due in here this morning?"

Phil looked around and shrugged his shoulders.

Linda said, "The waitresses will be in a few minutes. I think Stacey and Monica are on this morning, but I can check the schedule to be sure."

Kat motioned her to stay where she was and said, "We'll get to that in a bit."

Lake said, "So when Karen isn't here, who's in charge?"

Phil sat up and said, "Karen, she's the manager, but the owner is a guy named Ben Ferguson, he has a couple of places like this. I think he spends most of his time at the one across the river, in Rosslyn, on Lynn Street."

Al said, "Yeah, he called this morning and said he was coming over. Said he had to talk to us about something. I guess maybe it's about this, about Karen not being here."

Kat looked at Lake and said, "Yeah, well we have to talk a little more about that too. When will he get here?"

Al said, Well he called a little before you guys came in and he said he was leaving right then. So maybe he will get here in about fifteen or twenty minutes."

Lake said, "Okay let's cover a few things while we wait for Mr. Ferguson. Were any of you here last night after midnight?"

All three turned away from Kat to face Lake and Al said, "I left after the dinner rush, like around nine thirty, I guess."

Linda allowed that her boyfriend picked her up at about ten and they went home. Phil said, "Karen left at about one forty five and I locked the back door, then went out the front like always."

Kat looked at Phil, "So the last time you saw Karen was one forty five?"

Phil turned to face Kat, "Yeah, about that I'd guess. Then I walked down to the metro and caught a Blue line to go home."

"When Karen left, was she alone, or was someone with her," asked Lake?

Phil turned again to face Lake, "I didn't see anybody else out there, but I didn't really look. I just locked the door after she went out. She told me a long time ago to lock it as soon as she was outside. She wanted to hear the bolts locking the door before she got in her car." Phil looked very confused, "What's going on here, Where is Karen?" Phil started to get up.

Lake stood and said, "Sit down, we aren't done yet."

Phil sat, looked at Kat, "You guys are scaring me, where's Karen?"

"Karen was attacked in the alley last night," said Lake looking at Phil. "She won't be in today."

Phil settled a little and asked Lake, "Is she in the hospital, is she gonna' be okay?"

"Let's talk about last night," said Kat, "So like you said, she went out the back door, you didn't see anybody else in the alley so you closed and locked the door."

"Yeah, should I have gone out there with her?"

Kat continued, "Shoulda', coulda', woulda', that is not the question. What we have to know is what you did do. When she went out into the alley, where were you?"

"Let me show you," as he started to stand.

"No," said Lake, "Just tell us where you were."

Phil looked down, thinking , then he raised his head, looked at Lake and said, "I was next to the prep table, she said something about tomorrow morning as she opened the door, like we have to restock napkins, and something else — I think and she left."

"Then you closed the door?"

"No, she gave it a push from outside and it shut."

Lake sat down again, "Then what did you do?"

"Then I went out the front and locked that door from outside," said Phil.

"What about the bolts, you said before that she wanted to hear the bolts lock the door," asked Kat.

"Oh, well yeah, I pushed the bolts first then I went out the front."

Kat looked at Lake and said, "I'm not getting this, so Phil, help me out here, show me how this happened. Start at the beginning and don't leave anything out."

"Yeah, okay. Well we were closing up. I gave her the bag of receipts and cash and — ."

Lake put up his hand, "Whoa, wait a minute, you gave her what?"

"Well Karen is the boss. She tallies' up the money every night and takes it all with her so she can hit the bank on her way in the next morning."

Kat said, "She just takes the money and leaves?"

Phil stopped and looked at Lake, "No, we take all the cash out of the register over to that table," he said pointing to a small table in a corner, "You can't see that table from outside and the light is better than downstairs, so we do our final count of it over there."

Kat said, "When did that happen, like at what time did you count the money?"

Phil thought again, and again raised his head "I think that it was about one fifteen. We had closed the doors at one, nobody else was comin in then, and we started to clean up."

Kat said, "What's that entail, the clean up. Do you sweep up, wash the dishes, what do you do?"

"Well last night was kinda slow, so the kitchen crew was done by about twelve and gone. Everything was cleaned up in there, except the floor in the kitchen had to be mopped. I swept up the front room and ran the vacuum in the dining room."

Lake leaned forward, "Okay, so you take everything out of the register and bring it to this table. Then what."

Phil thought for a second and looked at Lake, "Then we count the money and write down the count, like how many ones, fives and tens, like that and Karen puts it all in her computer."

Kat said, "So you count the pennies, nickels and dimes also?"

"Oh, yeah, we count everything. Sometimes we have hundred dollar bills and fifties too. Then we count up all the charges. We do them by type, VISA, Master Card, like that and put it all in her computer."

Kat said, "What about checks?"

Phil said, "We don't seem to have too many checks. I'm not supposed to accept them at the bar. If someone wants to use a check, we call Karen and she handles it."

"After you have counted, what happens," asked Lake.

Phil again hung his head as he thought about what he was going to say, then he lifted his head, looked at Lake and said ,"When she has it all in her computer, she goes downstairs with it and I think she sends it to Ben. Then she comes up with the money pouch and takes off."

Lake said, "Okay so when you guys count up the money is anybody else around?"

"No, Karen waits until the last customer has left and the kitchen crew is gone. Sometimes Linda is still here, but everybody else is gone."

Kat touched Phil's shoulder and said, "So nobody else is ever around when the money is counted?"

Phil thought for a second again and said, "Well Brandon used to be here mopping and cleaning, but he doesn't work here anymore."

Lake sat up straight, "And who is Brandon?"

"He used to work here, washing the dishes and cleaning up."

Kat asked, "What's his last name and where is he now?"

Phil said, "I don't know his last name, you can ask Karen, she probably has it written down somewhere, but I have no idea. He used to talk about going to Florida, but I don't think he did."

"Why do you think that," asked Lake?

"Well about a week after she fired him — ."

"Okay, slow down here, she fired him, you mean Karen fired him," asked Kat.

"Yeah, it was about a month ago, maybe less. Brandon comes to me and says, 'Who's gonna' do the dishes,' like that," Phil said with a mock sad face.

"This was a month ago," asked Lake?

"Yeah about that, and the next day Karen had our old guy back in here doin' the dishes."

Lake looked at Phil, "And sweeping up?"

"No, well sorta, he did it a few times, but not like Brandon did it. Then he stopped doin it all together and Karen was thinkin' of tryin' to get somebody else again."

"What about getting Brandon back again," asked Kat.

"I don't think Karen liked him, I mean he was a little odd."

Kat pushed the point, "How do you mean 'odd'?"

Phil looked around at the others and they were both nodding as if to say they agreed with him. "He kept to himself mostly, didn't talk much, just worked."

Al added, "He wanted to work through the night, until the sun came up, like he didn't like the dark."

Kat looked at Al and said, "How do you know that?"

"A couple of times he would look outside and say something like, 'It's safe now,' or 'At last, I can go home,' and then he would leave, when it was light out."

Kat flipped the page in her notebook, "Tell me, how old is this Brandon with no last name?"

Phil knitted his brow, "I'd guess late twenties, maybe early thirties . . ."

Linda looked up and said, "He is twenty seven, I heard him say once to himself while he was washing dishes — like he was too old to be doing that kind of work."

"Okay," said Kat as she made a note, "What about hair color — ?"

All three replied in unison, "Black — ."

"Black as night, long and all over the place. I don't think he owns a comb," added Phil.

"How long," asked Lake, "Like down to his shoulders — ?"

Linda looked at Kat, "No, over his ears a little, but no more."

Kat was making notes, "Height — ?"

"Tall," said Linda, Very tall."

Al added, "He cleared the doorway, but he was close, I'd guess that he is six foot seven or eight."

"Yeah," said Phil, "I'm six two and he's a good six eight."

Linda chimed in again, "And very thin."

Kat looked up from her notes, "Eyes — ?"

Linda said, "Dark brown, big, dark and very sad — and no glasses."

As Kat continued to take notes, Lake said, "What about tattoos or scars, any identifying marks?"

Again all three responded, "No —."

Lake stood up and walked around, thinking. "Can we get some coffee?"

Linda stood up and went over to a waitress station and came back with several mugs and a pot of coffee, "Anyone want cream or sugar?"

Al looked at her and said, "Yeah, please."

Lake poured a mug full, took a swig and said, "Okay Phil, show me where you were when Karen went out the door."

"Okay," and Phil stood and walked to the kitchen door, "I was in here," he said as he went through the swinging door into the kitchen with Lake right behind him.

Al started to stand and Kat touched his arm, "No, you stay here, I have a few more questions for you."

In the kitchen, Phil walked over to the prep table about ten feet from the rear door and stood with his hand on a stainless shelf. "I was right here when she went out the door."

Lake walked to the door, pushed it open and looked outside. Then left it open and came over to where Phil was standing. You couldn't see her go down the stairs from here."

"No, but she pushed the door closed anyway, so I couldn't see out there much at all."

Lake took a step toward the door and said, "Were you moving toward the door when she closed it?"

"No, I stood here and when it was closed, I went over and pushed the bolts closed."

Lake pulled the door closed and said, "Show me how you did the bolts."

Phil walked over to the door, gave it a tug to make sure it was closed and pushed the top bolt across then bent over and pushed the lower bolt closed.

"You gave the door a little pull before you pushed the bolts, did you do that last night too," asked Lake?

"No, she pushed it pretty hard and it sounded like it was all the way closed when I did the bolts."

Lake slid the bolts back, opened the door and stepped out on the landing. The crime scene tape was still in place and a police officer was still at the site standing next to his vehicle at the alley's entrance. Lake whistled and called out to the officer. As Dan Carney turned and realized it was Lake he waved and walked toward the landing. "Morning Lake, how much longer do you guys want to hold this scene?"

"Morning Danny boy, we have a few odds and ends to clear up, shouldn't take more than an hour or so," said Lake. "Listen I want you to do something."

"Whatever you need detective."

"Yeah, okay. You are going to be like the victim. Walk out that door, push it closed and walk to your car."

"You mean her car, the victim's car?"

"Yeah, and then you are going to start talking in a normal voice, then raise your voice a little, then some more and keep getting louder until I open the door. You got that?"

"Yeah, I got it."

Dan waved at Frank and said, "Let me tell Frank what's happening here. I don't want him to come running and shooting."

Lake laughed, "Whatever," and went back inside the kitchen.

Dan came in and stood at the door, "Ready when you are Lake."

"Okay, now if I don't open the door keep getting louder till I do."

Dan looked around trying to see who else was there, "Okay should I go now?"

Lake knew who he was looking for and said, "She's in the front room Danny boy and we have work to do, now go on get moving."

Dan went out reciting the alphabet in a normal tone, pushed the door closed and continued down the stairs to the pavement. ". . . m, n, o, p, q, r, s, t, u, v, w, x, y, z. Did anybody hear that, I hope not cause I feel awful silly doing this." Then in a louder voice, he began again, "a, b, c, d, e, f, g, h, . . ."

Inside the kitchen Lake closed the bolts and listened. He moved closer to the door and could just hear Dan as he continued, . . . " i, j, k, l, m, n, o, p, q, r . . ." He opened the door and called out to Dan, "Okay Danny, bang a few things around, like it was a fight going on out here."

"Okay Lake," and he proceeded to shake a few dumpster lids and kicked the side of the dumpster.

Lake had closed the door and walked back into the dining room, stood quietly for a minute and said to Kat, "Do you hear anything outside?"

Kat listened for a second and said, "No, what should I hear?"

At that point Dan had dropped an empty metal trash can and hit the dumpster with a piece of wood. "I heard that," said Kat, "What's going on out there?"

"A test little lady, just a test," said Lake, "I'll go turn it off now," as he walked back through the kitchen to the alley.

"Danny, that's enough, we got what we need. Thanks."

Dan dropped the piece of wood, clapped his hands to shake off the dirt and dust and said, "Should I hold the scene longer?"

Lake was half in the door as he replied, "Give me a few minutes, I'll be back."

"Okay boss," and he walked back toward his car to let Frank know what was going on.

Kat looked at Linda and asked, "Did you think that Brandon was odd, or scary."

"He was strange, but I never felt unsafe around him. He was quiet but very polite and he didn't stare at me like some guys do."

"So he was nice to you," asked Kat?

Linda thought for a second and said, "It's not that he was nice, more like he was not mean or pushy, he was kinda like my brother you know like a person you didn't have to think about."

Kat moved on to Al, "You thought that he was odd, because he didn't like the dark. Was there anything else about him that you can tell us?"

"No," said Al, "Like Linda says he was here and you didn't have to think about him. He washed the dishes and swept up the place. Didn't talk much, didn't get in the way, he just quietly worked. I don't understand why Karen let him go."

The kitchen door opened and Dan came in. "Lake, where are you?"

"In here," answered Lake from the front room, "What's up?"

Dan walked into the front room and saw Lake, "There's a fella out back, want's to come in, name is Ferguson, Ben."

"Yeah, " said Lake, "We're expecting him. Let him come in."

Ben Ferguson was a middle aged, average size, harried looking man with glasses that kept sliding down his nose and thinning black and gray hair that was too long. He came into the front room and stood looking at the gathering. "So, you all know about Karen?"

Phil looked up and said, "Yeah, she got attacked and she's hurt."

Ben looked a little confused, looking at Lake he said, "I thought — ."

Lake put his hand on Ben's shoulder and said, "Why don't you sit down and we will tell you what we know."

Ben sat down next to Al and hung his head. Linda stood, walked to the waitress station, poured another cup of coffee and took it to Ben. Lake stayed on his feet, Kat got up from the table and stood next to Lake.

"Karen Pavia was attacked as she left this restaurant at about 1:45 this morning. She was severely beaten and succumbed to those injuries in the alley next to her car. The unidentified individual or individuals responsible for this act are not yet identified and this session is part of our investigation into this crime. We are not labeling anyone here as a suspect, we are gathering as much information as we can so that the investigation can proceed efficiently. In that vein we will ask you all questions that may seem pointless or even accusatory, but everything at this point is an attempt to completely understand the circumstances surrounding this event." Lake looked at Kat and continued, "Detective Murano and I will look into all sorts of scenarios, but again, there is no identified suspect or suspects."

Kat sat down at the table across from Ben and said, "Mr. Ferguson, where were you last night between midnight and 3:00 am?"

Ben raised his head and said, "I was at the other place in Rosslyn, we closed around 2:00 am and then I drove home. I live out in Fairfax County, in Middleridge."

"Lake put a foot on an empty chair, leaned forward and said, "You didn't come to this restaurant at all last night?"

"No, Karen had a slow night, she called at around 1:00 am and said they were shutting down. She was going to stop in the Rosslyn store this morning and we would go over the receipts and then one of us would go to the bank."

"We gathered some cash, some charge receipts and a tally sheet in the alley, but we have not counted it yet," said Lake, "After we check it out, we will give you the money bag, cash and all."

"Yeah, great," said Ben sarcastically, "Keep the damn money and get me Karen back."

Kat cleared her throat, leaned forward again and said, "Mr. Ferguson are you aware of anyone who would do harm to Karen Pavia, for any reason?"

"No, I mean she was a tough lady, ran a tight ship as they say, but no, nobody would do that to her. That's why I hired her six years ago, she was good at this business, and good with people."

Lake asked, "What about former employees, maybe someone she fired recently?"

Ben looked up, "You mean that skinny guy, the dishwasher?"

Kat said, "Tell us about him."

"Ben thought for a second, "His name is Brandon, not much to tell, he worked for her for a few months, on a part time basis, you know, for cash. He was pretty good, but he hung around all night sweeping and mopping. So we paid him, but he was just supposed to do the dishes. We couldn't get him to leave and Karen or Phil had to hang around until he left. He was more trouble than he was worth, so I told her to let him go and get someone else, I knew that our old dishwasher was available again, sober — ."

Lake asked, "What is Brandon's last name?"

"I don't know, she probably has it in the office, downstairs."

Kat got up and walked to the front of the room answering her phone, "Yeah, okay, you guys have all you need?" I'll tell the uniforms that they can release it." She walked back to the small gathering and looked at Lake, "CSI says they are done out back. I'll go tell Danny he can wrap it up."

Lake said, "Okay you talk to Danny and I'll go downstairs with Mr. Ferguson."

Kat walked through the kitchen to the back door with Ben and Lake following until they got to the stairs to the basement. "I'll come back in and see you in the front room," said Kat as she went out the door.

Ben stopped and said, "Just a minute, I should close down for a day or two while you guys get what you need and we get ourselves pulled together." He turned and called to Phil, "Phil make a sign to hang in the door, say we are closed , dealing with death in the family — something like that."

Phil nodded and went back to the front room. Ben looked up at Lake and nervously said, "Never had to deal with this sort of thing before," then he turned toward the stairs and led Lake down to the office. "This is pretty typical of these places, we don't want to waste space upstairs so we put the office down here with the coolers and storage room." He pointed across the basement to a small area where there were several lockers and a bench. "That's our locker room, I guess Brandon may have used one of the lockers, the guys up stairs would know." Ben opened a locked door, reached in to turn on a light and stepped into a small office. The room was no more than an eight foot square with a desk, a tall five drawer file cabinet, shelves with cook books and assorted samples of napkin holders salt and pepper shakers, dishes, glasses and mugs. A single two by four foot fluorescent fixture in the ceiling lit the room and a laptop computer sat on the desk along with an ink jet printer and a desk lamp. Ben went to the file cabinet and opened the top drawer. "I think she kept all the time cards and employee stuff in here." He fumbled through the files and finally said, "Ah, here it is, Brandon — but no last name, just Brandon. These are his time cards, May, June, July — she has each month stapled together through September, five months. Here you want to see them?"

Lake took the pile of time cards and said, "I would like to take these with me, but you will get them back."

"You need 'em, you got 'em, she most likely put all his info in her computer, so I don't need 'em anymore. Anything else that can help you down here, it's yours, just let me know what you need." Ben sat heavily in the office chair, "She's gone, son of a — , she's gone."

Lake looked around and said, "We would like to check out her computer — ."

Ben sat up straight, "Oh yeah, sure — take it with you if you want, she sends me an update every day with everything that I need. You keep it as long as you need it."

"Thanks," said Lake, "Let's go back upstairs and join the others."

"Sure," Ben said as they left the office and headed for the stairs. As they started up the stairs, Ben paused, "Do you think that Brandon did this?"

Lake turned and faced Ben, "Right now we are gathering information, the more, the better. We are eliminating everyone we can and if one or two people look a little more interesting, we dig a little deeper. This Brandon character is probably just like the rest of you, but we haven't seen him yet. Just as we wanted to talk to you, we want to talk to Brandon, and most likely eliminate him too. Any idea where we can find him?"

"Ben thought for a second and said, "No, I got a call from some guy, asking why he was let go — I told him that our old dish guy came back, so — ."

"And who was this that called?"

"I'm not sure that he said who he was. I just told him that Brandon was a quiet, hard worker. He never complains and he does not drink."

Kat asked, "You remember this guy's name or where he works . . . "

"No, nothing comes to me."

Lake asked the others about Brandon using a locker and Al said, "He rarely went downstairs, didn't like the dark. He usually just hung his coat behind the door."

Kat said , "We may be back to follow up on some things, but we have enough for now. If anyone remembers anything else, call us," as she handed a few of her cards to Phil.

Lake gathered up the laptop and the file of time cards and said, "Thanks for your cooperation. We will be seeing you again as we work through all of this." Then he and Kat walked out through the kitchen to the alley. "I want to get this laptop to the geeks and see what's in it."

*   *   *

T<small>WENTY</small> O<small>NE</small>

Thursday . . .   Tradin' up . . .

Brandon was walking to work with coffee and bagel in hand when Lake and Kat were driving in the opposite direction on Pennsylvania Avenue. They were on their way to the ME's office at the request of the photographer, Freddy. The sky was clear, the sun was bright and warm and Brandon blended in with the rest of the people walking the District's streets. Just another beautiful fall day and a guy on his way to or from work, dressed in khaki slacks, white running shoes, a bright yellow knit shirt and a dark blue jacket blending in with the rest of the mass of people constantly walking the streets of Washington.. Kat looked directly at him and gave no further thought to the six foot eight man who occasionally wore steel toed boots.

As he approached the Pub, Brandon finished his coffee, tossed the paper cup into a public trash can and ambled into the alley. "Good mornin' Brenda," he said as he walked in the alley door. "You are lookin' good this mornin. Something happening?"

"Very perceptive young man — I'll tell you later," she said as she lightly danced across the kitchen to the stairs leading to the basement and the office.

Brandon watched her disappear down the stairs, looked at George and said, "Okay, I guess I'll get started on these deliveries in the doorway and get 'em down to the coolers."

George laughed and got back to helping with the prep for lunch. The day progressed with an obvious light touch in the air, both Brenda and

Stu seeming to be in specially good moods. After the lunch rush, the Pub was all but empty and Stu called the crew together in the bar area.

"Everybody, I have a few things to say today. First, we have become aware of an incident about six blocks from here that kinda scare us a bit. A woman, the manager, was leaving Rozzonte's late or early in the morning and was murdered in the alley right behind the restaurant. No suspects, and from what I could tell, no clues. I want everybody to be a little more careful when leaving here and best if you are not alone. Brandon, you worked at Rizzonte's before you came here, did you know this lady?"

"Karen, yeah, I know — knew her. I mean she's the manager, are you sure it was her? What happened?"

"Stu replied, " Yeah, that's the name, Karen something and I have no idea what happened. I guess it coulda' been a robbery or. you know, like a sexual thing. But I really don't know."

Brandon looked shocked and sat on a bar stool looking as if he had just been punched. Wow, that's terrible. I should stop over and see — ." His voice trailed off.

"Now on a much happier note, this is a great day for me and I want you all to know that I think that I am the luckiest guy in town."

Brenda was standing next to Stu with a smile and a blush. She looked at Stu, he nodded and she said, " We are going to get married. Stu finally asked me last night and I can't wait. We will get all the paperwork in order and probably go to the JP over the weekend."

"I've wanted to do this for a while now and recently things have been going well here in the Pub. We now have a solid crew, so Brenda and I feel that we can disappear for a few days and leave it in your hands."

Brenda stepped forward and said, "We didn't want a big fuss — , just our close friends — , that's you guys — ."

Stu looked at George, "Will you bring your wife?"

George grinned, "You think she'd let me come alone — , she wouldn't miss this."

Stu looked at Steve, "Will you bring — ?"

"Linda —."

"Yeah, Linda — ."

"Sure, we have a standing Sunday date . . .   the only time we're both off at the same time."

Stu looked at Brandon, "Anyone you may want to bring?"

Brandon still looked a bit shaken and said, "I'll ask her — , so maybe — ."

Stu added, "Alright, wives, husbands and dates — and Brenda's sister in Philadelphia," as he put his arm around Brenda's shoulders and pulled her closer to himself.

Brenda added, "So we will have a little celebration on Sunday, here at noon and be done by 2:00. We would like it if you all could stop in for a few minutes — ."

Stu continued, "Yeah, and we will leave from here right after that for the harbor in Baltimore. We're taking a short cruise to Bermuda, five days in all. Back in town Friday night and we're going to take the weekend to move into a townhouse we found in Alexandria. Should be back to work on the following Monday, ready to get back at it. Steve will be running things while we are gone and we feel confident that there will be no problems."

Steve had twelve glasses lined up on the bar each with a taste of champagne . . . "Everybody take a glass, and let's have a toast to the Brickers, Brenda and Stu."

As all took their glasses with but a taste of champagne, Brandon felt very much a part of a family. A feeling that he had lost several years before, causing him to leave home in Detroit and head for Florida. Here he was appreciated, he was liked, admired and given the opportunity to better himself. Here he found peace and safety. Here he was a brother or a cousin to everyone from the busboys to the owners. He raised his glass and drank with all the others and spent the next half hour talking with his friends, laughing and congratulating the couple who were almost like a mom and dad to him. Brandon's life was improving every day that he knew them.

"Okay everybody, the evening crowd will be beating down the doors soon, so let's get back to work," said Stu as he gave Brenda a final hug and smile. "Later little lady, later — ."

Brandon put his glass on the bar and was about to retreat to the dish wash station when Steve said, "Hey, bartender aren't you gonna' clean that glass?"

Brandon looked puzzled, "I'll take the tray back —."

"Naw, why don't you do it here, behind the bar. You're gonna' need a little practice for next week. I will be doing a lot of different things and will need your help in this room."

"But what about the dishes — ?"

"Not to worry, we have been wanting to get a back up for you since you first got behind the bar. The fella that you replaced wandered back in last week and Stu told him that if he stayed clean for a week, he would give him another chance. So we have him, his name is Hank, starting part time today to do the dishes and you will come up front and tend bar."

"Today?"

"Yep, he just came in about five minutes ago, that okay with you?"

"Yeah, oh yeah, that'll be great — ."

"And you will spend most of your time up front over the next week, till Stu and Brenda get back. Then we're gonna' have to look at a number of things. Like maybe you take the day shift behind the bar and I'll cover nights for awhile. See how that works out. On the busier days, we will double up behind the bar."

"Steve, that sounds great, — just one thing. I may want to take a day for Karen's — whatever, funeral, I guess."

*   *   *

As they crossed 24th Street and headed into Washington Circle, Lake said, "I gotta watch where I'm goin' here — damn near hit a delivery truck last week stopping at one of these restaurants."

"Do be careful Lake, I'd like to live another day," said Kat. "What do you think the Doc has for us today?"

"No idea, he may just wanna' gaze into your big brown eyes, or maybe he has something we can chew on."

"Yeah, and maybe it's something 'Detective Freddy' found," she said with a smirk.

"Right, your future partner — ," said Lake as he turned into the center lane at 20th Street and passed a metro bus. He drove to 7th Street, turned onto Massachusetts Avenue and headed toward southeast and the ME's office. As they pulled into the parking lot he said, "We got anything else to check on as long as we're here?"

"Not on my list," said Kat as she opened her door.

They entered the building and spotted Dr Colburn walking through the reception area.

"Good morning Doc, what's new and exciting," said Lake.

"Good morning Kat, always a pleasure to see you," said Colburn as he apparently ignored Lake. "Did you bring your partner with you today, — what is his name again?"

"Very funny," said Lake as he caught Kat's eye. "If that's all, we gotta run, lots'a bad guys to catch today. C'mon 'Brown Eyes', let's move."

"Lake, there you are, let me show you what we found, or more appropriately what Freddy found," Said Dr. Colburn.

Kat smiled at Lake and quietly said "Tradin' up old man . . ."

"Okay, Doc what did Freddy find," asked Lake with a disgusted look on his face?

"C'mon downstairs, and we'll let him show you."

They took the elevator down two levels to a lab area. Freddy was sitting at a wide screen monitor running through pictures from the 'Pavia' murder scene.

"Freddy, the detectives are here, are you ready to run the pics for them?"

Freddy raised his head from the desk, turned and smiled nervously. "Hi guys, I think you should see this. Not exactly sure just what I got, that's for you to say — anyway, take a look at this." He typed in a command on his keyboard and the widescreen showed a series of partial dirty red smudges and smears. "These are all partials from the Pavia scene. When I combine them, like this," as he hit a few more keys and the six images melded into one, "I get a very fuzzy single footprint of a boot. About a size 14 boot." Freddy turned and looked at Lake and said, "It's not exact, and I don't have any definition of detail, but it sure looks familiar to me." He turned to the keyboard and with a few more strokes brought up another group of images. These are from the —"

"The Decker scene — ," said Lake.

"Yeah," and Freddy melded the images into one, "Another boot, but this one is a size 14-p, with a little more definition." He again hit a few keys and the two combined images appeared on screen next to each other. "The drug dealer and the nice restaurant lady, two prints, same size," as he superimposed the two images, "And as I said to the Doc, how many big foot kickers are there?"

"Freddy this is good stuff. Can you print this out and give me a little write up where it all comes from. Doc, we gotta run, this is good, real good and we gotta look at both files again. Kat let's get movin'." Lake and Kat hurried out the door and back to their car.

Freddy sat at his computer smiling and Dr. Colburn said, "Well, 'detective', don't just sit there, put that report together." He turned away from Freddy with a big smile a walked into the morgue.

Buckling her seat belt Kat said, "You think we got a link up here, these two cases?"

"Okay the kid is good, and yeah, this could be a big break — ," said Lake as he brought the big Ford out into traffic and headed back toward the precinct.

Kat grinned broadly, sank lower in her seat and just loud enough for Lake to hear she said, "Tradin' up — ."

*   *   *

T_{WENTY} T_{WO}

Friday . . .   I'm still a dish washer . . .

Autumn in Washington is as unpredictable as any other city. This day, the sky was clear of clouds, the sun shone through the thinning leaves on the branches of trees, the temperature was on its way into the low seventies and Brandon was enjoying the circus of birds and squirrels as they bounced about hunting for anything edible. His early morning walk took him to the coffee shop earlier than usual and he parked himself near the window where he could see everybody coming in the shop. Suzanne arrived about twenty minutes later looking just as Brandon remembered her. She saw him at his table as he stood to wave her over and she smiled putting a finger in the air and mouthing, "Coffee first — , be right there."

"Good morning, you are looking good this morning," said Brandon as he maneuvered a chair for Suzanne to sit, "I was hoping to see you here this morning."

"I almost didn't come in today, I'm running a little late, but glad that I did."

Brandon said, "I don't want to make you late, so let me ask you . . . how about having dinner with me on Sunday?"

"Sure, I'd love it —, what time?"

"Well we could make a day of it and finish with dinner — I have an invite to a little celebration at the restaurant, my boss is getting married and we're going to have a gathering at noon, we would be out of there by two and the rest of the day is ours."

146

"Okay, this is exciting, a wedding celebration."

"Great, how about I come by at eleven and we can walk over, then go see the monuments on the mall and see where we are at dinner time?"

"Eleven — I like that — but right now I have to run to work —."

"I'll see you Sunday — eleven — ."

Suzanne stood, touched Brandon's hand and said "Eleven —," smiled and hurried out the door.

Brandon sat in his chair, smiled and finished his coffee.

*   *   *

Freddy had written several book reports in high school and a few science reports. This one he patterned after one written for a senior level physics experiment. He listed the purpose of the report, the tools used, the sites where evidence was collected, the methods of measuring his graphics and the equipment used in comparing his findings. The report took Freddy the rest of that Friday, working into the night shift. Dr. Colburn looked over his shoulder periodically and allowed Freddy to forge ahead. The report would be over detailed and perhaps somewhat high school-ish, but it would be complete and convincing. As he was leaving for the day Dr. Colburn said, "Freddy, when you finish, put it on my desk and I'll read it over in the morning."

"Okay Doc, I may be here a little longer, but I should be done soon."

"I'll let the night crew know that you are busy down here and may be a while before you leave."

"Thanks Doc, see you in the morning."

"Good night Freddy," he said as he threw his coat over his shoulder and pushed the button for the elevator.

It was almost nine thirty when two people from the night shift came into the lab. "Hey Freddy, you spending the night or what," asked Jeff?

Freddy lifted his head looked at the clock and said, "I gotta finish this paperwork by morning for the detectives. It's taking longer than I thought it would, but I'll be finished soon and be outta here."

"Yeah, well I just needed a couple of new bags and some more tags, we got a nasty one over near the hill. See ya later," said Jeff as he and his partner picked up the clean body bags and hurried back to the stairs.

Freddy returned to his task, finally raising his head after mid-night with a sigh and a yawn. He looked at the clock and decided that one final read-thru would have him outside and on his way home in a matter of fifteen minutes. He walked into Dr. Colburn's office, sat in the Doctor's high back chair and started to read. Freddy was smiling and felt very proud of this little report and as he turned the third page, he leaned back in the chair and fell asleep.

*　　　*　　　*

Friday nights were always a little busier than the early week nights and Brandon was getting a taste of a busy night behind the bar. Steve was there, ready to jump in if needed, but Brandon was holding his own. Steve walked into the kitchen and elbowed Stu, "We got us a bartender, Stu. He's doing better than I expected he would. Maybe I'm just a great teacher —."

They both laughed and Stu said, "So you think you're going to have an easy week — ?"

"Never said that Stu, but it looks like it's working out as you hoped it might."

"Well Steve, good luck, just don't burn the joint down."

"We'll be fine. I'm gonna' run him outta here in a little bit, tell him to get a good night's rest, tomorrow will be the tough one and I'm sure we will both be behind the bar."

"By the way, Hank is also working out, at least for the time being," said Stu.

"You think he'll last?"

"No, not really, but we'll give him another chance. It'll be up to him."

Steve went back into the front room and stood at the end of the bar. "Brandon, how about a glass of soda water with a lime twist?"

Brandon quickly poured Steve his drink and set it in front of him, "This one's on me," he said with a grin.

"You having a good time back there?"

"I am, Steve this is fun. I am in constant motion, mixing and pouring drinks, wash a few glasses, take an order or two for stuff off the menu and I get to talk to people, and the time is flying by. I really like this."

"Well that's good, because you are doing it again tomorrow and the all of next week."

Brandon looked a little concerned and said, "How is Hank doing?"

"You know, he seems to be a little better than the last time he tied one on. Maybe this time he'll be able to stay away from the stuff, or at least longer than before."

"I hope so, for two reasons, him and me."

"Look, Brandon, you have to worry about yourself, not Hank. Stu, George and I will try to keep him straight, but you just keep yourself on track up here. By the way, if you need a half day or the whole thing, for the funeral, you're covered."

"Okay Steve, thanks and I am going to give it my best up here."

"I know you will, that's why you are getting this shot — ."

Brandon took an empty glass off the bar and walked toward the sinks and paused, staring at the bar, the bottles, the coolers, the beer taps and he turned toward Steve. "I should take care of this tray of glasses first, then —."

Steve smiled and said as he turned toward the kitchen, "Have at it Brandon, and scream if you need help, I'll be back in a little while." Steve disappeared into the kitchen and Brandon turned on the water in the sink.

"I'm still a dish washer ," he mumbled to himself with a grin and began washing the glasses.

*   *   *

Twenty Three

Saturday . . .   Well done Mr. Knolls . . .

Doctor Colburn pulled his car into his designated parking slot and noted that the lights were still on in his office. "Freddy must be early," he muttered. Colburn knew that Freddy would give this little report everything he had. It was a challenge for a kid with a high school education, writing a forensic type report that the police would make part of the file and if all went well, introduce it into evidence when the killer was caught and tried in a court of law. He was planning on reading the report and helping Freddy made corrections as needed to make it more presentable, "After all, Freddy is just a kid," Colburn said to himself as he opened the door.

Freddy was there when Doctor Colburn walked in, but he was not early, he was asleep in the good Doctor's chair. Colburn walked quietly around his desk and picked up the report that was half in Freddy's hand and draped across his lap. Colburn sat in his guest chair and with a red pen in hand began to read.

Twenty minutes later, the door opened as Sylvia, the admin assistant came in to let Doctor Colburn know that a fresh pot of coffee was ready in the break room. "What's Freddy doing," she blurted?

Doctor Colburn sat up straight with a finger raised and a "Shhh, he's asleep — ."

Freddy sat up with a stunned look on his face and with sleep in his voice and his eyes, "Hey — Doc — what are — ?"

"What am I doing, Freddy? Well I am watching you sleep in my chair and wondering how long it took you to write this report. Now what time did you fall asleep?"

"Doc, I — I just sat down to make sure it was done, and it was — I don't know, after twelve."

"Well it's almost 7:30 and we have work to do. First, I want you to make a few changes in this report. Then print out a fresh copy and let me see it. Then we will send it to the detectives and finally, you go home and get a little sleep. Here, I made some notes in red. Just make those changes and we're good to go." He handed the report to Freddy and started toward the break room.

Freddy went to his work station and opened the report. The first page had a note in large red letters, "Freddy, Add Cover Page . . . like this . . . one page, centered."

EXAMINATION OF FOOTPRINTS

CASE NUMBER 20100924.02 DECKER, PHILIP

AND

CASE NUMBER 20101004.01 PAVIA, KAREN

COMPARISON OF FOOTPRINTS FROM BOTH CRIME SCENES

SUBMITTED BY FREDERICK ARNOLD KNOLLS

APPROVED BY DR. ARTHUR COLBURN

18 OCTOBER 2010.

Freddy quickly went through the twenty pages of text and photos, there were no other comments except on the last page. "Well done Mr. Knolls." He quickly assembled the title page and printed the complete report, stapled it together and went back to Dr. Colburn's office. "You didn't change anything, Doc."

Dr. Colburn sat up in his chair, removed his glasses and said, "Freddy, remember that old rule, 'if it ain't broke, don't fix it'. Well this is a good piece of work and I don't have to change a thing. Now send it over to Lake and let them do what they can with it."

Freddy smiled, "Okay Doc, you got an e-mail address for Detective McLarry?"

Dr Colburn put his glasses back on and said, "It's in the system . . ."

Freddy turned toward the door, said, "Okay, I can find it," and went back to his work station.

Sylvia came back into Dr. Colburn's office, "What is Freddy so excited about?"

"He has written a report, first one for him, pretty good job," said Dr. Colburn as he continued to look at his desk.

Sylvia smiled and said, "You didn't Change anything, Doc. Was it really that good?"

"It is good, good enough to get the point across and the kid busted his butt putting it together. I was ready to make whatever changes were necessary, but after reading the thing, I didn't have to change anything."

"He's thrilled."

"Yeah, I know."

*   *   *

Lake turned on his computer and proceeded to go through the start up sequence when Kat walked into the squad room carrying two cups of coffee. "Hey partner, happy Saturday, have a little wake up juice," as she handed him one of the cups.

"Thanks Kat, did any one bring in bagels or doughnuts today?"

"There's a bag on the table in the break room, but neither of us should be dippin' into that stuff," she said with a finger pointing at Lake's waistline.

"Yeah, I heard about it again last night when I got home. Hey, I got something from Freddy," he said as he pulled up closer to his computer and opened an email. "Says, Lake, see the attached report on the two sets of footprints, Freddy." Lake opened the attachment. "Twenty one pages, I'll print it out and we can look it over."

The photographs, measurements and other similarities between the two cases made it apparent that the same boot on the same foot left the impressions at both sites. "I don't get this guy's angle. He doesn't take money, he doesn't rape or abuse the victims, there is no obvious connection between Pills Decker and Karen Pavia."

"Okay, Lake, both are killed in alleys, both in the early hours of the morning, both scenes are visited by a guy with big boots, size fourteen, no robbery, no sexual assault. Let's start with the time of day, between midnight and three a.m. Who would be out at that hour, like people coming home from a second shift at a construction site or maybe restaurant workers."

Lake perked up, "Hey, how many construction sites or restaurants back up to the two alleys where these two scenes are?"

Kat thought for a second and said, "I think that it's time for another walk about. This time we do both restaurants and construction sites."

"And any warehouse or loading dock where these boots might fit in," added Lake. "I'm gonna' refill my mug and I'm ready to go."

"Well I will make a quick trip to the powder room and I will be ready," said Kat.

"Good idea," said Lake, as he turned and headed for the men's room.

*   *   *

T WENTY F OUR

Saturday . . .   I said No, now leave me alone, . . .

Brandon carried a case of bottled beer up from the basement and set it behind the bar. As he was walking through the kitchen to the stairs to get another case he looked at George and said, "One down, two to go," and he continued down the stairs. The basement was dark save one hanging bulb that Brandon left on so he could find the next case. As he stooped to lift the case, he heard a rustling of feet in the darkened corner to his left. "Who's there," he demanded? No reply, but his mind heard a low whisper that sent a chill up his spine. He lifted the case and hurried back to the stairs. After depositing the second case behind the bar, he headed back to the basement. He slowly descended the stairs, listening and looking. No sounds, no movement and Brandon walked over to the last case of beer to be brought up the stairs. He lifted the case, turned and started for the stairs when he heard a very distinct laugh. A low, throaty laugh as if he was being watched and had been discovered. Fear rushed over him as he raced up the stairs and slammed the door.

"Hey, Brandon, easy on the hardware, that door has to last another couple of years," said George.

Brandon turned, faced George and his face relaxed from fear to frightened to confused and finally to ease. "Sorry George, guess I'm a little excited about working the bar today."

"Yeah, hey good luck man, you are gonna' be fine. Take it one draft at a time and before you know it, we'll be on our way home with a good night under our belts."

Brandon forced a smile, "You're right, I'll be okay." He went back into the front room, behind the bar and hefted the last case of beer to a shelf behind the bar, held it securely with one knee and began loading the contents into a cooler under the bar. He was dressed for the front room with a bright knit shirt, khaki slacks and his white running shoes. It was approaching the lunch hour and even though the Saturday crowd was not normally that large for a lunch, the evening crowd would be. He emptied all three cases that he had brought up from the basement into the coolers and saw that he could fit another full case in the coolers as well. A very short debate ensued within himself. Should he get another case or not. "Damn it, I have to be in control, I have to do this," he muttered. He took the empty cases and went back into the kitchen. "Hey George, I need one more case," he said as he opened the basement door. "Be right back," and he slowly stepped into the stair well. One step at a time, slowly, cautiously he descended again to the basement. He ducked his head as he reached the bottom step and surveyed the basement. Nothing, no sounds, no movement. He advanced toward the beer cases stacked about fifteen feet in front of him. As he bent to lift another case, a sound, a whisper. Brandon took a deep breath, lifted the case and scanned the basement. "No, no way am I gonna' run. You can go to hell." The whisper stopped, started and stopped again. Brandon slowly turned his back and walked to the stair. Sweat was beading on his forehead as he stepped up on the first stair. A hushed whisper. Brandon paused, "No," and the whisper stopped. A second step, slowly and another hushed whisper. Brandon stopped, turned on the stair and stepped back down. He stood at the base of the stairs looking into the basement. "I said No, now leave me alone," he turned again, slowly and took the stairs as slowly as he could. The whispers lessened until they were gone. As he stepped out of the stairwell and gently closed the door with his foot, he smiled at George, "Last one. This might get me through the night."

"Hey, are you okay?" I thought I heard you talking to someone down there. Listen, if you need any more cases, we can run down and grab 'em for you."

"Thanks George, Like I said, I think this might get me through the night." He went back to the bar , emptied the last case and started on slicing up lemons and limes.

"Good morning Brandon," said Steve as he came in the front door with a newspaper under his arm, "Are you ready for your lunch crowd?"

"Hey Steve, I think I'm in good shape here, just loaded up a few cases and have the next keg ready to slide in when this on dries up."

Steve put his newspaper on the bar and walked into the kitchen. Brandon opened the paper and began to scan the Metro section. Steve came back and said, " Do you have the sports section, I think that the Caps are playing tonight, are they going to be on television?"

Brandon put on his sad face, looked up and said, "I don't know, I'm checking the obits for Karen."

*   *   *

Lake pulled the cruiser into the alley where Pills had met his end. They sat in the car looking at the scene. "We covered this pretty thoroughly last week, I think we have to look at the Pavia scene the same way."

Kat thought for a second and said, "Okay, how many blocks away is it?"

Lake thought for a moment and said, "Maybe five, I'm not sure."

Kat reached into a pocket in the door and pulled up a city map book, "How long you been working these streets Lake?" She fluttered through a few pages and stopped. "Here we are, and there is the Pavia scene," she paused, then looked up, "Five Blocks from here with one jog to the left."

Lake was already moving the car through the alley and back into traffic. Kat was looking at the map and counting alleys that they could check out. "You know Lake, there are a lot of alleys in this town and if our guy is an alley dweller, we may require a little divine assistance to find him."

"Yeah, well this job is a high percentage of luck mixed with an equally high amounts of hard work, divine assistance and, never forget the paperwork . . . endless paperwork. The last time I fired my weapon, I was doing paperwork for weeks. One shot fired — , one, I didn't hit anyone and I generated a mountain of paper. So be advised, don't shoot anybody if you don't have to. You would be better off if you talked the bad guy to death —, you could handle that, right."

"Thanks Lake, I'll try to remember, — talk first, only shoot if he survives my speech."

They covered the few blocks to the alley where the Pavia scene was located. Lake turned into the alley, stopped the car, cut the engine and started counting, "Let's see, I count twelve doors. You ready for a little walk? I think we should split up, go around front again and check each business, then do the alley together."

Kat took a final sip of her coffee and said, "Ready when you are," and she pushed open her door. "I'll take the west side," and she turned toward the entrance to the alley.

Lake tossed his empty coffee into a dumpster and said, "Okay, I have the east side, and I'll wait for you at the other end."

Kat went around the corner and started to look at the several storefronts. The first was a bank. She walked inside and looked around when a man approached and said, "May I help you?"

Kat took out her identification and quietly said, "Just looking, we thought a person of interest might be in the area and we are looking for him."

The banker looked a little apprehensive and said, "Should we be concerned?"

"No, not at all. This man may have witnessed something and we just want to talk."

"Oh, I see, if you need access to the restricted areas, I'll be at that desk," said the man as he pointed to a corner cubicle and turned away.

Kat walked around the open area, stopped at the corner cubicle, waved to the man at the desk, said "Thanks," and walked out to the street. As she turned south, she muttered, "This is going to be fun."

The second door was an entrance to and office building with a door to an adjacent sandwich shop. Kat went to the security desk, showed her credentials and asked the guard, "Any construction goin' on in this building today or over the last few weeks?"

The guard looked bored and as blandly as he looked, he replied, "No."

"Well, has any construction work happened here in the last two months?"

The guard was now irritated, "No, I have never seen any construction work in this building in the time that I have been here."

"How long have you been working here," asked Kat?

"About six months, why?"

"Do you ever walk the building?"

"Yeah, every morning and night," he replied.

"The whole building, you walk each floor and shake all the doors?"

"Yeah, that's the job lady."

"And you have not seen any construction in this building in six months?"

"That's what I'm tellin' you. And if anyone wanted to do any of that work we have to have names of all the guys on the job, when they plan on being here, when the job starts and when it finishes."

"You get all that information?"

"Either we get it or they don't do the work. No exceptions."

"Okay, thanks," and she walked through the lobby to the sandwich shop. "Hi there, I have a few questions for you."

Kat was out to the street again. "Two down, and one, two — four to go," she mumbled as she walked to the next door. "Rizzonte's, this is where she worked," Kat thought. Maybe lake should be in on this one." She dialed his number and waited.

"Hey Kat, you got something," answered Lake?

"No, I am at Rizzonte's and thought that we should both do this one together."

"Yeah, look, I'm almost at the end of my side. You go in, grab a table and order some coffee, I'll be right there."

"Okay Lake, see you in a few minutes," and she hung up, walked inside and saw the bar tender.

"Your name is Phil, right," she said.

"Oh good morning detective, nice to see you again," said Phil with a forced smile. "We are going to close after lunch today. Karen's memorial service is scheduled for three this afternoon."

"We know about the service. We're just checking a few leads, nothing startling, just several routine things to check on. As long as we were in the area, thought we should stop in, see if anyone remembered anything new. Maybe ask a few more questions. Are you okay with that?"

"Oh sure detective, anything that we can do to help."

"Listen, my partner is around the corner, he will be here in a few minutes. Let's get a couple of coffees and we will sit down again for a few minutes."

"Yeah, okay, in fact Ben is downstairs. I'll get a fresh pot brewing and let him know that you are here."

Phil disappeared into the kitchen and Lake walked in the door. "Hey Kat, where is everybody?"

"Phil went downstairs to get Ben. Did you know that Karen's memorial service is today?"

"No, I probably did know, but — forgot," said Lake.

"Don't tell them that you forgot, show 'em that you care about this."

"Yeah, hey did you order coffee — ?"

"You're hopeless, Here they come."

Phil came back in the front room with Linda and Al. "Ben is coming up, he was on the phone with Karen's sister." Phil turned toward the waitress station and Linda said, I'll get that Phil."

Al and Phil sat at the large round table and Ben came into the room. "Good morning detectives. Is there any news about the — ?"

"The case?" Lake sat at the table and Ben joined them. "No nothing to talk about yet, but we have a few small leads."

Linda brought several mugs to the table and went to get the coffee pot. She returned with a bowl of creamers and the coffee.

Lake looked at Ben and said, "Mr. Ferguson, is there anything else that you can tell us about Monday night or Tuesday morning? anything at all?"

"No, nothing comes to mind, and please call me Ben. I looked for Brandon's name in the files and found nothing other than a file with 'Brandon C.' on it. No Social Security Number, no address, no work history, nothing. I think Karen had him on a straight cash basis. I know we are not supposed to do that, but it still happens."

"Okay, what else can you tell me about Brandon C, let's start with a description — ?"

Phil sat up and said, "Well he is about six foot six and thin as a rail, has wild dark hair, spooky eyes and always wears dark clothes. You know like black everything, pants, shirt, coat, like that."

Kat said, "Okay, that's good, what about his shoes, black also?"

"Yeah," said Phil, "I guess, black, or real dark brown."

Lake leaned forward and asked very calmly, "Shoes or boots — ?"

Nobody responded. Lake looked at Phil.

"I don't know. I'm tryin' but I just can't see them, they were dark color though," said Phil.

Al looked puzzled, "I got no idea, guess I didn't look at him much."

Linda said, "I never noticed his shoes, they could have been boots, or running shoes, but I really don't know."

"Let's change the subject," said Lake. "Are any of you aware of any construction going on around here in the last few months?"

Phil looked at Linda with a blank stare, Linda turned and looked at Al with a similar face and Al looked at Ben as he said, "About a year ago, there was some remodeling work going on in this building. Probably an office changing hands, but that's all I can remember. Karen fussed about the mess cutting into our margins, but between the three stores we run, we were in good shape."

Kat sat up and said, "You have three stores?"

Ben looked at Kat and said, "Yeah, three. This one of course, the store in Rosslyn and the third is out in Fairfax City. I try to spend a day a week at each one, but that doesn't always work out. Karen was good, I could let her run on her own and — no worries. She was good. I got over here when I could, but now, I guess it will be a lot more. Damn, I'm going to miss her."

Lake took a long drink of his coffee, leaned back in his chair and said, "Brandon C. Tall, skinny, dark hair, dishwasher, thinking about Florida — Kat, we gotta go. Ben, thanks for the coffee and when we have something solid, you guys will hear it from us."

Kat and Lake went out the door and Kat slowed Lake down, "Hey, what's brewin' in that little mind of yours, partner?"

"Dishwasher, that's what's brewin' kiddo. Any restaurant with a new dishwasher, we should look at," he said with a grin.

"A tall skinny dishwasher named Brandon, can't be that many."

They went back to their car and Lake said, "Let's cruise the strip here and see how many restaurants we have."

Kat sat up in her seat holding the seat belt, "You know, if this guy is a dishwasher, chances are he is more on foot than in a car. Dishwashers make minimum and so he probably walks more than rides the Metro."

Lake was listening as he started the car, "Click it kiddo . . . so the guy is on foot . . . so what are you thinking?"

"I'm thinking that rather than going from door to door, we find a nice comfortable bench and watch the people coming to work in the morning."

"Like around 10:00 am till noon . . . and which bench?"

"More like 9:00 or 9:30 till noon. So we pick a bench at McPherson Square and work that one first," said Kat.

"Okay, I'll go along. Why McPherson?"

"It's a cross roads for a lot of traffic. Any place we start is gonna' be a guess, and there's a coffee shop right there that we may visit a few times while we wait," she said with a grin.

"Okay, it's a little late for today, so we start this stakeout Monday morning."

"Yeah, let's wrap this up for today and try to enjoy the rest of the weekend."

*   *   *

T<small>WENTY</small> F<small>IVE</small>

Saturday . . .   I know that am alone down here . . .

The dinner crowd was a little better than average. It was approaching 7:00 pm and it was promising to be a good night for the Pub. Linda, one of the waitresses had taken over the hostess duties and squealed when the door opened and Stu and Brenda entered. "Congratulations," she said as she hugged Brenda. Stu walked over to Steve and said, "Just stopped in for a minute, remember, I'm on vacation."

Brandon laughed, "Time for a drink?"

Stu replied, "No, just enough time for a quick dinner and we have a load of things to do before tomorrow. Steve, Brandon, this is Kathy, Brenda's sister," he said as he guided an attractive young lady to the bar.

"I can see the resemblance, " Steve replied as he stepped forward.

Brandon smiled and moved back to his customers at the bar.

Stu grinned and said, "Her boy friend is coming in after he parks the car."

Steve looked toward the door, saw a tall, athletic looking man coming his way and said, "Is this the lucky guy?"

"Yeah," said Stu, "and he's loaded."

Stu lowered his voice, leaned toward Steve and said, "Is everything okay?"

"Stu, we have a great team. Everything is in good hands and we are looking at a decent night. Now go on in the other room, enjoy your dinner and don't worry." He looked at Linda and said, "Set up 301 for the group."

Linda looked at the first table in the second dining room, an eight top closest to the kitchen. "The four of them and anybody else?"

"Set it for four and put in an extra two chairs so we can all stop by for a second and have a little coffee or tea with the bosses. Oh and ask Brandon if he would get me a bottle of the 2009 Pinot Noir from Sonoma County, it's in the rack down stairs, he knows which one I mean."

Linda hurried back to the waitress station, saw Lisa and said, "Let's set up 301 and ask Stu if he wants to see menus. He may already know what they want, but give him the option." She then went to the bar and waved Brandon over. "Steve told me to ask you to get the 2009 Pinot Noir from the basement, said you'd know which one he was talking about."

"Yeah, okay," he replied as his knees felt a slight twinge. He turned back toward the bar noted everyone looked set and thought to himself, "I can do this." He hustled through the kitchen and to the basement door. It stood slightly ajar and he slowly pulled it open.

"Hey Brandon, you need another case from downstairs?" asked George. "We can grab it for you."

"Thanks George, but it's a bottle of wine that I'm after and I know exactly where it is," he replied. He stepped into the stair well and started down the stairs, slowly. All seemed quiet as his foot touched the basement floor. He reached for the switch and flicked on more lights than he needed and started across the floor towards the wine rack. As he touched the rack, he heard a shuffling sound as if someone was standing behind him. He turned, nobody was there. He heard a whispering sound across the room, but saw no one. "I know that I am alone down here and you can all go to hell. You want me, come out and stand in front of me."

Silence, as he stood there with sweat beading on his forehead, there was nothing but silence. "Just as I thought." He turned again toward the rack, found the 2009 Pinot Noir and was gently brushing off the dust when he heard a distinct whisper call his name.

"Brandon."

Fear was beginning to rise in him, his knees felt weak and his breathing deepened. He shivered, stood tall and said again, "Go to hell," and he slowly walked to the stairs and up to the kitchen.

George was looking puzzled, "Who were you talking to down there?"

Brandon, still sweating and breathing hard said, "Oh nobody, just me talking to myself."

George laughed, "You gotta get out more Brandon. Hey you left the lights on — , don't worry Hank will get 'em."

Brandon was walking toward the front room and said, "Oh thanks George."

He took the wine back to the bar and found the corkscrew. Standing behind the bar, staring at the wine, Brandon heard a distant voice, "Brandon, I need three light drafts and a glass of the house white."

He looked up to see Lisa standing at the waitress station, looking at him. "Are you okay," she asked, "you look a little pale?"

"Yeah, I'm okay, just came up the stairs a little too fast, — gotta catch my breath."

Lisa smiled and said, "I'll go put in the dinner order and be right back."

Brandon said, "Three light drafts and a house white — ?"

Lisa replied, "That'll do me," as she turned and walked into the kitchen with a smile.

Brandon pulled the three drafts, poured the wine and set it on her tray, ran her ticket through the register and picked up the wine and cork screw again. Lisa returned from the kitchen and said, "You sure that you're okay?"

Brandon took a deep breath and said, "I'm fine," winked at Lisa, surveyed the bar and said, "Gotta deliver this to the other room. Be right back," and he walked toward the dining room.

Steve saw Brandon approaching and made room for him to pour the wine at the table. Brandon cleared his head as much as he could, smiled and with a white towel over his left arm showed the label to Stu. As Stu was about to speak, Steve said, "You two both like this one and this is that special occasion that we might be saving this bottle for — ."

Stu looked at Brenda, she was smiling and he couldn't resist, "Okay Brandon, pop the cork."

Brandon carefully opened the bottle, gently poured a small amount in Stu's glass and waited for Stu to approve.

When the dinner was done and Brenda and Stu had taken off, the evening progressed as any other Saturday night. Busy, but not over loaded. It was a good night and at 2:00 am, Brandon was wiping down an empty bar when Steve came in and said, "Nice job tonight, Brandon. You're a natural back there. Now on Monday, get here around 2:00 and you can close. I will be in early and get us through lunch, then I'll take a break when you get here and come back for the dinner rush."

"Thanks Steve, I'm really enjoying it."

"So tell me Brandon, are you okay? Lisa said she was a little concerned that you might be getting sick or something."

"Brandon thought about the basement and said, "I'm fine. That Karen thing has been on my mind and I rushed up the stairs earlier and it took a minute to catch my breath, that's all. I appreciate the thought, but I am fine."

Steve pulled up a bar stool, sat and said, "Okay, but once again, we are family here, if you are a little down and need a break, that's not a problem. And, by the way, I think Lisa noticed you once you move up front. I think she kinda likes you."

Brandon lifted his head, looked pleased and said, "Lisa — , she is a nice kid, but I'm into someone else right now."

"Yeah, but it's always good to have options — . Are you gonna' stop in tomorrow?"

"I'm planning on it and I'll try to bring Suzanne with me," replied Brandon.

Steve took the bar towel from Brandon and said, "You go on home, you had a good day and tomorrow is actually here already. See you around 2:00 this afternoon."

Brandon was tentative, "You sure, I mean, I can stay, and — ."

Steve laughed, "No man, you've done a full day's work already, go get some rest."

Brandon thought, I can do this, I am in Control — , "Okay Steve, I'll see you at 2:00."

*   *   *

T WENTY S IX

Sunday . . .   Good morning, are you ready for a little coffee . . .

The streets were almost empty, Brandon walked half hunched over, pulling his coat tightly against himself. He had covered four blocks without a single strange sound and he began to relax. He raised his head and looked across the intersection at the traffic signal then glanced to his right looking for oncoming traffic. As he turned his head back toward the left, his eyes passed over a shop window behind the traffic light. A shape, dark, broad shoulders and a square shaped head in the shop seemed to move toward the window and stop. Brandon stared at the window, not thinking. Then a truck passed between Brandon and the window. The shape was gone, the traffic signal turned green and he slowly crossed the street, looking at the window. Nothing appeared in the window. He continued, once again pulling his coat tight around his gaunt frame. As he crossed the next intersection, a rustling of papers caught in a gentle breeze startled him. He turned, nothing was there. Brandon was remarkably alone on a city block, no one in sight. He started to walk again. A hushed whisper in a narrow alley between two buildings. He continued, the whisper seemed to follow him and another breeze rustled the street trash, mimicking a shuffling of feet. Brandon stopped, he raised his head, loosened his grip on his coat, straightened his back and turned toward the whispers. "If you are real, come out, come out and stand in front of me. If you are only in my head, go away, leave me alone."

He surveyed the scene, nothing, no sounds, only a gentle wind moving papers and leaves. As he relaxed, he turned to continue his walk home and saw a slow moving car approaching. The blue lights on the cars roof were blinking and the car stopped at the curb next to Brandon.

"Good morning'" said Officer Tollar, "Are you okay?"

"Sure," replied Brandon, "On my way home from work."

Dan Carney was paging through the on board computer and glanced at Brandon, then said to Frank, "Where does he work?"

Brandon heard the question and answered before Frank could repeat the question. "I'm a bar tender, work down at Stewarts Pub on — ."

"I know the place, thought Steve was the bartender there," said Frank.

"Yeah, he is, I back him up and we are gonna' split the duties starting next week," said Brandon.

Dan poked Frank, "We got something on 17th, let's move on it."

Frank looked at Brandon and said, "Be careful, we gotta run," and pulled away from the curb making a fast U-turn at the intersection and flipping on the siren.

Brandon continued walking, all the way home he was aware of little sounds, nothing threatening, just the normal sounds of the night.

*　　　*　　　*

The sun was shining and the air was clean and cool when Brandon left his apartment at noon. As he walked he periodically looked in shop windows at his own reflection. "Lookin' good," he frequently muttered to himself, "I do scrub up nicely." His hair was neatly combed, he was clean shaven, wearing a sky blue button down shirt, khaki slacks and brown loafers. He liked the way he looked and for the first time since he left Detroit, he felt a confidence in himself. A confidence that was growing as he thought about a real life free of fear. His step was light as he approached Suzanne's apartment building and he once again checked his wallet making sure that he had the money. He had that $150 that was owed to him and a little more from a good night behind the bar.

Suzanne was ready to go as soon a Brandon arrived, but invited him in. "Brandon, this is Deanna," she said looking at a tall, tanned, girl with a perfect smile. Suzanne turned as another young lady entered the room, "and this is Marcella," she continued, "my room-mates."

Brandon was amazed at the three of them, each one better looking than the other, each in her own way. "My pleasure — ." He was now at a loss for words.

Suzanne saved him saying, "We should probably go, we don't want to be late."

Saved by Suzanne, Brandon said, "Yeah, we gotta go — ," as they walked out the door. They went down the stairs to the first floor and out to the street. "Wow, the three of you — , look, Suzanne, I think that you are beautiful, but the three of you, wow, it's like a movie."

Suzanne smiled and said, "Don't get carried away young man, they may be my friends, my good friends, but I do not share. Understand?"

"Yeah, perfectly."

"Anyway they're both semi attached. It's a wonder which one will get married first."

Brandon flagged down a cab and they got in. "Stewart's Pub," he said, "It's on — ."

"Yep, I know the place," responded the driver as he pulled out into traffic.

"So you and the other two do modeling things — ?"

"We get a little job every now and then. We have one coming up in a week, at an industrial show at the convention center. I get to wear a new dress that I am allowed to keep and hand out brochures to people."

Brandon listened, looking at Suzanne and said, "Yeah, and smile, you do that very nicely."

The trip to the pub took about eight minutes, but they were there before either one said another word. Brandon handed the driver a ten and said, "Thanks," as he climbed out of the cab, "Keep the change."

The front door was unlocked but the sign said CLOSED. Brandon pulled the door holding it open for Suzanne. "Well, this is it — , my happy home." They walked into the dining room and saw Steve talking to George and Brenda. "Hey everybody, we made it," they walked closer and Brandon continued, "Brenda, Steve, George, this is Suzanne. Suzanne, these are my friends, and this lady," he said leading Suzanne to Brenda is the new bride."

"Congratulations, and it's a pleasure to meet you all," Suzanne said, "And where is the groom?"

"Good question," said Brandon, "I'll bet he's downstairs in the office working — ."

Brenda smiled and said, "I knew he would not be able to resist, so I told him to look now, because after we have a drink, a little cake and a little conversation, we are leaving, no later than 3:00."

The group laughed as Stu came in from the kitchen. "Brandon, glad you could make it. And who is this?" he said taking Suzanne's hand.

Brandon stood tall and proudly said, "Stu, this is Suzanne, my friend, my very special friend."

Stu smiled and led Suzanne to the table where the cake was set up and glasses ready for a taste of wine were waiting. Brenda rolled her eyes at Stu, smiled at Brandon, took his arm and walked back to the table.

The front door opened, Frank and Bill came in. As they were crossing the bar room floor, the door opened again and Hank entered. The group was assembling in the dining room and within the next ten minutes, there was more than twenty people milling about, talking laughing and sipping the wine.

The cake was cut, shared and the clock showed 2:56. Steve tapped the side of his glass drawing silence and he stood tall, smiled and said, "Everybody, let's raise our glasses to Brenda and Stu. They are our friends, they are our family. They are now one and here's to forever."

Glasses were raised and a round of congratulations filled the room. Stu stood and said, "I can't thank you enough for this, and if I don't get us to the boat on time, I may be in tomorrow. I drink to you and we gotta go."

There was laughter and applause as Brenda and Stu headed for the door. Steve watched them go through the door and said, "Okay folks, get outta here and enjoy the last little bit of the weekend. Tomorrow morning we are on our own and I for one want Stu to be happy when they return in a week. Don't worry about clean-up, I've got it covered."

The group dispersed leaving Steve in the Pub alone. As they walked down the street toward the Metro station, Suzanne looked up at Brandon and said, "That was very nice. You work with some nice people."

"Yeah, I was very lucky to find this job, and funny thing, it is like a family."

"What about Steve, he's there by himself cleaning up."

"Not to worry, he will probably take the rest of the cake home and he can clean up faster than most, he's alright."

They reached the Metro station and Brandon said, "Which way would you like to go? We could go to the mall and the monuments or go back to the zoo, I know that you liked the Panda exhibit. Whatever you like."

"Let's go to the mall, I really like the Lincoln Memorial. Every time I go there, I seem to be in a hurry, I've always wanted to spend more time there."

Brandon pulled out his wallet and withdrew two Metro tickets. "The Foggy Bottom station is just a few blocks that way, and the mall is like three or four stops up. Let's go, I have never been to the Lincoln Memorial, it's about time I went."

They walked quickly to the station, Brandon handed Suzanne a card, they went down the escalator, through the stiles and as they were going down the second escalator, an Orange line train pulled into the station. "Timing, timing is everything," said Brandon, "Well almost everything."

They boarded the train and stood at a pole even though there were numerous empty seats. "What station do we get off at?" asked Suzanne.

Brandon had ridden the trains before, from end to end on each line. "The Orange and Blue lines both stop at the Smithsonian station on the mall. We can walk from there."

Suzanne smiled, "Okay."

The ride was only a few minutes and they were up another escalator and standing on the National Mall. Brandon reached out, took Suzanne's hand and they walked down Independence Avenue toward the Washington Monument.

Suzanne said as she hurried her step to stay with Brandon, "I'd like to stop at each one of the monuments and spend time, but I really want to see Mr. Lincoln."

"We can see him today and come back another day to see more." They hurried past the obelisk, and skirted the pool arriving at the Lincoln Memorial at 4:00 in the afternoon. The sun was low in the western sky, just above the Memorial as they approached.

"Isn't that impressive?" said Suzanne as she started to climb the stairs.

Brandon paused, looked at the structure, shading his eyes and said, "I've never gone up there. In all my time in this city, I've never visited any of the monuments." He took Suzanne's hand and they both slowly walked up the stairs, taking in and savoring the view. The crowd around them seemed to disappear, their eyes were looking up at the seated Mr. Lincoln as they approached. The room was silent, Suzanne slowly turned her head, reading the engravings on the walls. "That's the Gettysburg address," she whispered.

Brandon followed her gaze and they walked across the floor stopping in front of the wall. "Four score . . . yeah," and Brandon quietly read the rest of the inscription in silence, standing next to Suzanne. He felt somehow more complete, not a lone individual, living in complete dread of those movie characters. Today was the absolute best day of his life. He was relaxed, happy and in the company of someone who provided that small piece of life that he had been missing for years.

They spent the next hour looking at the words carved in stone inside the building, then another hour outside on a bench as the sun disappeared behind Arlington Cemetery across the river. Happiness was his, and hers. They both drew something special from this simple date. They both felt comfortable and safe in the other's company. As they walked back toward the metro station, Brandon suggested dinner at the first place they saw that appealed to her. Suzanne smiled and said, "Well I have another idea. We could go back to my place and I could cook us a little dinner. Both of my roommates are out for the evening and we would have the place to ourselves."

Brandon could not refuse, saying, "Is there anything that you need from a store, I can — ."

"No, I have everything that I need," she said looking up and holding her hand out, "Rain, we are going to get wet."

Brandon squeezed her hand a little harder, glanced over his shoulder back toward the Lincoln Memorial and said, "Maybe not — ," as he raised his hand and waved down a cab."

It rained, bathing the entire city and washing away two weeks of dust and grime. Morning came and the air was fresh, cleansed by the nights rain. Brandon awoke in a brightly colored bedroom with the sun beaming in through the window. He sat up, looked around the room and saw an alarm clock on the opposite side of the bed. It was 7:36 am, then he heard a slight voice coming from beyond the closed door. A pleasant voice singing some tune he did not recognize. A happy tune. He rose, pulled on his slacks and his shirt and wandered into the sitting room where he had met Suzanne's roommates the day before. The voice was louder now and coming from the right. He turned, looked into the kitchen and saw Suzanne, dressed, ready to go to work and brewing coffee in a French press.

She saw Brandon, smiled and said, "Good morning, are you ready for a little coffee?"

Tucking in his shirt, he replied, "Oh, yeah. It smells great." He brushed back his hair with his hands, looked at his bare feet and let his eyes meet hers. "Suzanne, I — , I mean, ah — I think you are beautiful."

She was going to be late for work, but she didn't care. After letting the first batch of coffee go cold and brewing a second over an hour later, Suzanne was dancing down the stairs to the street with a paper cup in hand and a smile on her lips. It was 9:22 am.

*   *   *

Lake parked the cruiser at a meter and leaned against it as Kat wandered over to the coffee shop. Within a few minutes, a meter maid walked over to Lake and stopped. "You ain't gonna' feed the meter are you?"

Lake showed her his badge and said, "Nope, just wanted to let you know that we are going to be here for a few hours, till maybe noon." He stood up and continued, "We will be right over there on a bench, looking for someone."

"Tough job, who are you after?"

"A tall, skinny white dude. First name is Brandon, we don't know his last name, don't know where he is working, don't even know if he's still in the area. He was working as a dishwasher at Rizzonte's, but he hasn't been there for a few weeks. So if you see someone like that — ."

"You see what I do detective, I write tickets. Tell me what his car looks like and maybe I could help you."

"Yeah, well — dishwasher, probably is lucky if he has a friend with a car, much less one of his own. We figure that if he's still working this area, he is most likely on foot and may walk through this Square on his way to or from work. So we are gonna' set up here for a day, then try another high traffic location."

"We — , you mean you and little Suzy Q there with the coffee?"

Kat approached and handed Lake a cup. "Good morning — ," she said as she leaned closer to read the meter maid's name tag. "Miss Bennett — ."

"Well just so you know, I am not the only meter watcher working this area. There are two of us that are working the area today. She is doing the few blocks on the south side and I got the north. So she will probably be by sometime in the next hour or two. Good luck."

Lake and Kat walked over to a bench and sat down to watch the people passing by. "So tell me something new and exciting, Suzy Q — ," said Lake.

Kat sat up straight turned and stared at Lake, "Suzy who ?"

*　　　　*　　　　*

TWENTY SEVEN

Monday . . .   You are way too young to die . . .

Brandon stood in the shower for a few minutes before dressing, grabbing the coffee left for him in the kitchen and doing his own version of a dance down Suzanne's front steps to the street. He browsed several shops as he walked toward the Pub, not looking for anything in particular, but constantly thinking of Suzanne. He found himself walking down 23rd Street, crossing C Street near the tunnel. "I'm almost back at the mall," he thought and quickened his pace. He arrived at the Lincoln Memorial and went into the gift shop. It didn't take long for him to find a matted photograph of Mr. Lincoln that he was sure Suzanne would like. He bought the photo and a book about the Memorial and checked the time. It was almost 1:00 pm and he decided to head for the Pub. Along the way he stopped at a street vendor and bought hot dog and a soda. Walking, eating and enjoying the sunshine Brandon covered the distance to the Pub before long and walked in the front door. Steve was behind the bar talking to a customer and Lisa was standing at the hostess station stacking menus. Steve looked at Brandon and mockingly looked at his watch then said, "Brandon, you're early — ."

Brandon grinned, made an apologetic bow and said, "I just couldn't stay away." He walked over to the end of the bar and put his purchases on a shelf where they would be out of the way.

Steve walked over to the waitress station, refilled his coffee mug and said, "So what's the schedule for the funeral?"

Brandon had put Karen out of his mind for the last day and Steve just brought her back to the fore. "I have looked in the 'Post' every day since we heard and I must have missed the announcement. I think she was from Chicago or Cleveland and the family may have taken her home. I don't know, I think that it's time to move on."

Steve quickly changed the subject, "That was some good looking lady with you yesterday, young man."

Brandon went from a blank expression to a slight smile, then beamed at Steve's words and said, "Yeah, how lucky can I be, we had a terrific day and I really like her."

"Be careful now lad, don't start getting serious, you are way too young to die," Steve said with a smile.

Lisa walked over Steve and slapped him on the arm, "Steve, you shouldn't talk like that. She was very nice and they make a very cute couple," she said as she turned toward Brandon with a smile.

Brandon looked at Steve and Steve said, "She's right, she was very nice and you are a lucky guy."

Lisa took her coffee mug and walked back to the waitress station. As she passed by Brandon and Steve and they could no longer see her face, her smile disappeared.

*   *   *

David Gonzales was on his lunch break, getting coffee and a hamburger from a street vendor. As he paid for his lunch a tall, thin man got in line and was reading the menu. David looked at him and remembered the policeman he met almost two weeks before. "The police, they look for a tall skinny man," he muttered. "Maybe this is the one. Maybe not." He looked at the man's shoes. They were white running shoes, but they were large. David was thinking about calling the policeman to tell him about a tall man as he walked back to the job site where he was working today. "It's probably not the right guy," he mumbled to himself. David wanted to make the policeman happy, but he also knew what it was like to be looked at as a suspect even though he didn't do anything. He finished his burger, tossed the paper wrappers in a trash can and went back to his job.

*   *   *

Brenda and Stu were on their cruise, Steve was enjoying being in charge and Brandon was enjoying working behind the bar. The Pub was experiencing a normal day's business but the staff was hustling as if it were a banner day. The entire crew was in good spirits and Brandon was on a natural high, trying to remember the little tune that Suzanne was singing. He had never had a girl friend, never had a job with responsibility and never had a collection of friends who treated him like family. As he poured drafts and mixed drinks throughout the afternoon and into the evening, Brandon remembered the night before. Thoughts of Suzanne, the Lincoln Memorial and an evening like he had never experienced filled his head. The day passed with him trying to remember the tune she was singing, but he knew that he was not even close.

*   *   *

T<small>WENTY</small> E<small>IGHT</small>

Tuesday . . .   Saved by dispatch . . .

Brandon woke early on Tuesday. During the night he had dreamt about walking around the National Mall looking for someone that he could not find. He couldn't remember who it was that he was seeking. It was a disturbing dream, not one that instilled fear, rather one that raised concern. He assumed that Suzanne was his objective and couldn't find her. Uncertain, he wondered about her, was she alright, why was he looking for her. All questions that did not answer themselves. He looked at his watch, it was 6:45 in the morning. He stood, paced about his apartment and finally went into the bathroom, stood in the shower and dressed. He picked up the package from the day before with the photo of Mr. Lincoln, hurried out of his apartment and quickly walked to the coffee shop.

It was 8:15 when she walked through the door. Brandon saw her and felt half relieved. He stood to go over to her when she spotted him, smiled and waved. She held up a finger and placed her order, paid and came over to Brandon.

"Hi, I would have thought that you would still be sound asleep," she said as she hugged and kissed him.

"I woke up early and thought that I might be lucky and catch you before you go to work," he half lied. All of a sudden he felt relief and said, "Can you sit for a minute or two?"

Suzanne turned toward the counter as she said, "Let me get my coffee, I'll be right back."

Brandon watched as she glided across the floor and returned. He moved a chair into position for her and she sat down. They stared at each other smiling for a second and Suzanne said, "Sunday was wonderful. I want to do it again."

"Oh, that reminds me, — I thought that you might like this," he said as he handed her the bag.

Suzanne opened the bag and pulled out the photo. She smiled as she studied it and said, "Oh Brandon, I love it. I'll put it —, I think that I would like to hang it in my room."

"It needs a frame."

"I have a few older pictures about this size, maybe it would fit in one of those frames."

"How would you like to go back to the Lincoln — ?"

"I'd like that, but we could also go somewhere else if you would like. I have never been to Arlington Cemetery. Have you?"

Brandon was feeling much better and said, "We can remedy that this Sunday — ."

Suzanne looked a little disappointed and said, "Oh I have a show this weekend. Saturday and Sunday at the Convention Center. I think it's over at 7:00 on Sunday, that's kinda late, isn't it?"

Brandon thought for a second and said, "Why don't I meet you at 7:00 outside the Convention Center at 9th and H Streets and we could have dinner and — ."

"Dinner sounds great, There are a couple of places right there that are good — ."

Brandon smiled and said, "Whatever you would like, I would like."

"I would like to frame my picture after dinner — ."

*   *   *

Carney and Tollar were driving east on L Street when Dan saw David Gonzales carrying a tool box and heading into a building. David saw Dan and waved. He looked a little tentative, but Dan let it go. Frank noted the wave and said, "I'd turn that S.O.B. into the ICE guys."

Dan stopped for a traffic signal and said, "Yeah, you would and then the Latino community would never speak to you again." The light turned green and Dan said, "He looked a little tense, maybe he can hear you."

"Yeah, and maybe he found our guy, tall skinny L'il Abner type."

"Right, it's a quiet day, maybe I should go check it out."

Frank rolled his eyes and said, "You're drivin' partner, whatever you wanna' do."

As Dan was about to pull over to the curb, the radio squawked, "4075, please respond to alarm at 1566 L, see man named Gatlin, Leo Gatlin — . This is a non emergency."

Frank touched his radio as he said, "Saved by dispatch," he pushed a button, "Dispatch, this is 4075, will respond — Thanks."

The dispatch operator replied with a touch of confusion, "You're welcome — ."

Carney laughed, "Thanks — ?"

Tollar sat up straight, "Yep, and you're welcome."

*   *   *

Kat was sitting on a bench in Franklin Square, about two blocks from where they had spent the previous morning. Lake walked over carrying two fresh cups of coffee. Kat looked at him and said, "I'm gonna' start to shake if I drink any more coffee."

"Well I used their restroom and it only seemed fair to buy something," said Lake, "This isn't bearing any fruit today either, but I still think we try a few more locations before calling it a bad idea."

Kat was listening and looking across the square. There was a tall, thin man browsing the shop windows, stopping at each one and moving on. "Lake, take a look at the guy in the blue jacket across the way."

"Where," said Lake as he sat up? He looked at Kat to see where she was looking and followed her line of sight. "We got us a tall and skinny — . So those big brown eyes of yours do more than make guys fall apart."

"Very funny, let's take a walk."

Brandon was looking in a shop window at jewelry that he couldn't even begin to afford, couldn't half afford. As he was about to go on to the next window, a short and very attractive woman stepped in his path. She pulled something out of her pocket and showed it to Brandon.

"Good morning sir, my name is Detective Katrina Murano, and this," as she gestured toward Lake, "Is my partner, Detective Martin McLarry. Can we ask you a few questions?"

Brandon said, "Oh, the police, what did I do?"

Lake chimed in, "We just have a few questions, shouldn't take but a couple of minutes."

"Sure, whatever you need. What's this about?"

There were several tables set up as outdoor seating for a restaurant. Kat pointed to the table and said, "Let's sit down here for a minute."

They moved to the table and a waiter approached. Kat held up her badge and said, "We're only going to be a minute." Then she looked at Brandon and said, "First, what's your name?"

"My name is Brandon Croummer," he replied, noting that she was writing it down. "That's C - r - o - u - m - m - e - r."

"Okay Brandon," said Lake, "Where do you live?"

"I live in the Exeter Apartments on Third street, 1500 block."

"Okay," said Kat, "And where do you work?"

Brandon was proud to be able to say, "I'm a bartender at Stewart's Pub on Mass Ave."

Lake said, "I know the place. Okay, how long you been at Stewart's Pub?"

"About three weeks, before that I worked at Rizzonte's," Brandon responded.

Kat said, "Yeah, gotta ask you about that. You worked for a Karen Pavia?"

"Ah, her name is Karen, not sure about the last name."

"Were you tending bar there," asked Lake?

Brandon looked at Lake and said, "No, no there I was the dish washer. Until like three weeks ago, Karen says, we don't need you anymore."

"She fired you," asked Kat?

"Well, yeah, I guess — , funny thing is, I walked into this job at Stewart's the next morning. Best thing that ever happened to me."

"How's that," asked Lake.

"Stu is a great guy, and Brenda, she is a terrific lady. Then there's Steve, he's teaching me how to tend bar. Like I say, it's the best."

"Did you know that Karen was killed there about a week ago?"

"Yeah, we heard about that, what happened?"

Kat closed her notebook and said, "That's a long story. Do you know anyone who might want to hurt her?"

Brandon acted as if he knew nothing, "No, not that she was a saint, but she didn't have any enemies that I was aware of. You never know though."

"Okay and where were you on Monday, the fourth?"

"Monday, last Monday, I think that I was at work all day. I'm sure that I was. I was getting in a little early like around 9:00 am, help out a little with the stocking work, cleaning up, stuff like that. I figure that if I do a little extra, I'll keep this job a little longer, so I show up a little early, stick around a little late — , it's a win - win."

"So what time did you go home," asked Lake.

"Oh, I don't know, we shut down a little early one day last week, that mighta been Monday night, or more like Tuesday morning."

Kat was making notes again and asked, "So when you leave the pub, where do you go?"

"That's easy, I go home. Like where else can you go at that time of night. Anyway, by the time I finish at the Pub, all I wanna' do is hit the sack and sleep."

Lake said, "Did anybody see you leave the Pub that night?"

Brandon screwed up his face and said, "I guess that Steve might have seen me leave, but I don't know."

Kat then asked, "What were you wearing when you left?"

Brandon paused, shrugged and said, "Probably the same things that I have on now." He was lying, he knew exactly what he was wearing, where he went, what time it was. Everything, he knew everything, and he knew that he had to lie. He was ready for this encounter and wondered why it took them so long to find him. He had almost assumed that they had written the whole thing off to a robbery. He also knew that he had to appear as innocent as he could. It was like one of the many movies that he had seen. Act like you don't know and nobody could prove different. He knew that the clothes that he had worn on that day had to disappear. The shirt, pants, socks and coat had to be washed and tossed. The best place to dispose of old clothes is the salvation Army, or the Goodwill boxes. He had already washed and bleached those things twice. A third time would now not be feasible. Everything had to go now, including the shoes.

Lake came back with, "Steve?"

Brandon was relaxed, calm showing no signs of being threatened. "Yeah, Steve is the Bar Manager, I work for him and he has been teaching me how to work the bar."

Kat asked, "Did you get along with Karen?"

"I guess, I mean, I worked for her and she paid me. I came on as a dishwasher there and figured that after a few weeks, I would be going somewhere else. She paid me in cash and that helped me out, having cash and not checks."

Lake asked, "So do you still get paid in cash?"

"No, Stu is stickler for playing by the rules. We all get paid by check. So I opened a checking account at the bank down the street from the Pub and got a debit card. It's actually better than having to handle everything with cash."

Kat then said, "So you didn't get along with Karen and she fired you, right?"

"No, I didn't really deal with her, Karen. I did my job and she stayed away. Anyway, like I said, I figured that I was not going to be there for long and I think that the regular guy who did the dishes probably came back. I think he was in the hospital or something."

Lake came back with, "How long were you there at Rizzonte's?"

Brandon pretended to think, pausing he looked at his hand as if he was counting something and then he said, "I started there in May, and stayed until a few weeks ago, so that's like five months there and almost a month here, I mean at Stewart's."

Kat was making notes and Lake was thinking. Brandon saw his opportunity and said, "You said she was killed, Karen I mean. How did it happen, was it a robbery?" He looked concerned, puzzled. He played it to the hilt. "She wasn't the nicest person in the world, but she was decent to me."

Lake leaned forward and said, "She fired you, remember. She FIRED you. That is why we wanted to talk to you, you are at the top of our list of suspects."

Again Brandon played the role, "Oh, well , yeah, I guess that is what you might think, I guess." He looked at Lake and said, "Thing is — , she actually did me a favor. I got a better job, more money and now I'm not washing dishes, I'm tending bar."

Kat looked at Lake and shrugged her shoulders as if to say, I got nothing here. She looked at Brandon and said, "Do you have family in town?"

"Family, no, not really. I mean no relations, but I feel like I'm part of group of people that are kinda like family."

Lake picked up the scent again and asked, "Didn't I hear that you were talking about going to Florida and DC was just a stop on the road."

Brandon smiled, "Yeah, that was the plan a couple of years ago, but with this job and I met a girl that I really like, well, I'm not thinking about Florida anymore."

Again Kat felt like she was in a dead end alley. "Detective McLarry and I have a lot of questions to ask the people that you used to work with and the people that you work for today. Do you have a problem with that?"

"No, no problem at all. You guys have to find whoever did this to Karen. I know that I'm probably not crossed off your list of possible suspects yet, but that's okay. I mean, like you have a job to do and like you said, she fired me." He slumped in his chair and said quietly, "Karen's dead, wow, that's terrible." He stared straight ahead.

Lake said, "We will stop in at Stewart's Pub soon and talk to the people there. Is there a good time to do that?"

"To talk, yeah I guess in the morning before we get started. We usually do things like stock shelves, inventory stuff. When people start coming in, everybody is moving and busy, so yeah, mornings."

Kat readied her pen and asked, "Who is the manager at Stewarts Pub, that's where we would like to start?"

Brandon looked up and said, "Manager, that would be Stu Bricker, he's also the main owner. But he's gone until Friday. He and Brenda got married the other day and they're on a cruise. Steve is in charge until they get back, you could start with him. Brenda and Steve are the other two owners."

Lake asked, "And what is Steve's last name?"

Brandon still had a stunned look, as if Karen's death was disturbing him, "Steve, ah — Steve Benjamin."

Kat stood up, looked at Lake and said, "Brandon, thanks for talking to us. We will probably talk again. Like they say in the movies, it's routine."

Lake also stood and said, "You're not leaving town, right?"

Brandon stood and slightly shook his head, "No, I'm not going anywhere. Just to work." He looked at Lake and said, "You said she was killed on Tuesday, or was it Monday?"

Kat answered, "It was about 2 or 3 on Tuesday morning."

Brandon sat down again and stared ahead. Kat and Lake started to walk away, noticing Brandon's behavior. They crossed the plaza and when out of ear shot, Kat said, "I don't know Lake, in a sense he is looking good for this, in another, he looks clean."

"Yeah, well brown eyes, that's why we get the big bucks, we're gonna' figure this out."

*   *   *

TWENTY NINE

Thursday . . .   You tell me that everything is alright . . .

Lake and Kat arrived at the Pub at 9:30 in the morning. The front door was closed and locked, but there was activity inside. Lake knocked on the door and caught the attention of George as he was grabbing an apron. George walked to the front door waving at the early visitors and pointing to his wrist as if to indicate the time. He reached the door and said in a loud clear voice, "We don't open until 10:30."

Lake showed George his badge and said, "Open the door, we have a few questions for you."

George turned the lock on the door and stood aside as the two detectives entered the front room. "What can I do for you this morning officer?"

Kat responded, "Detective Katrina Murano, this is my partner Detective Martin McLarry, and you can answer a few questions. Are you Steve Benjamin?"

George looked a little relieved and answered, "No, I'm George Gombowski, Steve is the bar manager and I am the kitchen manager."

Lake sat on a bar stool and asked, "When do you expect Steve to get here?"

"Soon, I opened this morning and Steve will get in around 10:00. Brandon should be here by noon, Lisa will be here in about 45 minutes, — ."

Kat said, "Okay, so we will talk to you first. Let's sit down and take this slowly."

Lake walked over to a table and gestured to George to sit down. "Just a few easy questions."

George approached the table, "Yeah, okay. What can I tell you?"

Kat began, "How long have you been working here, George?"

George turned to look at Kat and replied, "About four years, I started when Stu opened this place. We go back a few years and I always enjoyed working with him."

"Tell us about Stu, said Kat.

"He's a good guy, is this about Stu, is he in some trouble — ?" George looked scared, "What about Brenda, is she okay?"

Lake leaned forward, "No problems with Stu or Brenda, let's skip them for a minute, tell us about Steve."

George relaxed a little and said, "Steve, he's a part owner. I guess he's a small part owner now cause Stu and Brenda got hitched on Saturday."

""Yeah, now what about Steve," pushed Lake?

"Steve is a good guy, he has been married and divorced, has a couple of kids. He works hard, but really likes to play around with the women. Probably why he is divorced."

"Okay, " said Kat, What about this — Brandon?"

"Brandon, oh he's new here, about a month. He's a good guy too. Works real hard, comes in early, works late. They hired him as a dishwasher, now he's tending bar. The kid is a prize."

"So where was this Brandon before he came here," asked Lake.

"He was at Rizzonte's, washing dishes. I think he said he was there about four or five months."

"Yeah, does he ever talk about this Rizzonte's place, like maybe why he left there?"

"The old dishwasher guy sobered up and came back. We got one of them here, Hank. He came back just last week and Brandon moved up to bar tending."

"So was Brandon maybe a little angry for getting fired at Rizzonte's," asked Kat.

George thought for a second and replied, "No, not that I recall. Brandon has always been upbeat. Well except for when he has to go down in the basement alone."

Lake perked up, "Whatta ya mean, basement, alone?"

"Oh you know, like the other day he needed a bottle of some wine from down there and he gets to the top of the stairs, turns on the lights and maybe says a little prayer before he goes down the stairs."

Kat was again making notes, "Tell me more."

"Well he goes down the stairs and I'm up here in the kitchen and I can hear him talking. He's down there by himself, then he comes up the stairs and leaves the light on. When I say, 'Hey, you left the light on,' he looks scared. Then I say, 'Don't worry, I'll get it', and he looks relieved. I figure it's a dark thing, some folks just don't like it when the lights are out."

As they were talking, Steve walked in through the kitchen. "Hey George, how are you this morning?" He walked over to the table where they were seated and looking directly at Kat, said, "Hi, I'm Steve Benjamin."

Kat was a little taken aback and said, "Hi, I'm Detective Katrina Murano and this is my partner, Lake McLarry."

Steve shook her hand while looking into her eyes, then turned toward Lake and shook his hand, still looking at Kat. "My pleasure, what's this all about?"

Lake took the lead while Kat gathered herself back together, "This is an investigation into something that happened a little over a week ago. We think that someone here may have seen something or be aware of something that may help us out."

"Really, wow, what happened — ?"

Lake said, "The manager at Rizzonte's was murdered — ."

Steve looked startled, "Rizzonte's, that's where — , ah — what was her name?"

Kat picked up the hook, "Karen Maria Pavia, and yes that's where Brandon used to work."

Steve looked confused, "So how can we help you?"

Lake pulled out a chair and said, "Sit down, and we will talk."

Steve sat in the chair and nervously said, "Brandon is a good guy. He's been here for a few weeks and we are breaking him in as a bartender. He's good with people — ."

Kat interrupted Steve asking, "Did you know why Brandon left Rizzonte's?"

"Ah, yeah, he was let go. I think that their regular dishwasher came back. We picked him up right away, so he never had a gap. Didn't miss a day's work, and we pay better."

Lake put his pencil down and said, "You seem to know a lot about what goes on over there at Rizzonte's."

Steve cleared his throat, "Yeah, well when Brandon came here and told us about working there, we decided to check him out. Stu called the owner, asked why he was on the street. The guy told him that the old guy returned. Brandon was a hard worker, and did a lot of extra stuff. Sometimes that extra stuff gets in the way."

Kat looked confused, "How so?"

Steve shrugged his shoulders and said, "Well, if he finishes the dishes, then sweeps up and then mops up, he could be here all night. I guess that was not what they wanted. They just wanted him to wash dishes and go home."

*   *   *

The day started for Brandon like most other days. Up at 9:00 am, stand in the shower for a few minutes, dress and head out to the coffee shop. He wished that he could finish earlier at the Pub some nights so that he could get up at 6:30 and maybe meet Suzanne for coffee in the morning. She tried to be at work by 8:00 and that was just not enough time for a breakfast meeting. He walked along the street with his cup of coffee, leisurely looking in shop windows and dreaming of having enough money to buy Suzanne another gift. He arrived at the Pub at 11:30 and hung his coat in the rear hallway.

"Good morning George, how's the day looking?"

George walked over to Brandon and ushered him to a corner where they could talk privately. "Brandon, a couple of cops were here this morning asking questions about you and that place where you used to work."

Brandon put his hand on George's shoulder and said, "Yeah, they talked to me yesterday and said they would stop by here. That's a scary thing, I mean Karen getting killed." He shivered and said, "I asked if it was a robbery and I don't think they answered me. Strange. I think it was though. She frequently had the day's cash in a bag in her purse and hit the bank in the morning."

George said, "They asked about you getting fired and did that make you mad."

"Sure, they have to ask all that kinda stuff from anybody that might be a suspect. They get answers and eliminate people, so maybe they are just eliminating me now. Anyway, not to worry, those guys are just doing their job."

He walked out to the bar area and Steve saw him. Brandon crossed the room, walked behind the bar and busied himself while Steve finished with a customer. When free, Brandon and Steve huddled at the end of the bar. "I hope this isn't changing anything here," said Brandon, "Those cops are just doing their jobs. They should look at me and everybody else that worked there for the last couple of years. That lady, Karen was pretty tough on people. Fair, but tough."

"Okay Brandon, you tell me that everything is alright with you and we are still in business."

"Thanks Steve, everything is alright, the police have a job to do and they have to finish."

Brandon completed his shift at 1:00 am and began his trek home. The night was dark, clouds in the sky prevented most of the light reflected off the moon from reaching and illuminating the streets. He walked at a steady, non-hurried pace, wrapping himself tightly with his coat and kept his eyes down on the pavement before him. Thinking as he walked, Brandon remembered a movie with the same type lighting. He also realized that it had been a while since he sat in a theater. He grinned, maybe he was breaking an old habit. Maybe this would forever erase the demons that had plagued him.

As he passed a dark doorway, a whisper called out to him, *"Brandon."*

He quickened his pace, another doorway and another whisper. Brandon cursed and said, "Leave me alone." He again hurried his step and covered the last five blocks to his apartment muttering curses to himself.

He entered his apartment, locked the door and turned on his television. There was an opened, half full bottle of soda in his refrigerator, a little cheese and bread. He ate, drank and tried to settle in watching the television.

There was another sound, this time from a window. A shadow passed the window and a door opened. A tall, heavyset man, in a dark rumpled suit walked through the door and toward Brandon. He could not move, he could not talk. The man came closer and Brandon could not see his face. The light behind the man was bright, and as he neared, he blocked out most it. The man stopped, studying Brandon from about four feet away. Still Brandon could not see his face, then as the man's eyes seemed to materialize, a noise, a loud crash made Brandon sit up straight, awake. He was still in his chair in front of the television, no longer dreaming. The sound had come from his television. Brandon was in a cold sweat. He stood, turned off the television, stripped, walked into the bathroom and turned on his shower. After several minutes in the stream of warm and cold water, Brandon dried himself off, laid down on his bed and noticed the time, it was 3:30 in the morning. He closed his eyes and fell asleep, laying on his bed, covered only with his damp towel.

*   *   *

T HIRTY

Friday . . .   Come out and stand in front of me . . .

Morning came suddenly, Brandon sat upright with a cold, damp towel draped across his lap. He stood, wiped the sleep from his eyes and walked into the shower again. Dried and dressed he left his apartment and walked to the coffee shop for his daily morning meal. As he walked to the Pub a construction worker was looking out a window. David Gonzales saw Brandon and wondered again, "Could that be the man the police are looking for?" He watched as Brandon passed by and out of sight. David returned to his drywall hanging chore of the morning.

Lake and Kat were involved in five different investigations and Brandon was pushed aside for the time being as they looked into another case where they had a concrete lead. As the lead panned out and an arrest was made, the detectives finished their paperwork and picked up another jacket with another murder in the district. Brandon slid another notch on the importance scale and nobody noticed or complained.

Brandon continued his daily routine, but now the others were slightly cautious around him. He was not accused, he was not arrested, but the seeds of doubt were planted and life became quieter, more serious, less fun. The turn of events also made his want to be early at the Pub, less desirable. He turned again to the movies. He found an all night theater playing an older version of a vampire movie. Brandon watched without clawing at himself, without feeling threatened. When the film ended and the house lights came up, he sat in his seat and stared into the screen. He stood, stared and slowly turned and walked out of the theater. He did not hunch over, did not pull his coat about himself and did not cast his eyes downward. He almost defied the demons to come after him. He showed no emotion as he walked casually past window, alley and darkened doorway. When he had covered about six of the city blocks on his fourteen block trek, the whispers began. Again he did not lower his eyes, he did not hurry his pace, he slowed and , looked around. No other person was in sight, the street was vacant. he stopped, stood tall and sought out the demons. Whispers and shuffling of feet but no one came out of the shadows. Brandon looked straight ahead and began to walk with a twisted grin. "Come out and stand in front of me," he muttered. He walked on, there was no visible movement. "Just as I thought, no guts, all noise and no substance."

The night was cold, and the walk home made Brandon shiver but he left his coat open. As he passed the last alley between his apartment and the building next door, he heard a very distinct whisper. Throaty, almost a growl the whisper called his name, *"Brandon."*

He stopped, turned and scanned the alley. Then he stepped in the direction of the alley. A slight wind moved the trash on the ground, no other sound. Brandon spit on the ground and turned to enter his building.

*   *   *

The night was calm, a slight misting rain, a gentle breeze, and the air was cool but not cold. Lying on his bed with eyes open, Brandon reflected on the last two days and especially the interview with two detectives. He knew what they were looking for and he knew that at the moment they did not have the necessary information to effect an arrest. He was the prime suspect, he might even be the only suspect. This presented a problem. Was he high enough on their priority list to merit observation? Could he walk the streets now, unnoticed, or were his actions being tracked? He thought about the whispers in the shadows. Were they aware of his predicament? Would they take advantage of that and force him to kill again?

Waiting was not an option. He had to know where he stood and what were to be his limitations. He thought about taking a walk now to see if he was being followed. Just a walk around a block or two, looking for marked or unmarked police cars or people hiding in shadows. As he thought and began to plan his route through several streets, noticing what was there and doubling back to see what had moved, he smiled at the plan, yes that would work, — .

He turned a corner and saw a police car and he continued, the officers were asleep, not looking, or were they pretending to be asleep. He walked to the corner and turned, then cut through an alley and came back to the corner where the police car was. He peered around the corner, the police car was gone. He looked up the street to where he had cut into the alley and saw the taillights of the police car disappear down the alley. Now, were there others? He didn't know. He waited and thought that the police car might return. He looked again and the police car pulled back into its previous location, the officers both leaned back on their headrests as if asleep.

Another test, he walked around the corner again and turned down the same alley but this time he turned right rather than left and went around a different block coming back to see the police car disappearing down the same alley. Then, almost a second later the police car raced past him with blue lights flashing — .

"I lost them," he thought aloud.

"Yes, you lost them," said the throaty whisper.

Brandon turned quickly to see who was there — . He almost fell out of bed. His alarm clock indicated that it was 9:54 am. "Another dream," he stood, walked about his apartment and dressed. As he left his apartment, he looked at the spot where he saw the police car in his dream. The spot was vacant, but the patch of dry pavement indicated that a car had been there through the night.

*   *   *

T HIRTY O NE

Saturday . . .   Yo, Davey, Que te pasa? . . .

A stop at the coffee shop and an unhurried walk across town had Brandon at the Pub just after 11:45. He was only 15 minutes early and the Pub was already busy. He hung up his coat and walked behind the bar as Steve was filling an order for one of the waitresses.

"Good morning Brandon, you look a little sleepy today. Are you okay?"

"Yeah, I'm fine. I read a little late last night and didn't get much sleep," he lied, "But I'm fine."

Steve picked up a towel, went to the sink and washed his hands, "Okay, you have the bar and I have to check on a few things downstairs. See you in a little bit." Steve walked past Brandon and into the kitchen.

"Hey, bartender can I get another — ?"

Brandon put on a smile and started his day, "What are you drinking, light or high test — ?"

The day passed without event. Brandon noticing every person who came into the restaurant, wondering if this one or that one was a cop. Some people came in and seemed to watch him all too closely, some seemed to obviously ignore him. He caught himself several times staring back at an individual or two and by day's end, he was exhausted. Lack of sleep and the stress of the day led him to a walk straight home after work and an extended shower before collapsing on his bed.

The sky was cloudless, the moon full and street lights were all working, but nobody was walking about. He looked at his watch, it was only mid night. "That's strange, I thought that I had worked until 1:00 am — ," he muttered. "Where am I?" He began to walk, "The streets are awfully clean, and where are all the cars?"

He walked on, block after block. It was all the same, street lights were on, there were no people, no cars and the streets were clean. "I think that I should go — , which way? I don't recognize this place. Where am I?"

"You are in my city now, Brandon," a deep voice half whispered.

He turned and saw the outline of a man standing about ten feet away. He was tall, heavy set, wearing a dark suit and a black tee shirt. His face was not well defined, a mass of grey with something moving as he spoke.

"I have been waiting for you," said the dark figure, *"Now that you are here, we can proceed."*

Brandon was not able to move, he wished his feet to take him back, but his legs couldn't move. "Who are you, what do you want?"

"We are you — ." As the figure spoke, another appeared, then another and another. *"We are all you — ."*

Brandon tried to turn and run but he couldn't. The men came closer, and closer. Then as they were about to reach out with their hands, a police car with siren and flashing lights came down the street. Brandon was suddenly able to turn and run. He woke in a cold sweat, looked at his alarm clock. It was 3:37 am. He got out of bed and pulled on his old jeans and dark shirt. He opened his closet and found his work boots. grabbing his raincoat, he walked out of his apartment and down to the street. He walked to the side of his building and ducked into the alley. There he peered out to the street looking for any sign of movement. He waited about 15 minutes and seeing no movement at all, he ventured out, walking with his hands in the pockets of his raincoat and holding it close as if he were cold. As he turned a corner a whisper in an alley made him stop, turn and defy the sound to speak again. Nothing happened and Brandon resumed his walk. Block after block was quiet, no rustling sounds, no whispers, just quiet. He looked at his watch, it was almost 5:00 am and he turned for home. An alley offered a shortcut to the next turn on his route and Brandon hurriedly stepped into the shaded canyon. He was about 200 feet into the alley when he heard a sound. It was not a whisper nor was it a voice, but a growl. He turned, looking and heard rustling of papers and another sound, another raspy choking sound. The dumpster to his right moved and Brandon saw a form come out of the shadow. He immediately looked for an escape route and saw a piece of metal on the ground. It was about 18 inches long and had one rounded end and one jagged end. He picked it up and turned again to face the dark figure.

Colin Coyle had been a marketing manager for an investment firm a few years ago but bad luck and unreasonable responses on the part of client and friend alike left him broken and drunk. From living in a 5,500 square foot home in McLean, Virginia to sleeping behind dumpsters in the District had been the result of his downfall. Colin saw nothing threatening in the man standing in front of him, and he 'needed a drink.' He stepped closer to Brandon and raised a hand to ask for money.

Brandon saw a tall dark figure step out of the shadows and move toward him. The figure uttered a sound that resembled a growl and when he raised his arm, Brandon swung the metal piece at the figures head.

Colin went down to his knees, groping for the pain in his head. Brandon swung the metal piece again and Colin saw no more of this world. His problems were now over and his body lie in an alley in a pool of blood and stinking trash.

Brandon stood over him, staring at the lifeless form. He realized that the man he had just killed was a harmless drunk and not a demon. He looked about to see if anyone else was there. As he walked out of the alley, Brandon still had the metal piece in his hand. He decided to keep it in case he encountered a real demon.

As he rounded a corner a group of five people were walking directly toward him. He side stepped the group and continued on his way. David Gonzales stopped and looked at the tall thin man walking away with something in his hand.

"Yo, Davey, Que te pasa?"

"Nada," he replied as he turned and caught up to the group.

They reached the building where they were working and turned in. David Gonzales paused, thought for a second, shook his head and followed the rest of his friends.

*   *   *

THIRTY TWO

Sunday . . .   He deposited the bagful in the bin . . .

"4075, see the man in Durbin Alley off 15th reporting a 10-84. This is a silent response"

Frank lifted the mic, "4075, that's a 10-4." He looked at his partner, "Nice way to start a Saturday shift, eh Dan."

Dan Carney looked for an opening in the morning rush hour traffic and made a lane change followed by a left turn at the next corner. "Yeah, well it makes the time pass faster."

They arrived at the alley and parked their car blocking the entrance. Dan said, "I'll tape off the other end and check the witness."

"He's all yours," said Frank.

Dan walked down the alley toward a man sitting on a step. "I'll be right there," he said as he passed the body lying on the ground, "Don't go away."

"No rush," said the man as he lit a cigarette and wondered if the cop was talking to him or the body, "I ain't goin' nowhere."

Dan tied off the tape to two handrails and returned to the man with the cigarette. "Are you the person who found our friend there?"

"Yeah, I go over to him to tell him that he's gonna' get runned over when da trucks come in here to de alley, you know," said the smoker, "And he don't move or nottin, so I get down there to look and there's blood and his eyes is all weird. So he ain't got no pulse and I go in to da kitchen there and call you guys."

"That's good," said Dan, "Now I have to ask a few questions, Is that okay with you?"

Smokey said, "Yeah, like I could say No to youse?"

"We appreciate your cooperation. So let's start with your name — ."

"Oh, yeah, my name is Garbin, Kenneth Garbin."

"Okay Ken, where do you live?"

*   *   *

Frank was watching the alley entrance when The Medical Examiner's van pulled up. He moved the patrol car and let them in then blocked the entrance again. Sal Benito brought the van to a stop and got out. Chuck and Freddy were getting out the passenger side when a pair of detectives arrived. Freddy approached the body looking at the ground, searching for any piece of anything that might be useful. Sal walked to the other side of the alley doing the same.

"Hey Freddy, I got a foot print, looks recent, and another one over here."

"I'll grab the camera, are they clear prints?"

"Not so much, a little fuzzy, like maybe the guy shuffled a little." Sal placed a yellow numbered marker at each print.

"Any more," asked Freddy as he photographed the first two?

"Don't see any more yet, still looking — ."

Chuck Barasso went directly to the body and began a preliminary examination. The two detectives stood back, awaiting clearance to approach. "Hey Chuck," said the older of the two, what do we have here?"

"Well he was loaded, with booze. Hit in two locations on his head. This one," he said pointing to an indentation in the man's skull, "Was probably the fatal blow. We can't be sure of that till we get him on the table."

"Anything missing — ?"

"You mean like a wallet, a wad of cash, keys to his caddy and his country club membership card?"

"Yeah, all that and his shoes, belt, stuff that another poor slob like this might have taken."

"Still has his shoes, his belt is still on. When we get him back to the house, I will inventory everything."

"Okay Chuck. Hey Sal, did you guy's find anything?"

Sal called out to Freddy, "Freddy, you got anything for our friendly neighborhood detectives?"

"Hey Carl," said Freddy as he lifted his head and saw the detective, "I got a couple of smudged footprints. These are big and we may have another case with the same prints."

"Oh yeah, who caught the other case," asked Carl Dempsey.

"McLarry and Murano," replied Freddy.

Dan Carney perked up at the mention of Murano's name. "I can take the preliminary info over to them for you detective."

"Yeah, I'll bet you will. I've seen McLarry's partner and if I was 30 years younger, I'd handle it myself. Here's my card, so they can call me when you finish drooling all over that babe."

"Detective, you are a gentleman. thanks."

"Hey Carney, be careful what you wish for, I've seen her work out with the judo guys. She's a tough little broad, probably kick your ass," Carl laughed as he and his partner continued to browse the scene.

Dan smiled and thought about what Carl said. He smiled again.

*　　　　*　　　　*

Brandon was up, showered clean shaven and ready to go to work at 9:30 in the morning. He thought about the man in the alley, the piece of metal and about his clothes. There was a chance of there being some kind of trace evidence on his clothes as well as the weapon. He put the clothes in a plastic bag and wiped down the metal. Every trace of evidence was either in the bag or went down the drain when he showered. He left his apartment with the bag and the metal. As he walked down the street, he noted a storm drain in the curb. The openings were big enough for the metal weapon and after looking around to see if anyone was looking, he dropped the piece of metal and gently kicked it into the sewer. As he passed a coin operated Laundromat, he went in and loaded a washer with everything except the shoes. He put the machine on hot water and inserted the required number of coins. The machine roared to life churning the mass of black clothing. After an hour, Brandon unloaded the dryer, packed the clothes in another clean plastic bag and left the Laundromat. He walked about six blocks from his apartment building to a church yard, where there was a Goodwill donation bin. He deposited the bagful in the bin and added the shoes.

Relief, as if a weight had come off his shoulders. Brandon walked on to the Pub and acted as if it were just another day. A bit more upbeat than the previous day, he tore into his work and put a smile on for everyone.

"Brandon, you know that Stu and Brenda are back in town. They may stop in for dinner tonight so I thought that you and I should have a little talk this afternoon when things are quiet."

"Sure Steve, whatever you say." Brandon was not sure what the subject was to be, but it was most likely going to include the visit by the police. As the day wore on and the crowd dwindled, Steve finally found an opening.

They sat at the table at the end of the bar so that Brandon could get up and take care of a customer if one came in. "Brandon, this bit about Karen Pavia being murdered is not good. You tell me that you are clean and tell the same to Stu and we will back you up to the hilt. He is a very fair guy and everything here thus far has been positive. Now if word gets around that you are a suspect, that could be bad for business. People are funny about stuff like that. They may come in just to see you and then leave. We really don't need that. Anyway, I've been thinking, if it gets dicey, you can move back into the kitchen till it blows over. If there's no show, we won't get the undesirable crowd. I hope you understand what I'm saying."

"I hear you Steve, do you think that the others here are okay with me? I mean yesterday was a little strained, you know. I felt uncomfortable, like everybody was thinking that maybe I did do it and I was dangerous."

"Well, let's face it, the possibility that you did kill her is going to be on everybody's mind. It's only natural. Even I thought like 'What if you did do it — .' Everybody has to go through that same sequence and then say to themselves, No, he wouldn't, no he didn't — ."

"I understand, but it's a terrible feeling when the people that you trust, don't trust you in return. Again, I understand and I guess that I have to ride this storm out to the end. I just hope that nobody loses faith in me in the process.

*   *   *

The dinner crowd started at around 4:30 in the afternoon. Brandon was busy behind the bar and the kitchen was ramping up. The line up at the door was soon hearing that there would be a 15 to 20 minute wait and still the line grew. Steve got behind the bar to help out and Lisa was on the phone calling in an additional waitress. It was looking like a banner night.

Brenda and Stu arrived at 6:15 coming in the kitchen entrance and entering the dining room next to the waitress station. Steve checked on a few patrons and refreshed two drinks and went back to see Stu.

"Man look at the crowd, we are on a roll here. Maybe you guys should get married more often." They all laughed and Stu said, "So any problems this week."

Steve obviously had something to say and was hesitant to open up. Stu suggested that they go down to the office and talk.

Brenda said, "It's been a while, but I'll give Brandon a hand behind the bar while you two talk." She put her purse under the waitress station, took off two rings from her right hand and stepped behind the bar. "Brandon, you are driving this bus, so tell me if I'm in your way or actually helping out. We gotta give the two boys time to talk."

Brandon smiled and said, "No problem, I am thankful for the help."

A customer who had a few in him already hearing the conversation said, "That lady could never be in the way. She is too good looking."

Brandon picked up his empty glass and said, "How about you have a cup of coffee next, on me?"

The man said, "Are you cutting me off?"

"Never, we're just shifting gears."

The man sat up straight and said, "That's okay, I'll have coffee."

Brenda smiled at the banter and thought to herself, "This guy is good. I think that we really lucked out with him."

Steve and Stu went down to the office and talked about the visit from the police detectives earlier in the week.

Stu came up from the basement and called Brandon off to the side. Steve went behind the bar with Brenda and gave them some time to talk. "Steve tells me that a couple of detectives were in here asking you about a murder."

Brandon was tense but tried to hide it. This was the man who had given him a break and let him move up. He did not want to lie to him, but the truth would be much worse. "Yeah, her name was Karen Pavia and she let me go from the other place. That's when I was passing by and saw your sign in the window."

"Brandon, I have to ask you one question and one only. Did you kill that lady?"Brandon pulled on all the acting strength that he had and even though the answer was tearing at him internally, he calmly replied, "No, I guess — ."

"I don't need an explanation, you answered my question and that's the end of it. Now why don't you get back to work and pour me and my little bride a little drink, bartender?"

Brandon was surprised that it had been that easy, one question and one answer and the matter was closed. "I believe that she likes a little white wine and you — , what is your pleasure?"

"Actually I never go beyond a glass of seltzer with a twist of lime."

*   *   *

Thirty Three

Monday . . .   I can't stay up to late . . .

When the sun rose the next morning, Brandon was already awake. He thought about his date with Suzanne and decided to do a little laundry, clean up his apartment and who knows maybe she would like to see where he lived. He was finished washing and cleaning by 2:00 pm, turned on his television and saw that the Redskins were not playing until that evening. The Capitols played the night before and baseball season was over. He decided to walk down to the convention center, browse through a few shops and be there at 7:00 pm when Suzanne finished her gig.

The walk to the convention center took him through Mount Vernon Square. The weather was pleasant, the temperature was around 70 degrees and the sun was shining. It was a perfect day to sit on a park bench, feed the little critters and watch the people pass by. At 6:35, he got up went over to a coffee shop and used the rest room. He looked in the mirror, combed his hair and finished off a small bottle of mouth wash. The walk to the convention center took only a few minutes and he waited patiently till she came out.

Dinner, a short walk and a cab ride had them back at Suzanne's apartment by 10:00 pm. "I have to get up in the morning, so I can't stay up too late," she said to Brandon with a smile that invited him once more to her bedroom.

The morning came all together too quickly and Brandon found himself back on the street wondering how the time passed so quickly. He thought about trying to get himself into a position of having either

Friday or Saturday night off. Saturday night would be best. that way they could have the night and the next day together. He walked back toward the Pub feeling good again.

*   *   *

T<small>HIRTY</small> F<small>OUR</small>

Tuesday . . .   That, detective, is the interesting part . . .

Freddy was looking at the photos of the Coyle crime scene trying to get the best composite of the footprints to compare to the Pavia and Decker files. He had been playing with it for only ten minutes when Dr. Colburn came into the lab. "What'cha got there Freddy?"

"Well, I am about to see if I have something or not. This is a picture of a footprint," he said as he put a photo on a monitor, "from the Coyle scene. And this, is a footprint from the Pavia scene," he said as he put a second print on an adjacent monitor screen. A little messy, but, they are the same size. Now this is a print," as he lit up a third monitor, "from the Decker scene. I'd say the Decker / Coyle ones are a slam dunk match."

"And the Pavia print matches them both as closely as they can," added the Medical Examiner. "Nice work Freddy, have you let the detectives know about this yet?"

"Well not exactly, I said to Detective Dempsey that I might have a match to another homicide. He said I should look at it and let him know."

"You know that you should have come back here first, then we let them know."

"Yeah, you mad at me?"

"No, you did some good work here, let's just do it by the book next time."

"Can I call Detective McLarry."

"Yeah, go ahead," said Dr. Colburn as he walked out of the room with a smile.

*   *   *

"Hey, brown eyes, just got a call from our friends at the ME's office. Let's take a ride," said Lake.

"Sure partner, what's the prize this time?"

"Don't know. Freddy says he has something for us," said Lake as he grabbed his coat and a new notebook.

Kat picked up her purse, slung it over her shoulder and followed Lake out of the squad room. They crossed town in under 15 minutes and were in the lobby when Freddy came up and got them. "Good morning detectives, I think that I have something interesting for you."

They went down to the lab room where Freddy had set up the monitors. He settled into a chair and as he was bringing up the first of the prints, Dr. Colburn came into the room.

"Well good morning Detective Murano. You are looking terrific today."

Kat replied, "Hey Doc, we're here to see what Freddy has found."

Dr. Colburn said, "Freddy, you're on."

"Okay folks, this print on the first monitor is from the Decker scene. The second one," as he brought up the picture, "is from the Pavia scene. And the third one is from the Coyle scene."

"Whoa," said Lake, "who the hell is this Coyle?"

"That, detective, is the interesting part," said Freddy. "A man found in an alley, off 15th street, is identified as one Colin Coyle. Death caused by BFT to the skull, Doc Colburn will fill you in on that, but back to the prints. On first glance, they are all about the same size. We have already figured that the Pavia and Decker cases are most likely related and this," as he pointed toward the third monitor, "This footprint is a nine point match to the Decker scene footprint."

Lake looked at Kat, "Strike three, we got us a serial creep."

"What the hell is this guy's game, a drug dealer, a restaurant manager and a vagrant?"

"All at night, all in alleys all different people — I'd guess that the guy is into killing and the victim is a matter of convenience, purely accidental in selection," said Dr. Colburn.

You turning psych on us Doc," asked Lake?

"No, Freddy told me — ."

Lake and Kat left the ME's office with Kat smirking and quietly singing, "Tradin' up, la la la, tradin' up."

*   *   *

Brandon arrived at work at 10:15 with his usual smile and helpful attitude. Stu was in full swing, unloading deliveries and stocking shelves. The kitchen crew was busy doing prep for the lunch crowd and the bar was unattended. Brandon went down the stairs to the basement to give Stu a hand and met Steve coming out of the office. "Good morning Steve, how are you today?"

Steve looked up and replied quietly, "You're looking better today, how was your day off?"

"It was great, but way too short. It would really be nice to have the Saturday night and the day Sunday together," said Brandon with a laugh.

"How could we work that out? Maybe we switch off alternate weekends or something — , let's talk to Stu about that, after we restock the bar and unload all these boxes," Steve said pointing at the pile at the base of the stairs. "Work first, then we talk about time off."

"Sounds good to me," replied Brandon as he walked over to the walk-in cooler, "Right after I check the kegs and the soda."

Steve smiled and turned to go up the stairs coming face to face with Stu.

"He seems alright to me," said Stu looking after Brandon as he disappeared into the cooler, "What's this about time off?"

Steve said, "I'd like him to be part of the conversation. He didn't ask for time, just said it would be nice to have a Saturday night and then the Sunday. I have thought that might work for everybody if we shifted weekends so that the Pub is always covered and half the crew is off one part of the weekend and the other half is off the next. Don't know if we have enough people or if it would work out."

Stu, pretended to scratch his chin and said, "Well we get a few minutes open before lunch and we can sit down and talk about it, the three of us. Oh, and Brenda, she'll be in a little later."

*   *   *

Stu brought the schedule for the next three weeks to the table and the four of them started talking at once. Stu raised a hand and said, "Okay, we all have some input so let me summarize a few things first. We all could use a decent weekend now and then."

The group nodded in agreement together.

Stu continued, "If we all took the weekend, we would have to shut the joint down and that ain't gonna' happen. So I think that we consider different folks taking different days off. Brenda and I would want to be off at the same time and we should both be here on our busy days and nights along with a crew that can keep us in business."

Once again the group nodded in agreement.

"Steve or I should be here every day that we are open. George should be here on the busy days and Bill can handle the easier days with a little help from me or Steve. Brandon, well Brandon has a girl friend who has weekends off and he would prefer that. As long as the bar is covered, both Brenda and I have experience back there — ."

Again, agreement. "So that being the case, I propose that we start with George getting this Saturday off giving him a two day weekend. Brandon, you take the next Saturday, that's the 30th, then Steve will take the following Saturday, the 6th, and the following weekend, Brenda and I will take off. That brings us to November 13th and George gets that one again and we continue the rotation."

Brenda cleared her throat, sat up straight and said, "That's good, now we have to schedule the rest of the days off so that nobody is over working. I figure that we should each have two days each week off and with Sunday as the given, we just covered Saturdays, we should look at Mondays. That is a slow day to begin with and we could tolerate a lighter crew. I would like to take a crack at this on my computer and have it ready to talk about next Monday."

Stu leaned back in his chair with a big smile, Steve looked at Brenda and nodded, George put his hands behind his head and leaned back with a grin and Brandon smiled, looked at the bar and said, "This is great, and I have a customer — ."

Stu said, "Okay that's it for now, let's get at it."

The group broke up, Brandon was behind the bar, George was in the kitchen, Steve went back to the basement and Stu and Brenda sat at the table looking very pleased.

*   *   *

Lake pulled the big Ford into an open slot on 21st Street and the two detectives walked to the Pub. "I want to cover the same turf with the owner, what's his name — ," said Lake.

Kat had her notebook open and replied, "Bricker, Stewart Bricker, and his new wife, also a part owner, Brenda."

"Yeah, you want to do them together or split them up?"

"I think that the two together will work, let's see how they act."

The pub was still making preparations for lunch when Lake and Kat arrived. They walked in and approached the bar seeing Brandon busily cutting garnishes and sat down. Lake grinned and said, "Good morning Brandon, how are you today?"

"Hey, detectives, I'm good, what can I get for you?"

Lake looked up at the ceiling and said, "I'd really like a cold draft — ."

Kat cut him off and said, "We could both use a cup of coffee."

"Yes ma'am, Coming right up," said Brandon as Lisa came to the end of the bar. "Hey, Lisa, could you get the detectives some coffee?"

Lisa turned toward the waitress station, "Sure, and it's a fresh pot."

Lake screwed up his face looking at Kat and said to Brandon, "Is Stu Bricker here?"

"Yeah, that's Stu and Brenda at the last table near the kitchen," said Brandon. He wiped his hands on a bar towel and walked to the opposite end of the bar near the Bricker's table and introduced them to the detectives. "Stu, Brenda, these detectives were here last week and would like to talk to you."

Stu stood up and extended a hand to Lake, "Sure, I'm Stu Bricker and this is my wife, Brenda."

"I'm Detective Martin McLarry and this is my partner Detective Kat Murano, may we join you for a few minutes?"

Brenda reached a hand toward Kat and said, "Please, sit down and —." As she was about to offer them coffee, Lisa came over with two mugs and the coffee pot. "Thanks Lisa, just leave the pot and I'll put it back."

Lisa smiled and went back to the waitress station and Brenda poured coffee for all four.

"What can we do for you," detective asked Stu?

"Just a few questions about an incident a few weeks ago, on the 4th of this month," said Lake.

"You're referring to the manager at Rizzonte's being murdered. Yeah, we heard about that. It made me a little more aware about our people leaving here late at night. I am also aware that Brandon worked there before coming here. Is that what we are going to talk about?"

Kat had taken a sip of her coffee, "This is good, much better than the swill we have at the station."

Stu smiled and said, "Thanks, we order it special from our supplier, it's a blend of three or four Columbian beans."

Lake then asked if either Stu or Brenda could verify Brandon's presence on the 4th of the month. Stu answered by asking if that was the Monday was two weeks ago.

Kat took another sip and said, "Yes, two weeks ago, was Brandon working that day?"

Brenda was thinking and said, "I'm sure he was, it was a Monday and he has not missed a day since he started here."

Lake looked at Stu and said, "Do you know what time he left here that night?"

Brenda sat upright and said, "I remember, that's the night that we," as she looked at Stu, "Took off a little early. It was raining and things were slow so Stu and I left Steve in charge and went — , ah, we went out, or home, to my place."

"What time was that," asked Kat?

Coulda' been 6:30 or 8:30, I can't remember," said Stu.

Brenda looked at Kat and said "It was before 8:00, we got to my place just as 'Jeopardy' was ending, and we settled in to watch a movie."

Lake looked at Stu and said, "Well then how long does it take to get to your place from here?"

Stu said, "Actually we went to her old apartment, from here it takes about twenty to twenty five minutes from the time we walk out the door till we are in her place."

"Okay," said Kat, "that makes it around 7:30, plus or minus a nickel, when you left here."

Stu said, "Yeah, that sounds about right."

Steve was half listening as he approached from the kitchen. "You mean that night when you two left early?"

Brenda looked at Steve, "Yes."

"Yeah, it was 7:30. I remember thinking that he had a great four hours at the bar by himself that night and I chased him outta here at midnight. Told him to go home, get a good night's sleep and be ready for some work the next day."

"That was at mid-night," said Kat questioningly?

"Yep, mid-night."

"Do you remember what he was wearing when he left here," asked Lake.

Steve turned, looked at Brandon behind the bar at the opposite end of the room and said quietly, "Same thing he has on now. He's got a limited wardrobe. Payday is Friday and he said yesterday that he was going shopping this weekend for another outfit."

"Same shoes and all," asked Kat?

"Shoes, he wears a running shoe, I kidded him about that. Told him that he was going to need those shoes with all the running he would be doing behind the bar."

Lake was writing notes in his book and without looking up he said, "Does he always wear those white running shoes?"

"Hey, detective, I don't spend my time constantly looking at Brandon's shoes. I don't remember him in anything but those shoes. Shoes?"

"Yeah, shoes, like has he ever worn boots, or work boots," asked Kat?

Brenda said, "I remember that he was wearing all black when he first came here. Then a week or so later when we said he could train behind the bar, he started to dress lighter. You know the khakis and the knit shirt. He looks so much better that way."

"So that night, what was he wearing? Was it all black or what he has on now?"

Steve answered, "He was working behind the bar and he was dressed like he is now."

They all glanced at Brandon and he noted that he was being observed. "You need me for something," he asked as he walked the length of the bar?

"Just wondering what you were wearing when you left here that Monday night," said Lake.

Brandon came a little closer, "You mean the night that I left early, around 12:00? I remember, because I got soaked. I got home and hung everything up in my bathroom and it still took a tumble in the dryer to dry them all out."

Kat asked, "To dry what out?"

Brandon stepped backward and held his hands out to his sides, "What you see."

"You were wearing the exact same thing," quizzed Kat as she picked up her cell phone as if it were ringing and set it to take a photograph..

Brandon looked down at his outfit, thought for a moment and answered, "Pretty much, maybe my other shoes, but this shirt for sure."

"What other shoes are we talking about," asked Kat as she snapped three pictures in a row and put the phone away?

"Another pair like these, I wear these or the others like these to work every day " Brandon answered as he gestured at his feet.

Brandon was catching on. There was something about the boots that he wore on the night that he saw Karen. He had seen enough 'Cops and Robbers' movies to know that a simple thing like a foot print could be very costly. He was pleased that he had gotten rid of his old clothes and those old black boots. He also remembered that they were a size smaller than the shoes he was wearing.

"What time did you get home that night," asked Lake.

"Oh, I don't know. I mean it takes about twenty minutes to walk it, so 12:30 or maybe 12:45. I got home, took off the wet stuff and hung it up, took a shower and hit the sack. I was beat, so I didn't even turn on the television."

"You remember all that," quizzed Kat.

"Yeah, well you get wet like that and it sticks in your head."

Lake looked at Stu and asked, "Have you ever met Karen Pavia?"

Stu replied, "No, we never met that I can recall, of course she could have been in here a dozen times and I wouldn't know. We talked on the phone once about Brandon and that was it."

Kat raised an eyebrow and asked, "What did she say about him?"

Stu thought for a second, "I can't remember the exact conversation, but it was not negative, I mean, I hired the guy. I do remember that she said that he was always there, working, like he didn't have an off switch, and I liked that. Since he's been a part of our team here, he has not disappointed me, shows up early, works hard and efficiently and is never anxious to leave. The guy is a prize in my book."

Lake put his notebook down on the table and put his pen in his pocket, "You all understand that we have to check out every possible lead in a case like this. The lady was not robbed, not assaulted sexually, just killed."

Kat added, "It's as though someone killed her just to see her dead, no reason, no logic that we can see."

Stu sat up straight, "Perhaps she had a disagreement with someone and it escalated — something personal or business related — ."

Kat put her notebook and pen in her purse, "Yeah, someone like an employee she fired."

*　　　*　　　*

THIRTY FIVE

Thursday . . .   I got a picture of Brandon . . .

Dan was driving east on Constitution Avenue and Frank was sitting quietly , looking out the window. As they passed a street vendor selling hot dogs, Dan noticed a short man with a hard hat hanging from his tool belt. The man saw Dan at the same time and looked as if he wanted to say something. "I gotta check this out," said Dan.

Frank looked at his partner and rolled his eyes mumbling, "And it was such a nice peaceful day — ."

Dan pulled the cruiser over to the curb and got out leaving Frank in the car. "Good morning David."

"Hey, Mr. Dan, You lookin' good, healthy."

"Yeah, thanks David. So how have you been?"

"Hey, I'm doin okay, you know." David looked around to see if anybody was watching, then he said, "Listen man, I see this tall dude, with big feet, you know. He's not doin nothin, but I think maybe I should tell you. Then I think, maybe he is not the guy and I don't want to give nobody trouble, so I shouldn't say nothin, you know."

"Okay, I hear you, but if you see someone that fits the description, you can tell me and I'm not going to shoot him. I just want to talk to him. If he is clean, that should be the end of it, He goes his way and I go mine. You understand that, right David?"

"Si, yo comprendo, I mean yes, Mr. Dan."

"Look I have to get going, you take care of yourself and don't hesitate to call me."

"Si, Mr. Dan, but I see this man again and this time he carries a stick or something. But I still don't know if he is the man you look for, so I don't say nothin."

"When did you see him that time?"

"It was on Saturday, early in the morning, like about 5:00 o'clock, but this time I think you want to know. He was near the alley where a guy got killed that morning, and he was carryin a stick, you know."

"You should have called me right away, David."

"Yeah, you right, but I don't know about the dead guy until we leave the job that afternoon. Then I hear about a dead guy in the alley and I don't figure it out. Then this morning when I'm comin to the job, I remember about the tall man, the stick and maybe you want to see him because maybe he is killin people. you know."

"Okay, David, tell me more about the stick that he was carrying. How big was it, what color was it, was it wood or what — ?"

David sat down on a low wall and thought, "I don't know, it had a funny shape, and it was about this long," he said holding his hands about 18 inches apart, "and it was a dark color, but I don't know if it's wood or somethin else."

"This is all good stuff, David. Now tell me, where exactly did you see him and where was he going?"

"Okay, he was walkin on 15th street, near the alley where the dead guy was and he was walkin toward the Post Building."

This was about 5:00 am?"

"Yeah. we was goin' to work about that time."

"David. I would like you to come to the station and talk with a couple of detectives, maybe look at some pictures."

David stood up and started to fidget about. "Oh man I really don't want to go to no Police station. They see me and I get sent away again."

Dan thought for a minute and said, "Okay, here's how we take care of that. Your name now is Raoul, you are an informant that I use. You can't be seen in the station because other people would see you there and that could get in the way of information getting to me. Do you understand that, David?"

"Si, sure, so we meet them out here on the street?"

"That's what I'm saying, we meet out here and we don't use your real name. You are now Raoul Ramierez."

"When do we do this thing?"

"We can do it right now, if you have the time," said Dan.

David stopped fidgeting and looked around again, "Okay, but I gotta get back to my job in a little bit. Like in about fifteen minutes."

"I don't think the detectives can get here that fast. Where are you working this week?"

David sat down again, "We doin a remodel in the Marlin Building over there."

"Okay David, what time do you get off work?"

"Today we stop at like about 3:30 in the afternoon."

Dan stood up, shook David's hand and said, "Okay, I will be right here at 3:30 with the detectives. When you get off, you come right to me, okay."

"Si, Mr. Dan, I can do that."

"Good David, very good."

*   *   *

Kat came into the squad room with a large brown envelope and smiled when she saw Lake.

"What's with the grin, Brown eyes?"

"Like they say in the movies, I got art — ,"she replied and tossed the envelope on Lake's desk.

Lake opened the envelope and as he was looking at a series of four 8 x 10 photographs of Brandon, Kat said, "I got a picture or two of Brandon on my cell while you all were talking this morning."

"I didn't see you take any pics — ."

"Yeah well when I answered my phone, I was not answering my phone, I was snapping as many pics of our friend as I could. A couple of them are good enough for talking to people around the different crime scenes."

"Not bad kiddo."

"Yeah, well I had them zoom in on his face and printed out the best of the lot," said Kat.

As Lake was looking at the photographs his phone rang. "These are pretty good for cell phone photos," he said to Kat and picked up the phone, "Detective McLarry," he listened for a second and turned toward Kat. "Yeah we're interested Danny boy. 3:30, the Ellipse. We'll see you there. Hey Danny, nice work."

"Kat, we got a lead. Some guy saw a tall thin man leaving the Coyle crime scene on Saturday. Those pictures are just in time."

"Is he bringing him in?"

"No, the guy is a confidential informant, police stations make him nervous. So we will meet on the street this afternoon. We are going to call him Raoul."

"Raoul — , is that his name?"

"No, this is Danny's informant and we are gonna' play along with 'Raoul', is that okay with you?"

Kat picked up the photos and said, "I gotta get some others mix in with these and see if 'Raoul' picks out our favorite bartender." As she was pulling similar copies of other tall, thin men from a file, Kat said, "Freddy finds footprints, Danny finds witnesses, what are we doing?"

Lake sipped the last of his coffee, grinned and said, "We're the smart guys who tie the whole mess together and hand it to the DA's office."

"Yeah, smart is good, when do we meet this witness?"

"3:30 at the Ellipse, 15th Street side. Let me see the picture array that you pulled together."

*　　　*　　　*

Dan and Frank were parked on 15th street behind a hot dog vendor, waiting for 3:30 and their meeting with David. An unmarked car pulled in behind the cruiser, Lake and Kat got out and joined the two uniformed policemen.

"Danny boy, where did you find this guy, 'Raoul'?"

"Long story cousin, you buy me a beer and I'll tell you," smiled Dan.

Frank rolled his eyes and Kat said to Frank, "Cute little kids, ain't they?"

Frank laughed as Dan stood up and said to Lake, "Here's our guy now."

David came across the street directly to Dan. "Hey Mr. Dan, I tole you I'm comin' here at 3:30, and here I am."

Dan cleared his throat and said, "Okay Raoul, these two detectives have some questions for you, this is Detective McLarry and this is Detective Murano. Detectives, this is Raoul Ramirez."

David shook Lake's hand and then turned to Kat and said, "Mucho gusto. Encantado — ." He held her hand for a few seconds while looking into her eyes and smiling.

Lake broke the trance saying, "Raoul, tell us what you saw Saturday morning."

David released Kat's hand and turned toward Lake, "Like I say to Mr. Dan, this tall skinny guy is walking from that alley of 15th Street with a stick in his hand. I don't know if this is the guy you look for, but when I hear that a dead guy is in the alley, I think maybe I should tell Mr. Dan."

Kat began to open the envelope and said "Tell us what this tall man looks like."

David smiled at Kat and said, "Sure, he is very tall, more tall than Mr. Dan. He is skinny, you know like a stick. A tall , skinny, white dude, you know."

Lake was making notes and asked, "Yeah, I know, now what color was his hair?"

"It was dark, very dark hair and messy, long and messy maybe black hair."

Kat looked at Lake and said, "Long hair?"

David replied before Lake could say anything, "Maybe not so long, but messy."

Lake relaxed and said, "Okay, Raoul, what was this guy wearing when you saw him?"

"Oh, I think he was wearin black clothes that was all too small for him, you know. Like the coat was too short and the pants was way tight and did no cover his boots."

Kat perked up and said, "Boots, what color were the boots, Raoul?"

"They was kinda dark grey, they was one time black but they was old."

Lake took his turn, "What else can you tell us, Raoul?"

"I tell Mr. Dan that this man carries a stick kinda thing."

"Can you describe this stick," asked Kat?

"Okay, sure, it was about this long," he said with his hands about 18 inches apart, and it was funny shape. Like maybe one end is skinny and the other end is wider and kinda flat."

Lake inquired, "Was it a wooden stick?"

"Hey man, I don't get too close, I don't know what it is made of. When I see the dude he is walking away from me, you know."

Kat stepped closer to David and said, "Raoul, we have some pictures of different people. I would like you to look at these people and show me which one looks most like the guy that you saw."

David smiled at her and said, "Sure, I look — ."

Dan was standing back out of the way and mumbled to himself, "Look at the pictures, 'Raoul.'"

Kat pulled the photo array out of the envelope and showed it to David, "Do you see anyone that looks like the man you saw on Saturday?"

David flipped through the six photos and stopped cold at the picture of Brandon. He stared at the photo not saying anything.

Kat leaned forward and said quietly, "Do you see something, Raoul?"

Lake stayed back, letting Kat work the fact that David was a very healthy young man wanting to please the very attractive detective.

David lifted his head, "This is the man — ."

Kat smiled and again quietly said, "You think that this looks like the man — ?"

"No, no this is the man, this is the guy that I saw and I see him here one day too."

Kat looked surprised, "You mean here at this hot dog stand?"

"Si, — yes, I see him here buying a hot dog and I think this is a tall man like what Mr. Dan looks for — , but I don't want to make trouble for some guy, you know, like I don't know if this is the right guy."

Dan stepped closer and said, "I asked him if he had seen a tall man with black work boots — , what he saw then was a tall man, no work boots. So he didn't report it to me."

Kat held up the picture to Lake and Dan, "This is guy that he saw near the alley and here. Same guy. Our guy."

Lake was looking at David and said, "Still not enough to get a warrant. But it is enough for us to put all other possibles on a back burner. Your guy is a little nervous, Dan. You want to let him take off, as long as you know how to grab him up again, that's ok with us," As he looked at Kat.

Kat shrugged her shoulders and said, "Yeah, sure. I think we got more than we thought we would.

*   *   *

Freddy and Sal pulled their van into the unloading area at the ME's office and wheeled another victim of poor driving, partially from cell phone activity. Dr. Colburn happened to be in the dock area and saw Sal.

"Sal, what'cha got there?"

"Hey Doc, guy makin a right on red with a cell phone in his left ear. The other guy movin at about light speed, T-bones this dude and tried to push the phone out his right ear. Guy never saw it, probably never heard it and never felt it. Even I can figure this guy died on impact."

Dr. Colburn pulled the zipper down enough to see the man's head, winced and said, "Yeah, on initial look, I fully agree."

Freddy walked over to the two of them, shook his head and said, "They took the other guy to GW for a look see. He was banged up some but not like this," as he pulled the zipper back up. "By the way Doc, did the detectives ever pick up that stick for blood analysis," he said referring to the blood smear on the piece of wood from the Pavia murder scene.

"No, but you could remind them, Freddy," he said as he walked back toward the morgue entrance, "Give McLarry a call."

Freddy helped push the gurney into the holding area outside the morgue entrance, looked at Sal and said, "I'm gonna' do that, as soon as we put this goof-burger in the cooler."

*   *   *

Kat's phone rang, "Detective Murano, yes, oh how you doin' Freddy?"

237

Kat sat down at her desk and picked up a pen, tapping it on her note pad, "The stick, no we didn't ask for any tests yet, but we now have a lead that makes me want to run some science on this case."

Freddy pushed the point, "I can pick it up and take it to the lab for you guys. We can probably get some DNA from the several blood stains on the stick, and — ."

"And, Freddy, my friend, we now have a suspect to compare the DNA to. It is starting to come together, thanks to your footprint pictures."

Freddy grinned, "So what do you need that you could get from me?"

"How about some DNA from our suspect," answered Kat.

"Give me a name and an address and I will get you some DNA . . ."

*   *   *

Lake looked up from the photos and said, "What's up with Freddy? Did you say DNA?"

"Yeah, can we ask this Brandon guy for a sample of his DNA, Freddy has a blood smear on a stick from the Pavia scene?"

"Not yet, I mean he could easily refuse and this 'Raoul' didn't see Brandon do anything. The guy was just in the wrong place at the wrong time."

"You sound like the guy's attorney."

Lake had a goofy expression on his face as he said, "Well detective, as soon as you have some real evidence, we will consider giving you what you want so that you could put my client away for the rest of his rotten life."

*   *   *

THIRTY SIX

Friday . . .   I need an excuse and you may be it . . .

Freddy was up and at the lab early in the morning, cleaning and stocking the van with fresh supplies when Dr. Colburn arrived. "Good morning Freddy, you have been busy." As he turned to walk away, Dr. Colburn stopped looked up, turned and said, "You want something, don't you Freddy, you want to do something that you aren't supposed to do, right?"

Freddy grinned, "Well Doc, there's this guy, see, and he doesn't have to give up his DNA and it could really help the detectives if they had his DNA and we can get it from a whole bunch of places like cigarette butts, or soda cans or even a napkin that he wipes his mouth with. And I would like to kinda follow him around a little and see if he drops something or — ."

"Freddy, the detectives should do that. You have enough other things to keep you busy and out of trouble here."

"Yeah, you're right Doc. I mean I am a part of the crime scene team and I know how to secure and handle evidence and I probably would do it better that the average detective and it could make or break a case and, Doc, I really, really want to do this."

"Okay, you clear it with the detectives and you are not to put yourself in any danger. No danger, is that clear?"

"Clear, thanks Doc." Freddy practically ran to the phone and called Lake. "Good morning Detective, can I ask you a favor?"

"Ask away Freddy, I owe you a few favors — ."

Freddy ran the case for himself doing a little detective work. and Lake listened. "Freddy, you make a good point, I mean the guy has never seen you, at least not as a cop or a CSI, so you could be right on top of the guy and — , I like it, Freddy, I like it."

Lake switched hands with his phone, waved across the room to Kat and picked up a pen. "Freddy, it's almost 8:40 am and this guy usually gets to work around 10:00 to 10:15. If you were hanging around outside his apartment and followed him with us a block or two behind. This could work. Why don't we pick you up in about 20 minutes?"

Kat came over with two cups of coffee, "Who we pickin up partner?"

Lake grinned, "Your favorite draft choice — ."

Kat smiled, "I like Freddy, maybe that coffee is for him."

Lake was reaching for his coat, "Freddy, you can steal my partner, but you can't have my coffee," he picked up the coffee mug and took a big swallow. "Whoa, fresh pot, I'm takin this to go."

They went to the car with coffee, photos and a simple wire device so Freddy could be in touch with them. Lake again brought the Big sedan out into traffic and started across town.

Freddy was at the main entrance with a paper shopping bag in hand and was in the car as soon as Lake brought it to a stop. "Good morning guys, I have something for you," as he handed Kat a small walkie talkie unit. "I'm wired so you can talk to me when you need to."

Kat looked at Lake, "La la la, tradin day is a comin . . ."

Freddy looked a little confused and Lake said "Ignore her she's having one of those female moments." He pulled out into traffic again and headed toward Brandon's apartment building.

Kat turned around and said, "What else you got in the bag, Freddy?'

"I have two hats, different colors and a blue pull-over, In case he sees me and I gotta make a quick change."

"Lake, the man is loaded for bear, he is ready," said Kat.

They drove across town with no real delays and pulled around a corner heading toward Brandon's building only two more blocks away.

Kat saw a tall thin man exit a building wearing a blue jacket, khaki pants and white shoes. ""Timing, timing is everything. There's our man now Freddy he's already on the move."

Lake said, "Okay Freddy, I'm gonna' get about two blocks ahead of him and drop you off. Leave the bag in the car, if you need a change, I'll be right behind you. Did you two do a sound check on that talkie thing?"

Kat turned it on and heard a confusing mass of sound. "We're too close, but it seems to be working."

Lake turned left twice and sped up three blocks and let Freddy out. "We don't let him get in any trouble, Kat."

"Not even close, I agree."

Freddy's voice came over the walkie talkie "Hey guys' I can hear you fine and don't worry about me, I've been living on these streets a long time and know how to stay out of the way."

"Read you loud and clear Freddy," said Kat.

"I see him, stay with me I gotta slow down here or I'll be in his pocket."

"We're gonna' be one block over and about even with you Freddy," said Kat.

"This is cool, watchin a guy like this, I'm gonna' be quiet for a while, don't want to look goofy to the population by talking to thin air."

"Cough or sneeze once in a while so we know you are still there."

"Relax detective, I'm okay."

They covered three blocks when Freddy chimed in again. "Bingo, we have a potential winner here. Your man just entered a coffee shop. I'm gonna' sit down on a bench for a minute. I'll let you know when he is on the move again."

Kat smiled and looked at Lake, "He's pretty good at this tailing someone business."

"Yeah, he blends in nicely, doesn't look at all threatening. Brandon may not make him even if he looked right at him."

*   *   *

Brandon was feeling semi confident in his situation, He had gotten rid of his old boots that seemed to be of interest to the police and they had no way to connect him to any of the killings. He stepped into the coffee shop and after scanning for a Suzanne sighting, he ordered his usual coffee and a bagel. "Thanks Angie, see you tomorrow," he said to the lady behind the counter. He sipped his coffee and slowly walked outside munching on his bagel and sipping his coffee. He walked about half a block and sat on a park bench, set his coffee next to him and began to break off little pieces of his bagel tossing them to the birds.

Finally after sharing the last bits of his bagel, Brandon stood and began walking again with coffee in hand.

*   *   *

"Little birdies ate all that evidence Lake," joked Freddy. "He's on the move, taking his time. This could last a while. I'm movin'."

Kat looked at Lake, "If he tosses that coffee cup — ."

"I'll be all over it mom, not to worry," said Freddy.

Brandon covered the next several blocks at a very relaxed pace as if he was deep in thought, not paying much attention to the time. Then as he rounded a corner about five blocks from the Pub, he hurried his pace and almost lost Freddy.

"Man that guy can walk. His one step takes me about three or four — ."

Kat picked up the mic, "Do you still have him in view, Freddy?"

"Yeah, I got him, he's about half a block ahead of me and movin, excuse me while I put on my track shoes."

"Freddy, you are about three blocks from the Pub, time to close the gap, but not too much."

"I'm movin in. He's still got that cup in his hand. You say it's only three blocks to go?"

"Closer to two now Freddy," said Kat.

"I'm about thirty feet behind now, don't want to get any closer."

"You're good Freddy, we are going to turn left again and should see you any second now," said Lake.

Kat was scanning the street, "There's the target almost home — ."

Lake chimed in, "I see Freddy, he's on him."

Brandon reached the corner in front of the Pub and waited for the light to change. Freddy came up behind him, close enough to touch him and waited. The light turned, Brandon stepped off the curb and walked across the street.

Freddy saw a trash can set up in front of the Pub and looked at Brandon. "Come on man, toss the cup — ."

Brandon reached the opposite side stepped toward the trash can and flipped the cup in the can, turned and walked toward the alley. Freddy walked over to the trash can, looked in and saw one coffee cup on top of a mound of other trash. He reached into his pocket and pulled out a large plastic bag, turned it inside out over his hand and reached into the trash bin securing the coffee cup.

"Detectives, we have a coffee cup, the only one on top of the trash. I have it bagged and ready to be tagged. Wanna' come pick me up?"

Lake drove across the street and picked Freddy up on the corner. "Did anyone see you retrieve the cup, Freddy?"

"If they did, they didn't say anything."

Freddy opened his shopping bag and pulled out an evidence bag, placed the plastic bag with the cup in it in the evidence bag and sealed it. He wrote the appropriate information on the bag and handed it to Kat. "All yours, detective. Now we have something to run against the blood smear on that stick."

Kat looked at Lake, "When's the tradin deadline?"

*   *   *

Brandon worked until 1:30 in the morning. The activity at the bar was unusual, but much appreciated and the tips were an indication that he was doing a good job. Counting his tip money, Brandon was surprised that he had made almost $500.

He called Lisa over and handed her $50 and the same to two other waitresses, then he went into the kitchen and gave Hank $50 and walked out the back door.

The walk home was quiet at first and until a breeze blew some leaves from a tree. The wind seemed to whisper and the leaves fluttering across the ground sounded like foot steps behind him. Brandon looked in windows for confirmation that he was alone on the street, but even though he could not see anything, he could hear them. The whispers grew louder with each step and by the time he reached his apartment, they were calling his name in gravely voices louder than a whisper.

He locked his door, turned on the lights, grabbed a heavy blanket and curled up in his chair staring at the television. The infomercials ran all night and they distracted him enough to allow him to fall asleep.

The street was empty, the wind calm. The sky was cloudless and the moon was full. Brandon could clearly see the dirty red brick walls surrounding him and as he turned, windows appeared. Then doors, then shadow figures in the windows and then through the doors walking directly at him, whispering his name at first then in deep hoarse voices, louder and louder *'Brandon'*. Their faces were only inches away and their eyes were little more than lighter shades of grey in their faces.

As their large, grey hands reached for him, Brandon awoke. He sat up right and looked at the time, it was 3:57 in the morning. He stood, looked out his window and tried to reason what he should do. "I cannot allow these dreams to control everything that I do," he mumbled, "I have to stop them. Stop them now." He picked up his coat and walked out into the street.

As he walked, he thought, he remembered. "I killed that little man with the knife and they went away, I killed Karen and they went away, but I cannot keep on killing to keep them away." His walk took him into an area frequented by a number of people of the evening. People who lived in shadows themselves and did not think twice about leaving you for dead if attacked. Brandon rounded a corner and bumped into a man leaning against a wall, counting his money.

"Hey, watch where you're going, mutha — " But before he could finish his words, Brandon pushed him deeper into the alley.

"Don't threaten me you miserable piece of crap," he said as he tried to walk past the man. Then he heard that familiar metallic clicking of a switchblade knife being opened. He turned and said, "The last man to do that spent the next few days in the morgue. You want to try your luck, come on, I need an excuse and you may be it."

The man stepped back, pocketed his money and slowly walked backwards toward the street at the end of the alley. Brandon stood there amazed at what he had just done. His knees suddenly felt weak and as the man turned at the corner and ran from the scene, Brandon looked for something to brace himself. A handrail at a back door to some shop met his need and he took a few minutes to catch his breath and allow his heart to slow to a normal pace. He stood and continued his walk, no sounds of the night invaded his thoughts, no whispers, no footsteps. He was exhausted and he turned for home and his bed.

*　　　*　　　*

Thirty Seven

Saturday ... The guy almost jumped outta his big black shoes ...

Brandon slept till 10:00 am and he woke to a misting rain and a slight wind. He showered and dressed, pulled on his heavy jacket and put on the blue baseball cap that he had gotten a few weeks earlier at the ball game. The walk to work included his usual stop for coffee and a bagel. Once inside, he decided to finish his bagel there, then continue his trek to the Pub in the rain with coffee in hand.

As he approached the Pub, Brandon tossed his cup in the trash and ambled toward the back alley and the kitchen door. "Hey, George, did you order this rain?"

"Good morning Brandon, you look like a drowned rat. There are some towels in front of the lockers downstairs, dry yourself off before you come back up, and toss the towel in the laundry bag at the bottom of the stairs."

"Thanks George, see you in a minute or two." Brandon went down the stairs more easily than he had in the past when he was alone. Drying his hair he looked around the dark basement and covered his head with the towel for a final wipe down. He tossed the towel in the laundry bag, opened his locker and retrieved a comb. Looking in the mirror he smiled, finished combing his thick locks, turned to go up the stairs and heard a whisper, *"Brandon."* He stopped, turned scanned the basement and quietly mumbled, "Not today, not today. We are done and you can go back to hell." He turned again and slowly walked up the stairs.

*   *   *

Freddy had taken the coffee cup and the stick to the lab and was anxious for results. "Freddy, you'll have to relax, this stuff takes time," said Ben Chemen, the lab tech who checked the evidence in. "We will call you when we have something."

Freddy was in the ME's lab early Saturday morning, nervously pacing back and forth. Dr. Colburn came in most days if for no other reason than to check on the flow of the work. "Good morning Freddy, I didn't realize you were on this weekend."

"Hi Doc, well I'm not on, but I want to be here in case anything comes up on the stuff that I took over to the DNA geeks."

"Did they give you a time estimate when it may be ready?"

"Yeah, he said about two weeks, but it could come in earlier, so — , well I didn't have anything else going on today."

"Freddy, relax, go home, go to a movie, chase a cute girl, you are not doing yourself any favors hanging around here. I'll leave word that you should be contacted when the results come in. And Freddy, figure that it will be at least two weeks, and probably a day or two more. Now get outta here, go enjoy something."

*   *   *

Lake was sitting at home with his son, trying to build a volcano on a piece of foam-core. "Marty, how big do you want to make this volcano?"

"Not so big, it'll just make it harder to carry to school. I guess that we should make it — this high," he said as he held his hand about 4 inches above the surface, "And we can put some little trees and a river in here," he said pointing at the foam-core."

"Okay," said Lake as the phone rang.

"I'll get it," called his wife from the kitchen. "Lake, it's your other wife."

"Thanks, I have the extension right here." He picked up the phone, "Hey Kat, what's up?"

"Lake, the guy that we are lookin at, Brandon — , what's his face, was on television a few weeks ago at a ball game. It was on a Sunday, the 26th, and he jumped out of the way of a foul ball. I don't know if it means anything, but, it drew some attention, made a highlight reel and the clip has been played a bunch since. I called the Network that does the ball games and they just sent me that clip. I can forward it to you."

Lake grinned, "Marty and I were watching that game on television and I do remember seeing a tall skinny guy jump outta the way of a liner into the crowd."

"Yeah, like I said, I got it about ten minutes ago and I can forward it to you now."

"Yeah, I'd like to see it, " said Lake as he went over to his computer.

"Done," said Kat, It's on the way."

"Thanks brown eyes, I'll see you Monday morning bright and early."

Little Marty came into the study where his father was down-loading the video clip that Kat had just sent. "Hey dad, we gotta make the volcano a little higher — , what'cha doin?"

"Marty, do you remember this," he said as the video began to play?

Marty watched for a few seconds and said, "Sure, the skinny guy almost got hit."

Lake let the video finish and he watched it again. Marty was anxious to get back to his volcano and Lake said, "I'll turn this off and watch it later, okay buddy."

"Sure dad."

"Okay, let's build a mountain."

Shelly was passing the door to the study and said, "What did Kat have for you?"

"She's at the station, squaring away some paperwork and we got a video of a suspect in a case. She sent it over for me to see. I'll check it out later when Marty has gone to bed."

"Is it bad?"

"No, nothing like that. It's a video that the television network has played a number of times. Our suspect is at a ball game and almost got hit by a foul ball."

"Yeah," said Marty, "It was funny. The guy almost jumped outta his big black shoes."

"Lake paused, looked at his son, "Big black shoes — ?"

"Yeah dad, remember, his feet were almost straight up in the air and he was wearing big black shoes."

*   *   *

Brandon finished the evening, wiping down the bar and checking the levels in the liquor bottles. Satisfied that there was enough to get a start on Monday morning, he decided to bring a few new bottles up from the basement to replace the three that were at very low levels. He checked two more bottles and was thinking, as he walked to the basement stairs. George came up the stairs with an empty box and started to load the items he wanted to leave in the walk-in cooler over the next day.

"Hey George, need any help?"

"Thanks Brandon, but I got this one," and he continued to load the box.

Brandon walked down the stairs thinking about the bottles that he was going to bring up. At the bottom of the stairs he turned toward the liquor room and flipped a switch lighting that area of the basement. "Let me see, I need one of these," as he pulled a bottle of gin from a shelf, "And one of these," as he pulled a bottle of scotch from another shelf, "And — hmmm, oh yeah, one of these," as he took a bottle of vodka from another shelf. He paused, thinking about the other two bottles that he might take and he heard a footstep behind him.

"Hey George, I didn't hear you come down — ," he said as he turned toward the stairs. No one was there. The light in the kitchen was on and he could see a shadow of someone moving about. "I'm letting it get to me again — ," he mumbled as he stepped toward the stairs.

"Brandon, you forgot something," said a deep throaty whisper.

He turned again and saw a shadow move behind a shelf. "Who is that, what do you want?"

There was no reply, the shadow did not move again. Brandon waited, thought, then he walked toward the shelf and looked behind. Nothing, no one was there. He was alone in the basement and now about five steps farther away from the stairs. He raised his voice, "Is anyone down here with me?" Again, no answer. He walked to the stairs and as he put his foot on the bottom step, he heard a footstep behind him. He took the first two stairs slowly and then took the rest two and three at a time.

"Whoa Brandon, slow down on the stairs man, you are carrying liquid gold there," grinned George. "Hey are you okay, look a little queasy like my cooking didn't agree with you?"

Brandon slowed to a stop, "I'm okay, just in a little hurry."

"Yeah, Saturday night, or Sunday morning — you gonna' see that pretty lady of yours when you get outta here?"

"Probably in the morning," he said as he walked out to the bar.

As he left the Pub and began his walk home, Brandon was thinking about Suzanne. What could they do together tomorrow? He hadn't talked to her in a few days and had not planned anything. That troubled him. He should have called her and made some arrangements for the day. He thought about getting a cell phone so he could talk to her. The best he could hope for now would be to go to her place and if the lights were on, maybe knock on the door. As he debated, his feet found their way to Suzanne's apartment.

The lights were on, the as he was looking up, one of the lights went out. He looked at the other two windows and saw a figure pass by the window and another light went out. Then a second, taller figure passed in front of the last window and the light went out.

Was that Suzanne, or one of her roommates? He didn't know. He turned and started walking toward his place. He walked several blocks thinking and brooding over what he had seen. Was that Suzanne with someone else?

"Brandon," said the whisper, *"It is time — ."*

He stopped and spun around looking for the source of the voice. Nothing was there. He was completely alone on a street. No people, no cars, no dogs, cats or rats. He was alone.

"Time, Brandon, it is time — ."

"Time for what?"

"You know what you must do."

"No, no I won't do that again."

The whispers in the shadows began again. The wind made the trees move and the shadows moved along with the wind. Brandon began to walk. He was already upset about the uncertainty about Suzanne and the voices, the whispers made it all worse. The whispers were punctuated with laughter, laughter from the darkened alleys, the sewers, from behind parked cars. He walked faster, trying to get away, but the whispers and the laughter were everywhere. It grew louder and louder and he walked faster and faster.

He turned into an alley and bumped into a man hurrying in the opposite direction. Both were startled at the sight of the other and the man turned and ran. Brandon stopped, panting he watched the man run.

"You know what you must do — ."

"No, I said no, and I mean it."

He turned again to continue his trek and saw a woman stagger out of a doorway twenty feet away. She was partially dressed, apparently drunk and looked as if she had been beaten. As he came closer to her she looked up, she saw Brandon, raised her right hand gripping a rock and screamed.

Brandon was about to try to calm her — .

"You know what you must do — ."

She was bleeding from several cuts on her face and arms, her clothes that remained on her were ripped. She screamed again and Brandon tried to tell her that he would not hurt her. She threw the rock at Brandon hitting him on his left shoulder. He backed up against a wall.

"You know what you must do — ."

She hurled herself at him flailing her fists, striking him in the chest and face. Brandon pushed back and she stumbled backward, loosing balance and falling to the ground. He touched the shoulder where the rock had made contact, it was numb, the pain was just setting in and as he moved to a light to see the damage, the woman picked up another rock and was struggling to her feet.

"I'll kill you," she screamed.

Brandon looked up as she took a step in his direction. "Wait," he said as he put up his right hand. The guy that hurt you just ran outta here, it was not me — ."

"Liar," she said as she launched the second rock.

It struck Brandon on his hip as he turned to avoid contact. The woman looked for another rock and Brandon started to back away from her. She looked up and started to come at him without a weapon and Brandon thought that he now had the edge. He grabbed both of her wrists and tried to talk to her, but she screamed again and tried to kick him.

He pushed her back across the alley against a wall and said, "The guy that did whatever he did, ran out of here as I was coming in . . . I did not hurt you."

"Liar," she screamed and bit his arm.

Brandon yelped and pulled his arm away. She then started at him again and he reacted with a fist to her head. He could hear the cracking sound of bones being broken and as he looked at her falling back against the wall her eyes were already empty.

"You did what you had to do — ."

The woman lay on the ground twisted, battered and dead. Brandon was bruised but not bleeding, and alive. He looked at her and said, "I was not the guy, why didn't you listen?"

"You did what you had to do — ."

Brandon angrily replied, "Leave me alone — ."

He looked around wondering if anyone had heard the screams, wondering if the guy who ran out of the alley was still around. He saw no one, He was safe and he had to get out of there as soon as he could. He ran to the opposite end of the alley and peered around the corners. Again, empty streets, he proceeded. The whispers were still following him but the laughter had stopped. When he arrived at his apartment building, he stopped to look around one more time.

"Do it again — ."

*   *   *

T<small>HIRTY</small> E<small>IGHT</small>

Sunday . . .   Lake, it's always a pleasure to hand you a case . . .

The sun rose and shed light on the morning dew, Saturday night's litter in the streets and a body twisted and cold in an alley. The man who discovered the victim was pushing a shopping cart, looking for bottles to return for the deposit and any other valuable items that may have been lost the night before. The lady that he found was already half naked, stripped of her purse, watch and jewelry, leaving Norman little to scavenge but a possible reward for calling the police.

The patrol officers, Paul Evers and Stan Dorsch, who were first on the scene thought that a call to Dan Carney might be in order in that Dan and his partner had had several recent 'Alley Discoveries' over the last few weeks that might be connected. Dan did not answer his phone but Paul left a message.

"Dan, this is Paul Evers, hey I just responded to a '10-84' in Slater's Alley off of M Street. I already have a team of D's on the way and the ME's Office ought to be here any minute. Just thought that you might want to know about this one. See you at roll call."

Detective Carl Dempsey walked into the alley and approached Officer Evers as he was tying off the last of the crime scene tape to a stair railing. "Hey Paul, what'cha got for me?"

"Carl, looks like a bunch of things, she's been beaten, maybe raped, clothes ripped and no purse, jewelry, watch — ."

"Lights out — ?"

Paul looked down at the victim, sighed and said, "Yeah, lights out."

Mark Portman and his partner Shirley Devers arrived at the scene a few seconds after the detectives. Paul opened the tape barrier to allow the CSI van into the alley and tied off the tape again. Mark approached Paul, "Mornin' Paul, Carl. What's the word?"

Carl looked at Paul and deferred to his version. "Well, we were flagged down by that fellow over there with Stan, at 7:14 am, he stated that there was a body in the alley. The guy's name is — Norman Byzanski. He stated that he was looking for bottles in this alley when he found the victim. Says he didn't touch anything, but I think he probably poked around for a few minutes before he came out to look for us. We were on M street when we saw him, he waved us down and we took a fast look and called it in. It is now 7:36 and I am handing this site over to Carl and Mark. Stan and I will stay as long as you need us."

"Thanks Paul. You know we answered a call about a week ago in an alley — ."

"Oh yeah, I was talking to Dan Carney the other day and he mentioned a couple of 'Alley killings'. I gave him a call, thought they might be connected. So you are the detectives on those cases?"

Carl grinned, "Nope, and this one may also wind up in McLarry's bucket with the others."

*   *   *

"Lake, this is Carl Dempsey, I may have another one for you. I'm in an alley off M Street. We are finishing up but, if you want to have a look, I'll keep the tape up till you get here. Give me a call."

*   *   *

Lake rolled over in bed groping for his phone and pushed it onto the floor. By the time he picked it up and tried to answer, the caller had been pushed to his voice mail box. He held the phone, looking at the screen and grumbled, "It's Sunday, 8:45 am, so much for sleeping in."

Shelly poked him, "You have to go in?"

"Don't have to, but I should check this out. Could be nothing, could be something — ."

"You won't know till you get there, right?"

"Yeah, right."

"I'll start the coffee."

"Thanks babe, I'll be right down." Lake got out of bed went into the bathroom and looked in the mirror. He picked up his tooth brush and began his day off as a day on — .

*   *   *

"Lake, it's always a pleasure to hand you a case that I now won't have to write up."

"Very funny Carl. What happened here?"

"Not exactly sure, could have been a simple robbery that went a little off. Or maybe an attempted rape that didn't get that far. The most interesting thing is this over here." Carl led Lake to the taped outline of the victim and pointed to a mix of footprints in a small patch of damp dirt next to the outline. "There, those are some large shoes."

"Did the CSI guys photo these?"

"Yeah, her name is Shirley Devers. She shot the whole scene, kinda like Freddy does . . . If in doubt, shoot it two times, or three. I think she has it covered."

Lake stood and stared at the foot prints. Carl reached into his pocket and pulled out his wallet. He took a one dollar bill and laid it on the ground next to the footprint and used his phone to photograph the footprint and the dollar. "I saw that in a movie — ."

Lake grinned, "Carl you're not only cute, you're clever, well at least clever. Send that to me and I'll give it to Freddy — ."

"I'll just send it to both of y'all."

*   *   *

Brandon woke to the sound of a barker on his television, screaming the great advantage of his cleaning product over all others. He stood, turned off the television and started to stretch when the two encounters with a rock reminded him of the previous night. He thought about it and turned the television on again looking for a news program. An all news channel was running a story about some political meeting and he turned his attention again to his aches and pains.

His clothes were covered with blood stains and his face hurt. He pulled off his shirt and pants and walked into the bathroom, looked in the mirror and realized that the blood was not his. His shoulder was bruised, as was his hip and there were a series of teeth marks on his arm where she had bitten him, but no open wounds, no blood. He stood in the shower allowing the hot water to wash over him then the colder water and the hot again. He stepped out of the shower and started to dry himself off. His bloodied clothes were in a pile on his floor and as he dried himself, he wondered if the police would be questioning him about this.

The news program began with a story about a woman found in alley — he walked over to the television and listened.

" . . . The woman has not yet been identified and the Medical Examiner's office is not releasing any further information until her identity is determined and the family has been notified."

Brandon turned away from the television, dressed in clean clothes and took his bloodied clothes into the bathroom. He held the shirt under the cold water shower wringing the stains out as much as he could, then the same with his pants. He decided that he needed to run these through the laundry at least once and maybe more to get the remnants of blood out.

His Laundromat was open 24/7 and he took all his cleaning from the previous week to make a clean sweep. After he ran his clothes through once, he put the shirt and pants in for a second washing and then a third.

Home and satisfied that he had wiped out all trace of the woman's blood, Brandon changed his clothes again putting on the same outfit that he was wearing the night before.

"Shoes, the police were looking at my shoes before and these could be a problem. It may be time for another new pair." He looked closely at the shoes for blood stains and found none. It didn't matter, he was going to get another pair, these were going to the Good Will donation box in the church yard six blocks away.

*   *   *

Suzanne was sitting in her apartment wondering if her new friend was going to call her. She had not seen or heard from him since the previous weekend and she wondered if this was going to be the end of something she envisioned as promising. "This is his day off," she muttered to herself as she poured herself a cup of coffee.

Deanna came into the kitchen and asked, "Is there enough in the pot for two more?"

Suzanne looked a little troubled and said, "Sure, I just made it and I have all I want."

Deanna poured two cups and started to walk to her bedroom. "Hey Suzz, are you okay?"

"Yeah, just a little disappointed. I thought he would at least call — ."

"The day is still young, he works late and I would give a little more time before writing him off."

*   *   *

Brandon made sure he had Suzanne's number in his wallet and left his apartment heading in her direction, which took him past the Good Will box. He found a pay phone and dialed her number.

"Are you open today, I am going to go to a store and get a cell phone and could use some company?"

"And lunch — ?"

"Yeah, and lunch."

*   *   *

T HIRTY N INE

Monday . . .   Let's go see the judge

Freddy arrived at the ME's office at 7:15 am, ready to start a new week and still anxious about the DNA testing. He walked into the lab area, turned on his computer and helped it through it's start-up cycle. He stood and looked at the screen as it went through a few exercises and decided to get his first coffee of the day. As he was passing the administration area, he saw Dr. Colburn sitting at his desk getting his calendar arranged for the day. "Good morning Doc."

"Freddy, come in here. You're early today."

"Yeah, well there could be a lot to do, and — ."

"And I told you it would take at least two weeks."

"I hear you, but that's not the only case that we have open — ."

"As a matter of fact, it's not. We got a new murder victim in yesterday morning. We are still in the process of identifying her and I would like you to get a few good pictures of her face for identification purposes. She was beat up pretty badly, so we have a little cleanup to do first."

"Okay Doc, I'll get tuned in out there then come down stairs and help get her ready. See you in a minute or two.' Freddy stepped out of Dr. Colburn's office. "Hey Doc, I'm headin' for the coffee pot, you want one?"

"Oh thanks Freddy, I just put a new pot on, it may be ready by now."

"I'll bring it with me."

Freddy poured two cups of coffee and went back to his computer on his way to the morgue. He had 14 messages in his in box and clicked on the icon to see the list. One was from Carl Dempsey with an attachment. He opened the message, then opened the attachment.

"Coffee Doc, get while it's hot."

"Thanks Freddy." Dr. Colburn pulled a gurney under a light and folded the drape down to Jane Doe's shoulders. "Looks like a broken neck, probably from a BFT to the side of her head, possibly with a fist. We will know more as we open her up. Anyway, before we do that, let's clean up the cuts and photograph her."

"Should I get a few before and then do the after?"

"Yeah, please," and Dr Colburn backed away from the table, allowing Freddy to shoot a series of her. When Freddy finished, Dr. Colburn again approached the table, turned on the recorder and started to clean the facial wounds.

Freddy was reading the information clip board attached to this Jane Doe and he said, "Doc, I got a message from Carl Dempsey and a photo of some footprints that he thought I should look at. Those prints are from this lady's scene."

"Why did he send them to you?"

"Actually to me and Lake McLarry."

"Oh, I see. Let's get through this first and then you can attack the footprints. You picked a good day to come in early my friend."

"Yeah, let's hope it leads us to some answers."

*   *   *

Lake and Kat were looking at the video clip of Brandon diving out of the way of the foul ball and finally decided to call Freddy and see if he could do something with the clarity.

"Freddy, Lake McLarry. I want to send you a video clip and see if we can get a better pic of some details."

"Sure Lake. Hey I got the picture of the footprints, nice work."

"Yeah, I'll tell Carl, his idea, his photograph."

"I'm on my way back to my desk now, so as soon as I finish a few touch-up photos of our Jane Doe, I'll jump on the footprints. You wanna' send me the clip or are you and Kat comin over?"

"We'll be there in about an hour. It's almost 8:30 now so I'll look for you at 9:30 and I'll put on a fresh pot of coffee."

*   *   *

Brandon woke and walked into Suzanne's kitchen. Coffee was made, she was dressed and ready to go to work.

"I have your number and you have mine, so we can talk anytime. This is much better than wondering if I should sit by the phone . . ."

Brandon sipped his coffee, "You can call me any time and if I am busy, I'll call you back when I'm not busy."

"Great, now I have to get to work."

Brandon said, "Give me a few seconds and I'll walk out with you."

*   *   *

Lake and Kat arrived at the ME's office and found Freddy immediately. Lake was anxious to see the blow-ups that Freddy could do with Brandon's shoes and he wanted to see if the new footprints tied the several cases together.

Freddy was ready with the foot print comparison and had the equipment set for the video clip review.

"We photographed Lady Slater this morning and I touched up the pics so she is not so beat up looking. You guys wanna' see?" Freddy was very proud of the work he had done and rightfully so.

Kat looked interested and said, "Sure, Freddy, let's see what she looks like."

Freddy pulled up a series of photos and picked out a very nice looking photo of a young lady. "This is a picture of our victim," said Freddy, "She looks like a nice lady."

"This is good Freddy. Let's get this to a facial recognition in all three areas, The District, Maryland and Virginia."

Freddy said, "Let's hope she has a license." He stood and walked over to another table, "You have that video clip."

Lake handed him a memory stick, "This is it, Freddy."

Dr. Colburn walked in as Freddy was loading the clip into memory. "Good morning Detective," he said looking at Kat, "You're looking good this morning."

Freddy cleared his throat, "Ready when you are."

Lake said, "Let the show begin."

Dr. Colburn then said, "Oh hi Lake, I didn't see you there."

"Yeah, Yeah, good morning Doc."

Freddy ran the clip up to the point where Brandon went upside down. "why don't y'all go get some coffee and let me play with this for a little bit. Go on, get outta here."

Dr. Colburn said, "When he gets into something, we give him his space and see what pops out. You guys ready for coffee?"

Less than an hour later Dr. Colburn's phone rang. The three of them came back to the lab and Freddy's video set-up.

"First, the footprints. These were made by a larger shoe that the ones at the other scenes, but that doesn't mean much. It's a different manufacturer and a different type shoe. So the smaller boot may fit as well as the larger athletic shoe."

"So we're nowhere on that one — ."

Kat looked at Lake and said, "Maybe not Lake, it's still a small group of people that would wear that size or those sizes and as Freddy said, the boot and the tenny could both fit the same foot."

"Yeah, okay, so Freddy, could you zoom in on the shoes when the dude was upside down or down side up, my system at home left them very fuzzy."

Freddy grinned and began fiddling with the key board. The image on the screen grew larger and again larger. "I'll start to lose clarity as I move in closer, but the detail at this level tells us a lot. See that guy on his right?"

Lake nodded and Kat was staring at the big screen.

Freddy continued, "He's holding a cup of beer, and his change from a vendor."

Lake and Kat nodded again.

"Fortunately, he is holding a dollar bill such that I can measure it from end to end and top to bottom. See, six and an eighth inches by two and five eighths inches."

"Okay," said Lake, "So what is that telling us?"

266

Freddy drew a block around the dollar bill and moved the curser dragging the block next to Brandon's shoe. Then he drew a second block around Brandon's left foot and dragged the two boxes off to the side over a clear space and printed the two blocks. "You see Lake, the shoe is longer than the dollar bill, longer than two dollar bills. These shoes are at least a size thirteen and most likely, one size bigger."

Lake looked slightly puzzled, "That doesn't help much Freddy, but thanks."

"Lake, I'm not done. Look at this." Freddy pulled up a picture of a pair of boots saying, "This is a 'Frontier' boot, it happens to be one of their best sellers and they have not changed anything in their design or manufacture of these boots in the last several years. They use the same tread pattern and stitching today that they used ten years ago. This is the boot that was at the Decker and Pavia scenes. Now look at the boot on Brandon's foot, the stitching the cut of the leather, the soles, from the side. They all match, this is the boot that Brandon was wearing at the ball game that day and this is the same boot that walked through the mud and blood at the crime scenes. Is that enough to pull a warrant and search his place?"

"It may well be, Freddy. We are gonna' find out. Let's go see the judge, Kat."

Freddy was excited about the information he had just passed along and added, "Hey Lake, it's gonna' take at least two weeks for the DNA to come back, so nothing on that front yet."

Lake responded, "No surprise there. Maybe we could get one of those television labs to knock this out overnight . . . like on NCIS."

The group laughed and Kat started her quiet singing about trading up.

*   *   *

Thirty Nine

Tuesday ...   "Brandon, again — ."

"Our 'Jane Doe' from Slater's Alley has been identified, Freddy. Her name is Donna Markus Newberry. She lived with her husband and two teen aged kids in Fairfax, out near the George Mason campus."

Freddy looked sad, "Two kids, teenagers, man that really sucks — ."

"Lake called this morning, there was a missing persons report and she is a match. The husband is coming in for an identification. Should be here in about an hour, depending on traffic."

"Is Lake going to be here."

"Yeah, and Kat. This is the hard part of their job. Apparently she was in town for a meeting with some teachers group and she never made it home. Everything seems to fit, the pictures you took matched up with her Virginia driver's license, height, weight, the clothes she was wearing — . Her husband identified her picture and what she was wearing, He listed a necklace, watch and a wedding ring, but that was not found. Kind'a leads to a robbery gone bad."

The clock read 9:47 am when Lake and Kat pulled into the ME's parking lot. As they were getting out of their car another car pulled in and a very tired looking man got out. He approached Lake, "Excuse me, is this where I should go in to see a Dr. Colburn?"

Lake looked at Kat, then at the man, "Yes sir, would you happen to be Dan Newberry?'

"Yes, yes I am, are you Dr. — ?"

"No sir I am Detective Martin McLarry and this is my partner Detective Katrina Murano. We are handling this investigation. Let's go inside."

Kat led the way opening the door and letting Dan Newberry into the reception area. She walked past Dan and said to the receptionist, "Please let Dr. Colburn that Mr. Newberry is here and we will be in the little conference room speaking with him."

"Will do, detective."

Lake led the man into a small conference room and asked him to sit. "The Doc will be out in a minute or two and we will go to the identification room right away."

Newberry looked confused, tired and scared all at once. Lake offered him coffee or water and he declined. "No, I just want to see my wife."

*   *   *

Brandon was up and ready for a new day. He was feeling good about himself. The woman that he had killed was really an accident, or maybe self defense. He wasn't sure but he was sure that he felt fine. He hadn't broken any laws or hurt anyone that he didn't have to. He was good. He had his morning coffee, his bagel with cream cheese and his new cell phone. As he crossed through McPherson Square, he flipped open his new phone and pushed the number 1.

"Hello," said Suzanne, "Shouldn't you be on your way to work?"

"I am, gorgeous, just finished my bagel and now I'm talking to you while I finish my coffee and walk to work." The world was perfect as he walked. It could have been raining and he still would have been happy. When he arrived at the Pub, he got right into the routine of checking supplies, wiping down the bar and making sure he had a supply of glasses. "I'm going down to check the soda system," he said to Steve as he passed through the kitchen. He opened the basement door and locked it against the wall to keep it open and headed down the stairs. He turned on the lights at the top of the stairs and was about to turn on the light at the bottom when he heard the whisper,

"Do it again — ."

He paused, thought and with determination in his eyes and voice he said, "No way, I'm done with you — ," as he moved toward the walk-in cooler.

"No — , not done — ."

He paused again, then he continued to the cooler.

"You must do it again — ."

He stood straight and turned around looking for the speaker, but no one was there. "Where are you?" There was no answer. Brandon continued into the cooler, adjusted the several soda bottles, checking the temperature and pressures. He finished and exited the cooler, pulling the large door closed and started up the stairs.

"Again — , do it again — ."

"I will not do it again, I am finished, through — ." Then he heard laughter in the distance as if it were coming from the basement but from farther away than the basement would allow. He again paused, trying to decide if he should confront these demons or run from them. In the past, he would have lowered his head, hurried up the stairs and tried to ignore the damn things. He heard his name again and he turned, stepped back into the basement, hands on hips and head held high, "I don't see you, you hide from me, you fear me. Maybe you are not here at all."

"We are here — ."

"Right, where — ?"

"Here, with you, always with you."

"No, I don't believe you. Your voice is here, but you are not. He turned again toward the stairs as he said, "Now leave me alone."

"We are with you − ."

"Go away," he said one more time as he again started up the stairs.

As he stepped out of the stairwell, George looked at him and said, "Brandon, are you feeling okay? I could hear you downstairs. Who are you talking to − ?"

Brandon looked at George and said, "I'm just muttering to myself. Old habit, I guess it makes me look a little silly."

George shrugged his shoulders and got back to his prep work for the lunch hour. Brandon also shrugged his shoulders and walked straight to the bar. Alone behind the bar, he busied himself, arranging bottles of beer in the bar coolers, wiping down the bar between other little chores. He mumbled to himself, "They just won't leave me alone." This time nobody heard him.

Four men entered the bar through the front door and took up position at a table half way to the kitchen. Their choice of location was based on privacy. they needed about five minutes to complete their conference and lunch was their reward for finishing the several thoughts that each brought to the table.

Brandon was relieved that someone was there for him to wait on and he leaned on the bar toward them. "Gentlemen, what can I get for you?"

"Let's do a round of coffee first," said the apparent leader of this band of business suits, "while we finish our discussion and then we'll see about a little lunch."

"Comin' right up," said Brandon

He walked over to the waitress station and was checking on the status of the coffee when Lisa came in and approached with a smile. "Hey Brandon, are you trying to take my job?"

"No way," he replied, "Just need some coffee for table three, there are four guys trying to finish their business before they order lunch. You handle the coffee and I'll grab a pitcher of water and fill their glasses."

Lisa smiled, "Yes sir."

Lunch was busy, the voices were quiet and there was no laughter. Brandon was confused, why was he hearing voices? And why did they leave when others were around?"

The day passed without further incident and Brandon was feeling good. At about 9:50 in the evening, he again had occasion to descend into the basement and he did so without reservation. One of the soda bottles was running out and a new one had to be installed. As he finished his chore and was moving once again to the stairs, the voice spoke, *"Again — ."*

"No, not again," he responded. He stood tall, turned slowly around and scanned the basement. No one, only him. "I am alone — ."

"We are here — ."

"No. No you are not. You are just my imagination gone a little overboard." There was no reply. There was only silence. Brandon went back up the stairs and finished the night without so much as a whisper. Three blocks into his walk home, he heard a single sound then silence for the next three blocks. Again a sound, a hushed whisper two or three words and then again, silence. Home and tired, he stripped and lay on his bed. The walls were about six or seven stories high. there were no windows, no doors and he could not see an entry, worse, he could not see an exit. It was night, the pavement was damp and cold, the air had a chill and he was looking at the clouded sky when a whisper drew his attention toward the intersection of two walls. The corner was not lit, the voice grew louder and a figure stepped out of the shadows. A tall hulking man in a dark suit. As he approached and the moon light illuminated his face, Brandon saw the grey blank expression, the empty grey eyes and a mouth that moved very slowly emitting a whisper that became more audible as he approached. *"Brandon — ."*

Brandon turned looking for a way out and saw another man, then a third and a fourth.

"Brandon — ," each man said over and over.

Brandon turned again and tried to run. As he turned he fell from his bed and woke in his apartment, sweating, exhausted and shaking. "Dreaming, I'm dreaming. These things are not real. He stood, walked into his bathroom and stood in the shower. Hot then cold, then hot again. As he was drying himself off,

"Brandon, again — ."

He did not respond. He took a blanket from his bed, wrapped himself and turned on his television. Nothing was on that satisfied him and he delved into his collection of old films.

Once again the Frankenstein monster walked across the set with rigid, awkward steps, opening and closing his large grey hands. Brandon watched and slowly began to sleep.

*   *   *

F ORTY

Lake was sitting at his desk shuffling through the crime scene photographs and wondering if they were on the wrong trail. The prime suspect was Brandon Croummer, but what was his motive? Why was this one a robbery and, it appeared, a sexual attack as well. The differences in the several cases were troubling.

Kat walked into the room carrying an envelope and handed it to Lake. "Ya wanna' go pick up our suspect, take a peek at his apartment, poke around his closet, check for a pair of Frontier boots — ?"

"You got a warrant," said Lake, more as a statement than a question.

"Yeah, I got it, so let's go . . . "

They covered the distance to Brandon's apartment in less than 15 minutes and as they got out of their car, the time was 9:37 am.

Lake looked at the mail boxes. Croummer was lettered in permanent marker on the box for apartment 3D. "Third floor, let's go."

They knocked and after a brief pause the door slowly opened. Brandon stood wrapped in a blanket looking very tired.

"Good morning Mr. Croummer. We have a warrant to search your apartment. Are you going to let us in?"

Brandon stared, then said, "Yeah, sure, come on in. What is it that you are looking for?"

Lake stood next to Brandon as Kat walked to the closet next to the bed. She opened it and shined her flashlight into the corners. The

274

closet was neat, not as clean as Kat would keep her's, but neater. Shirts and pants were hung on hangers. A box on the floor held a pair of old athletic shoes. "White, well at one time white. Probably not what we are looking for," she mumbled.

"What are you guys looking for," asked Brandon. He knew the answer, but played the game. "I don't have much, so I know where everything is."

"You have a pair of black work boots," asked Kat?

"Not anymore," answered Brandon, "they were shot, coming apart and I got new shoes, about, oh I guess three maybe four weeks ago."

"Really," said Kat, "What kind were they?"

"Brandon smiled, "Old and coming apart, they were cheap and I had them for a few years. I don't remember where I got them, I mean it was around here somewhere, at a second hand store that happened to have my size."

Lake said, "Were they 'Timberlands'?"

"No, those are the expensive ones, I got something for a lot less. I think they were 'Frontier's.'"

"They're not that cheap, are you sure of that brand?"

"I think so, anyway, they lasted for a couple of years and when I got these running shoes, well the boots got booted."

Kat continued her search and found nothing of interest. "You're into old movies," she posed as a question?

"Yeah, have been for years. I think that I have about fifty films on DVDs on that shelf."

Kat casually looked through his collection, "These are all on the dark side, Frankenstein, Dracula, Wolfman — ."

"Yeah, I find the play of black and white films using shadows and subtle sounds very interesting."

Lake asked Brandon to sit down and answer a few questions. Brandon complied. After a routine pass through his apartment by Lake as Kat sat and talked to Brandon, the detectives left, empty handed.

"Nothing, not a shoelace out of place, not a speck of dirt that we could use, nothing," complained Lake.

"So he tossed his shoes. Frontiers, well he's not denying anything, like trying to hide something from us. Maybe we should just ask him to confess, save us all a lot of time and energy."

*   *   *

Brandon walked into the pub at 10:15. Brenda was standing at the end of the bar talking to Steve and looking more serious than usual. "Good morning all, is everything okay, " he said looking at the two of them?

Brenda half smiled and said, "Yes everything is okay, Stu has a bit of a cold and I don't want him to push it too hard today. Actually, I'd like him to go home and rest."

"Well we can all pick it up a bit and leave him with nothing to do," offered Brandon.

"That's exactly what we were discussing," said Steve. "You take care of the bar and let me handle the rest. Brenda, I can get Lisa to take the front door and you can haul that big lug home."

"Thanks guys, I appreciate this," said Brenda as she went toward the kitchen and the stairs to the office in the basement.

Steve found Lisa and suggested she run home and change into a hostess outfit and come back as quickly as she could. He then went into the bar area and talked to Brandon about getting him a break as needed and suggested that Brandon take lunch when the bar was quiet.

"We're going to be fine," he said to Steve. "Look at all the practice we had when they went on the cruise."

"You're right Brandon. Do you need anything before I run downstairs?"

"No, I'm good," he replied.

*   *   *

Carl Dempsey and his partner responded to a 10-84 in a cheap hotel on the east side. The ME's office was notified, dragging Freddy and Sal out into the misting rain. The DOA was tentatively identified as one William Albert Furnald, a two time visitor to the facilities at Lorton before it was converted from a prison to an Art Center. He had overdosed on some bad crack and found in his possession was a wedding ring that not only did not fit, but bore the inscription *'DRM & DBN August 21, 1993'*.

The ring was soon identified as being the property of Donna Newberry. Her husband verified the identification and showed the detective his matching ring with the same inscription. Lake and Kat were notified that this case was now probably not tied to their prime suspect, Brandon Croummer.

*   *   *

Brandon and Suzanne talked several times a day and planned on another small adventure for the weekend. "This time I want to take you to the Art Museum," he proposed.

"I have not been there in years, what a great idea," she replied. It was set, he would meet her at the corner of Constitution and Seventh at 9:00 am Sunday and the day would be theirs. Suzanne was excited and Brandon was again feeling good.

*   *   *

The remainder of the week was a series of highs and lows. At one minute, Brandon was confident, sure about everything, the next, he would hear a sound, a whisper and he would want to hide. The rising and ebbing of his tides of fear were becoming more radical and the difference between those extremes was enough to describe him as two different people. Fortunately, these low points were confined to his visits to the basement, his walks home and his dreams. In the company of others he was normal, or so he appeared.

By the time Saturday rolled around, Brandon had survived a three day roller coaster ride of peaks and valleys that left him drained. His eyes were darkened and bloodshot. His speech was slurred and disjointed and his ability to work behind the bar was gone.

*   *   *

Lake and Kat decided to check on Brandon's locker at work, perhaps he was mistaken and he had left his old shoes at the Pub.

"We need a break somewhere in this one Kat," said Lake, "Something, anything and we won't find it if we are not there where he is."

"Eee Haw, road trip," squealed Kat, mockingly, "You're right, we need something, just wish we knew what it was — ."

The two detectives went to their car to head over to the pub and check Brandon's locker.

*   *   *

Steve had noted Brandon's slump on Friday and noted it was worse on Saturday. He took Brandon aside and said, "Hey, you look terrible. You may have whatever Stu had earlier this week. Maybe it's time we gave you a break. Why don't you take the rest of the day, go home, sleep and if you are better on Monday, then you come back."

Brandon was relieved to have the opportunity to get some rest, if the demons would allow. As he walked into the kitchen to get his coat, George was cutting meat in preparation for the evening's special.

He looked at George, nodded and said, I'm gonna' go home and try to get some sleep."

George said, "Hey man, you need something to make you sleep. I got some stuff from my doctor a couple of months ago. Still got four or five pills. You want 'em?"

"That would be great, George. Thanks."

George said, "I'll get 'em, they're in my locker," as he hurried down the stairs with a meat cleaver still in his hand. He returned almost immediately, handed Brandon a small pill bottle and said, "Wait till you get home, these little suckers will put you on your butt, knock you out cold. So get home, get in bed and take one, only one and lay down."

Brandon smiled weakly and said, "Thanks man." As he turned to go out the door, he remembered his coat and went toward the stairs to go down.

George said, "Hey where did I put that meat cleaver?"

Brandon paused then moved toward the stairs again. At the base of the stairs, Brandon saw George's meat cleaver and hollered back up, "George, I found it, I'll bring it right up."

"Thanks Brandon, no rush, I got another."

The kitchen door opened, "Another what," said Stu in a raspy voice?

George smiled, "Hey boss you feelin' better, you still sound like sh — , you know."

Stu chuckled and coughed lightly, "Don't make me laugh. Where's Brandon, I hear that he may have what I got?"

He went down to get his coat, he's gonna' go home and get some sleep. I gave him some pills that a doctor prescribed for me a few months ago, they will help him sleep."

"That's a nice thought George, but maybe he should go to a doctor and get a check up before he puts some strange drugs in his body." Stu started for the stairs with a slight cough again.

Brandon picked up the cleaver and walked toward his locker setting the cleaver on the middle shelf. As he was pulling his coat on he thought that he heard a whisper, or a cough, he wasn't sure. He heard footsteps behind him, he dropped his coat and picked up the cleaver, then he heard a deep throaty whisper,

"Brandon, I can take you — ."

Brandon swung around to his left raising the cleaver in his right hand and brought it down on the large hulking figure in the shadows behind him, striking the demon in the neck and shoulder. Blood spurted from the wound, covering Brandon's hand and striking his arm and torso.

The figure stopped, staggered, grasped at his neck and made a hideous gurgling sound as he fell back into the lighted stairwell. Stu lay on the stair, blood flowing from his neck. The sound stopped, his hand loosened it's hold and fell to his side, his eyes rolled up and his body lost all control of function. He was dead.

Brandon stood looking at Stu, eyes widening and the tide of fear rising again. The whispers turned to screams and the voices no longer called his name, they cursed him.

George came to the top of the stairs and looked down. He saw Stu and Brandon, the blood, he panicked and ran out to the alley.

Brandon started up the stairs with the cleaver still in his hand blood dripping from it's edge.

Lake and Kat arrived in the alley, got out of their car and moved toward the back door to the Pub. George came out the door looking terrified. Lake grabbed him as he tried to run and said, "Hey what's wrong? Where are you going?"

"He's crazy, he just cut Stu — he's crazy — he's crazy — ."

Lake held onto George and pushed him up against Stu's car, "Who's crazy, who cut Stu — ?"

"Brandon, he has my meat cleaver, he cut Stu — ."

Kat carefully reached for her weapon. Lake nodded to her and looked at George. "Okay, where is he now, Brandon where is he?"

"He was in the basement and Stu went down to talk to him and he cut him, he cut Stu. He's just laying there and the blood is all over the place."

Lake said, "Okay, you get in the car and stay there." He opened the back door to his car and George got in.

Kat was watching the door of the pub and said, " Hey Lake, should we get back-up.?"

"Hell yes," he said as he reached in his car for the radio and called for assistance.

As they approached the door to the Pub, Dan Carney pulled his police vehicle into the alley. Frank was speaking into his radio and the two came over to Lake and Kat.

"Lake, what's the play here?"

"We have a reported victim in the basement, apparently attacked by a man with a meat cleaver."

"Do we know his condition?"

Lake looked at Kat and said, "A meat cleaver, I hope he's alive but we don't know. Frank, you and Kat go to the front, clear people out quietly and Danny and I will go in this way. I'll give you — ," he paused and thought, "twenty seconds to get in front, then we are going in this end. You guys are wired?"

Dan looked at Frank, "Yeah, up and running."

"Let's do it."

Kat followed Frank around the building to the front door and walked calmly in with their fire arms down. The people in the restaurant were quietly hustled out the door from the front room. As they made their way through the two dining rooms more people were led outside.

Frank clicked his radio, "Three front rooms clear, proceeding to the kitchen doors. Hold — hold, I got movement in the kitchen." He approached the kitchen door peering through the glass panel. "Tall, thin, white male, holding a meat cleaver, covered in blood, pacing, looks confused, scared, can't see others in kitchen. He is moving away from this door, we have access capability."

Dan replied, "We are at the alley door, can only see the opposite open door to the basement. Make a sound, draw him away from this exit, and we can enter, don't want him going down stairs."

"Copy, we have two doors to cover I will move to the middle door, Kat has the door to the bar area. Give me five." He nodded at Kat she returned the nod and Frank moved toward the middle door. "Four . . . Three . . . Two . . . One . . ."

On cue, Kat moved a chair up against the swinging kitchen doors making a sound that was heard in the kitchen. Brandon moved toward the sound.

Frank saw Brandon turn and move toward the bar. "Dan, he has turned, enter now." Dan and Lake entered the kitchen with weapons up. Brandon turned and saw them then turned again crashing into the swinging doors. As he threw open the door he pushed a chair into Kat's hand holding her gun. He raised his hand and started to swing the meat cleaver down. Dan fired, striking Brandon in the left shoulder.

Brandon spun around and threw the meat cleaver. Dan and Lake each fired their weapons. The cleaver crossed the kitchen and struck Dan in the chest. His body armor prevented the cleaver from cutting Dan's chest but as it dropped to the floor, the cleaver tore open his pants and slashed a deep wound in Dan's leg on the way.

*   *   *

Forty One

Sunday . . .   I figure that this is better than tradin up

Suzanne stood on the corner of Constitution and Seventh and waited. She waited for two hours and tried to call Brandon on his cell phone. No answer. No Brandon It started to rain, she moved under a tree. It rained harder and she finally gave up and took a cab home.

*   *   *

Freddy answered his cell phone. "Freddy, this is Ben at the lab, looks like you got a match buddy, I'll fax the results over right away."

He thanked Ben and dialed Dr. Colburn. There was no answer and he left a brief message, "Doc, I'm goin' over to the office. The lab guy called and they have results on the DNA match. This Brandon is our guy. Fast results, a little late, but faster tha we expected."

*   *   *

Brandon was dead, Stewart Bricker was dead. The family that once was Stewarts pub was now dead. This one man with a fear of demons from the movies had ended five lives and caused his own to be taken.

Dan lay in a hospital bed with a ten inch gash in his left thigh stitched, draining and healing. Lake and Kat came into his room and tried to decide if he was awake.

Groggily, Dan opened his eyes and said, "Hey guys, what's happening?"

Kat looked confused, "I thought that Frank would be here."

Dan half laughed, "Yeah well the advantage is he didn't get hit, the disadvantage is he gets to do all the paperwork."

Lake grinned, "Yeah me too. I tried to tell this little lady that she should have talked him into submission, but . . . well — ."

Kat cut him off, "Thanks Dan, that guy was going to chop me up. I owe you a big one."

Dan grinned, "How about dinner, just you and me?"

Kat said, "Pick a day, I'll make it work."

"As soon as I can walk again, Doctor said about a week and I will be able to come in and do my desk duty, so dinner should be okay by then."

"You're on," Kat replied with a smile.

Lake rolled his eyes, looked at Kat and said, "He's a good man, brown eyes. Advantage for you, all of us are on desk duty till the shooting investigation is complete."

"Yeah, well Freddy is still a terrific kid, but, I figure I should take this trade instead and give you another chance."

"Freddy will probably be around longer than the two of us," said Lake.

"Yeah, he'll be the one doin' the tradin' up."

END

*   *   *

ABOUT THE AUTHOR

John B. Wren is a consulting engineer, living in Northern Virginia with his wife, Lois and two younger children. He grew up in a large Irish-Catholic family in western New York. **"Killing His Fear"** is his second published novel. His first, **"To Probe A Beating Heart"** was published in July of 2011 and his next novel is in the developmental process with an anticipated publication date in early 2013.

Made in the USA
Charleston, SC
15 May 2013